This Way Home

This Way Home

MARCIA KING-GAMBLE

sepia

★BET BOOKS™

BET Publications, LLC
http://www.bet.com

SEPIA BOOKS are published by

BET Publications, LLC
c/o BET BOOKS
One BET Plaza
1900 W Place NE
Washington, DC 20018-1211

All Kensington Titles, Imprints, and Distributed Lines are available at special quantity discounts for bulk purchases for sales promotions, premiums, fund-raising, and educational or institutional use. Special book excerpts or customized printings can also be created to fit specific needs. For details, write or phone the office of the Kensington special sales manager: Kensington Publishing Corp., 850 Third Avenue, New York, NY 10022, attn: Special Sales Department, Phone: 1-800-221-2647.

BET Books is a trademark of Black Entertainment Television, Inc. SEPIA and the SEPIA logo are trademarks of BET Books and the BET BOOKS logo is a registered trademark.

ISBN 1-58314-298-3

First Printing: October 2003
10 9 8 7 6 5 4 3 2 1

Printed in the United States of America

Special thanks to my wonderful agent, Helen Breitwieser, and my supportive editor, Glenda Howard.

Thank you for believing in me. You made this book possible.

1

The old woman's face came clearly into focus. Lined mahogany skin and tired red eyes pleaded with Liza. Her lips were cracked and dry and her stained headdress had shifted to reveal nappy hair below. Sweat trickled into the rivulets around her mouth. She wore a long skirt and soiled apron—clothing from another time and place. It was evident from her panting breaths and disheveled appearance she was on the run.

The clip-clop of hooves came closer, an ominous sound. Dogs bayed in the distance, their nails digging into the parched ground. Wearily the woman looked around for a place to hide and spotted the old shack. She shuffled toward it.

Liza's heart pounded as the shouts of men and panting dogs permeated the air. In minutes, the woman would be caught unless she did something. That thought propelled her into motion. Opening her door, she called out, "Come, you will find a safe haven here."

The woman angled her head. You could only see the whites of her eyeballs. Stumbling, she changed direction and headed for the house. She practically fell through the open door. Liza grabbed her, saving her from the shot that whizzed by, shattering the mahogany breakfront. Glass flew everywhere.

Liza's entire body trembled and her eyes flickered open. The dream had been so real, just like the others. She brought a trembling hand to her heart, and took a deep breath. Her chest felt tight and her pulse raced. The T-shirt she'd worn to bed was drenched in sweat.

She focused on the periwinkle walls of her bedroom and the contrasting ivory trim. This house was reality, not these dreams that drew her into the past. Dreams that had all started the moment she moved back to Syracuse and took over the downstairs consignment shop.

The clock on the dresser ticked off the minutes. It was time to get out of bed, shower, and get dressed.

An hour later, Liza, hair in a ponytail, raced downstairs prepared to roll up the green and white awnings on the old Victorian house. The first floor had been converted into a store. The second floor was where she lived.

"Morning. Looks like it's going to be a nice day," Delilah Kincaid, the owner of the small florist shop next door and her friend, greeted her. "Pray we make money today, honey. Holidays are coming and God knows we need it." She rolled her eyes skyward.

"From your lips to God," Liza said, about to go to work on the awnings. "Want to have a cup of coffee before our day starts?"

Delilah, a divorcée, placed her hands on sizeable hips and nodded. "You know it, honey. We have forty minutes to sit down at Ned's and catch up. Everyone's yakking about Erik Price, your stepbrother. He inherited Malcolm's place and occasionally comes into Ned's. If he's not there this morning, I'll take him a pie and check out the merchandise myself."

Her stepfather's place was a sore subject. By rights the house should have gone to her mother, who'd endured five hellish years with that man. It had been a fortunate thing that Liza had won a modeling contest, because it had enabled her to leave Syracuse in a hurry, heading for the bright lights of New York City. That had been the turning point in her life.

Delilah waddled toward her in buttercup-yellow capris that

were at least two sizes too small. She didn't cook, so the pie would be purchased from Sweet Eats up the street.

"Come on, honey, let's go," she said, taking Liza's arm.

Inside Ned's, the usual assortment of locals gathered. The drone of conversation almost drowned out the sound of a television newscaster busy announcing the latest calamity. Liza inhaled the scent of sizzling bacon and freshly scrambled eggs and the smell of freshly perked coffee that Kelli, one of Ned's two granddaughters, poured.

Liza had grown up in the upstate New York town and knew most of the people seated in the banquettes. She greeted them with a nod and a wide smile. Her wide smile and inner confidence had earned her the label of girl most likely to succeed. And for a short time she had. She'd been a supermodel—up until the accident.

Liza preferred to refer to it as an accident, but in truth it hadn't been. She'd been mugged in Central Park. Her assailant had left her battered and scarred, ensuring that she would never model again. The moment her physical scars had healed and she'd gotten her head together, she'd packed up her things. She'd returned to Syracuse where the only outrageous thing happening was the next-door neighbor running off with his best friend's wife.

Lucky for Liza, Blanche Lucas's store and home had been up for sale. She'd used her sizeable savings to acquire the property and start a new life. Visage, her store, specialized in vintage clothing and unusual costume jewelry, items the college kids and young professionals loved. After she had put three months of her heart and soul into it, the store was finally realizing a small profit.

"Hey," a voice that Liza recognized as Cassie's, the owner of Sweet Eats, called from a red pleather booth. "Over here."

Liza and Delilah joined two laughing, chattering women, who didn't seem the least concerned about cholesterol or gaining weight. They chowed down on copious amounts of pancakes, bacon and eggs, waving forks in the air to punctuate their points.

Ned's other granddaughter, Tiffani, came over, pouring coffee and quickly taking their orders: waffles, cream, and Canadian bacon for Delilah, and a fruit plate for Liza. The women went on about the upcoming Labor Day weekend, the last opportunity to make money off the tourists. Cassie and her breakfast companion, Rona, were also small business owners. Both had at one time or another left the upstate town but returned, because of divorce and the desire to raise their children in an environment considered safe.

"How's Alexia and Jamal doing?" Liza asked Rona.

"Loving every moment of visiting their dad and that hussy in North Carolina. I'm happy because I have the house to myself. As far as I'm concerned that's heaven in and of itself."

The front door swung open with a clang and every head swiveled. The new arrival, a tall man wearing baggy jeans and a paint-stained T-shirt, seemed oblivious to the impact he made. He scanned the dated interior with hooded eyes, looking for an available table.

"Ummmm, hmmm, ummm, that man is fine," Cassie said, gaping at him openly.

Delilah elbowed Liza. "That's who I was talking about, Erik Price. Old man Mitchell's illegitimate son, your stepbrother. How come you've never met him?"

Liza shrugged. "Malcolm never had any inclination to discuss his past. He barely tolerated me. He died a bitter old man. As far as I was concerned my mother did the right thing by leaving him. At the end, after going through several young wives, he died alone. The last wife walked out, too, taking with her three children."

"Ummm, hmmmm, ummmm. Lord have mercy. Man just couldn't keep it in his pants." Delilah wagged her head sagely.

When the banquette in front of them emptied, Kelli picked up the dirty dishes and beckoned Erik Price over.

"My, my," Delilah gasped, fanning herself with an open

hand while watching Erik sit down. "A woman can only take so much of seeing that man up close and personal."

Liza smothered a chuckle. Erik Price wouldn't win any points with her; he'd stolen her mother's house. Still, he was a dead ringer for Rick Fox of the Los Angles Lakers, the finest of men. Just the breadth of his shoulders and his wide column of a neck had women salivating. She wished Delilah a lot of luck. Men like that brought with them a whole lot of trouble.

Liza attacked her fruit plate and tried to ignore the man whose aura practically shouted sex. When the conversations around them resumed, she remembered the dream that had been so real.

Ned Lewis, using his cane, hobbled out of a back room. He spotted Erik Price and headed over.

"How's it going, son?" he shouted, angling his body into the booth and sitting opposite Erik. He beckoned Kelli over. "Coffee for both of us."

Liza thought it strange that ornery Ned, who rarely made an appearance these days, had come out to greet the new arrival. Then she remembered he'd been buddies with Malcolm Mitchell. Mesmerized, she stared in the direction of the twosome and connected with a pair of unblinking hazel eyes.

Erik's unshaven face added to his mystique. His high cheekbones and almost aquiline nose bespoke of an Afro/Native-American heritage, as did the jet-black hair that curled around his collar. When he smiled at her, the women seated next to her sighed.

"Morning, ladies," Erik Price said, flashing them another killer smile.

Ned Lewis turned up his hearing aid and looked around. "Morning, girls," he growled.

Liza couldn't resist giving him a smile back. It had been a while since she'd been called a girl but at age twenty-eight it was flattering. Her friends, all in their thirties, batted their eyes at the old man but the flirting was really meant for Erik.

Ned ignored them and returned to his conversation. "You

need to get out more often, boy. Meet some of the townsfolk, like those available ladies seated back there. A boy with your looks shouldn't have any problems getting those women into bed."

Liza wanted to sink into the upholstery and die. Did she have desperate written all over her forehead? She hadn't been with a man since the attack. Since then she'd sworn off men altogether. Her fiancé, unable to deal with a face that was no longer perfect, had left her to face months of plastic surgery alone. What that ordeal had taught her was that she didn't need a man to survive.

"Boyfriend can park those size twelves under my bed anytime," Rona muttered, loud enough for Erik to hear.

"More like fourteens," Delilah muttered.

She was the expert on men and had gone through every available and not so available man in town.

Erik sipped on his coffee and blushed. He'd overheard their conversation.

"See what I told you?" Ned said, smiling slyly, his hearing apparently not as bad as he pretended. "You've got them drooling. You getting any sleep, boy?"

"I sleep," Erik growled. "Just don't need as much as the average man." His voice held a tinge of a New York City accent.

"Every man needs sleep. You can't expect to stay up painting all night. Not even if some fancy New York gallery wants your stuff."

Liza listened shamelessly. Initially she hadn't made the connection. Inwardly she scolded herself for just now registering that her stepbrother was the hot new Erik Price the Soho galleries were raving about. He was considered to be *the* black Andy Warhol.

"I've turned into an insomniac since I moved here," Erik answered. "When I shut my eyes I have the strangest dreams. It's as if I'm thrown back in time. I'm chased by people I can't see. Dogs bay at my heels and men keep shouting at me. Then a woman comes to a window, or at times it's a door. She lets me in moments before I'm captured. Sheesh, I'm beginning to think my father didn't do me a favor by leaving me his house. The damn place seems to be haunted."

"Could be," Ned said. "You're not the first to say that. Malcolm just learned to live with those ghosts."

Liza continued to eavesdrop, drawn to what she was hearing.

"What kind of ghosts? Real or imagined?" Erik asked.

"The ghosts of those people whose lives he'd turned into a living hell, as well as that of the ancestors."

"Uh, Liza," Delilah called, waving a hand in front of her face. "Come back to us."

Liza's attention turned back to her friends. She'd been so fascinated with Erik and Ned's conversation that she'd totally tuned out her breakfast companions. But she couldn't believe that Erik Price was having dreams similar to hers. She wasn't crazy. If she wasn't so resentful she'd go over and ask him questions, to see if they could compare notes.

For the first time in a long time, Liza was conscious of her hastily thrown together appearance and of the ten pounds she'd gained. She hadn't worn any makeup and her scars were pronounced. What had possessed her to pull on the wrinkled peasant blouse and rumpled linen skirt, and tuck her wild hair under a hat? There wasn't the remote chance of her showing up in a tabloid as a fashion do. But after ten years of being a beautiful person, it felt good not having to worry about how she looked. Liza Hamilton was yesterday's news.

"It's ten to nine," Rona said pointedly and signaled to Tiffani. "Check, please."

They divided the bill up equally and prepared to leave. As they walked by Ned and Erik's table, Ned tapped his cane to get their attention.

"Just a moment, girls. I want to introduce you to Erik here."

Delilah's beaded braids swung furiously back and forth. She bent over the table, giving Erik a full view of her considerable assets.

"I'm Delilah Kincaid," she said, batting her eyelashes furiously and offering Erik her hand. "Welcome to town. I'd planned on stopping by and dropping off one of my pies."

His smile firmly in place, Erik clasped the proffered hand and shook it. "I'll look forward to that pie," he said, giving Delilah another killer smile.

One by one the women were introduced. Finally it was Liza's turn. Erik's hazel eyes appraised her. "Do I know you from somewhere?" he asked.

Liza wasn't about to tell him that she was his stepsister and that her face had once adorned the covers of several popular magazines. Besides, he would never believe her. The Liza that had emerged after the mugging was very different from the long, tall, glamorous babe most people remembered. She had a purpose.

Flustered, she tried to remove her hand from his, but Erik would have none of it. "Ned tells me that you own a consignment shop," he said.

"Yes, on Main Street."

"I'll make a point of stopping by some time."

Liza didn't know what to say. She didn't want Erik Price in her store. He'd done nothing to her except inherit a house that should have been her mother's or sister's by right. Elizabeth Price had scoured that house from top to bottom while waiting hand and foot on that old man. She'd gotten little from the divorce, and depended totally on her new husband for financial support.

"Certainly, if you like," Liza managed to say, and could promptly kick herself. But deep down she wanted to hear more about his dreams. Maybe question him.

Cassie cleared her throat and Liza tugged her hand away, breaking the connection. As they left she heard Ned say, "See what I told you, boy, you need to get out more. You never even met your own stepsister."

A group of college kids waited on the verandah as Liza unlocked the store. They made a beeline for a rack of peasant skirts that had been popular in the seventies.

"How much is this one?" a blond coed asked, holding up a ruffled print skirt whose tag clearly read fifteen dollars.

"The price is on the tag," Liza said firmly.

She was used to the kids wanting to bargain. Her clothing was priced dirt cheap and she'd been told that she was practically giving the stuff away.

The blonde grimaced. "Fifteen dollars. I only have ten."

"Come on, give us a break," her freckled, red-haired friend said. "We're poor college students living on an allowance." The girl held up a velvet beret. "What about this? Can you go any lower?"

Five dollars was as low as she intended to go. Liza faced them. "Why don't you put them on layaway? You can pay a small amount every week, then pick up your clothes."

The students huddled together, conducting a whispered conversation. Liza turned her attention to a pile of clothing that hadn't yet been priced. She flipped on her computer, verified the buying price paid, then set about putting tags on the clothing.

Another of the students approached, clutching items from the sales rack. Liza rang them up, accepted payment, and carefully folded the items. She added a pair of retro earrings, gratis, tied a bright red bow around the brown paper package, and handed it to the girl.

"Enjoy," she said. "The earrings are on me."

The student thanked her profusely. Her friends, after another whispered conversation, decided to put their merchandise on layaway. Laughing, they let themselves out.

Liza had just completed the task of tagging the new merchandise when the bell at the front door jingled. She looked up to see Erik Price strolling in. He brought with him the smell of summer. She tugged on the paper rose adorning the front of her hat and willed herself to breathe.

The sheer ruggedness of Erik made the merchandise surrounding him look silly. For the second time that day Liza wished she'd taken the time to put herself together. Nervously, her fingers stroked her cheek, outlining the almost faded scars that ran in jagged paths across her cheek.

"I decided to take you up on your invitation," Erik said, looking about him. "What a wonderful use of colors." He sniffed the air appreciatively, "And scents."

She hadn't invited him. He'd invited himself.

The walls were painted lavender and pink. Lime-green tulle draped from the moldings and huge cabbage roses rimmed the room. Headless mannequins sported a mishmash of vintage clothing. Liza had stenciled vines and lilacs on fabric umbrellas, strategically placing them to hide the worn spots on the faded carpeting. The overall effect was a Victorian haven designed specifically with women in mind, a place that shoppers would wile away time and hopefully spend some money.

Erik Price cleared his throat, waiting for an acknowledgment.

"Thank you," Liza said when she was finally able to formulate the words. "What you're seeing is a labor of love. I'm very proud of what I've done with this place."

"And you have every reason to be," Erik said, propping an elbow on the counter separating them, and staring into her face. "Give yourself credit. Most people just talk but never produce. Something tells me Liza Hamilton does what she wants and no one and nothing can stop her."

The conversation had grown personal in an amazingly short time. She needed a distraction, something to temper this burning physical attraction for a man she had just met. She turned her back on him and debated whether to offer the tea that sat in a chipped Rosenthal pot. But she couldn't imagine those huge hands clasping the ridiculously small cup.

"Would you like some water?" she asked, turning back to him.

Erik shook his head. "No, thanks. How did you get those scars?" His hazel eyes remained on her face.

God, he was blunt. Most strangers never asked; they simply wondered. She had to admire the man. He got to the point.

"I was mugged," she said, not making an apology for her appearance. She was long past that.

"Here? In this town?"

"No, in New York. Central Park to be exact. I did something stupid. I'd had a fight with my fiancé and decided to take a walk."

Erik leaned across the counter and cupped her chin, turning her face this way and that. Liza suppressed the tremor that the warmth of his palms produced. Let him look. She stared back at him, her golden eyes steady.

"You're a beauty, always have been," he said authoritatively and released her abruptly. "I may want to paint you sometime. Ned tells me you're my stepsister."

Liza simply gawked. When the silence spoke louder than words, she said the first thing that came into her head. "I just found out myself. Listen, I overheard you talking to Ned this morning. You mentioned you were having strange dreams."

"That I am. They started the minute I moved into that old house."

"I'm having a similar experience. I wonder what that's about. I was tempted to come over and ask you about yours, but I thought you'd think I was . . . being a bit forward."

"Why would I think that?" He wiped a paint-stained hand on his pants and seemed to reflect, then with a flash of perfect white teeth said, "Tell me about these dreams of yours."

Before she could tell him, the doorbell jangled and two elderly ladies entered.

Liza had a sneaking suspicion that it wasn't the merchandise that interested them; more likely it was Erik Price whom they'd spotted through the clear glass windows.

"You're Malcolm Mitchell's boy," one of the two women said. "The one he surprised everyone by leaving his house to."

Erik smiled but his eyes flashed fire. The ladies, oblivious of his anger, didn't seem to care.

The other one added, "We'd heard of you. Everyone in town heard about Malcolm getting another young thing pregnant, but the fool went to his grave with a closed mouth."

"I can see why he would," Erik muttered, pushing off the counter and sauntering by them. He turned back to Liza. "Let's continue our conversation over brunch. I'll be by on Sunday at one to pick you up."

"He's definitely Malcolm's son. Got an eye for pretty ladies, even if one of them is his stepsister," the first one said.

Pretending he didn't hear them, Erik opened the door and let himself out.

2

"I must be losing my mind," Erik muttered, a paintbrush held between clenched teeth, as he examined the weathered face on the canvas.

A turbaned woman with a red bandanna tied around her neck stared back with haunted eyes. Her expression said it all. Life had been hard.

Erik thought he might be hallucinating. He'd left a blank canvas on his easel and this portrait just wasn't his style. Where could it have come from? Frowning, he pushed open the huge attic window and breathed in the stifling August air. Liza Hamilton, from the moment he'd met her, had distracted him. His mind was muddled and his attention elsewhere. Even now he still pictured her beautiful face, perfect in its imperfection.

Determined to make the most of the afternoon sun, Erik removed a fresh canvas from the pile on the floor and went to place it on the easel. He rubbed his eyes realizing that the portrait of the old lady was gone. He knew he had not moved it, but strange things had been happening ever since he'd moved into this house. It wasn't just bizarre dreams. There were images of a young woman in the mirror, then with a blink of an eye they were gone.

Erik grabbed a handful of brushes and his oils, and for several hours he lost himself in painting. The first chance he got he would sit Ned Lewis down and ask him about the history of this house. It was clear that he was not the only one living here. The question was, were they good spirits or bad?

The phone rang as he was cleaning his brushes. Erik let the machine pick it up.

A woman came on the line, chattering about a pie she wanted to bring over. It was one of the women he'd met at Ned's. She'd been with Liza.

Time to clean up and get himself the hell out of there.

Sam O'Reilly was having another one of his spells. He could tell by his light-headedness and his queasy stomach. His heart beat rapidly as he stumbled around the old carriage house searching for his chair and muttering under his breath. Damn those ghosts for moving his furniture. They so enjoyed playing tricks on him.

It had taken him a while to adjust but Sam was now comfortable living in darkness. It wasn't always so. Initially he'd cursed the blindness that afflicted him late in life; now, a decade later, his senses heightened, he considered it a gift. Life, what little there was left, would be boring if not for the noises in his head and the visions that came to him with such clarity.

Sam found the old armchair and sank into it just as the spell took force. His head lolled to the side and his body convulsed. He saw the first explosion of bright white light as he was transported back into time. He was outside in a field, working alongside the slaves, the only white man in sight other than the overseer. The ruddy, sweating man referred to as Master barked orders and brandished a whip. The welts on the back of the black man next to him signified the whip was used plentifully and often. Children, their frail bodies bent under the baskets of ripe produce, shuffled by, their eyes vacant and lifeless.

Suddenly a noise broke out as a male slave broke free and headed toward the underbrush. Work ceased temporarily as his companions leaned on their hoes and in astonishment stared.

"Get back to work," the overseer bellowed, summoning reinforcements to chase after the runaway slave. All hell broke loose as a slew of hound dogs arrived. A posse of men guided them through the bushes in search of the slave.

The scene changed to an old church where men's and women's heads were bowed in prayer, black and white joined together. Sam recognized the church as the one he'd cared for. It had been established as a safe haven for those who had escaped.

The minister, leading the prayer, had been a fugitive slave who'd escaped to Canada. Later, he'd settled near Syracuse, establishing Underground Railroad stations, one at his home and the other in this church. Now the church was no more. It had been demolished twenty-odd years ago and a nursery school stood in its place.

The congregation began to sing one of the more popular Negro spirituals. Over the singing, Sam heard three loud knocks. Immediately, the crowd hushed and the minister bellowed, "Who's there?"

"A friend with friends," the secret reply came.

Hearing the familiar signal, he threw the church door wide open. A Quaker entered, half carrying a black man who looked more dead than alive. A terrified-looking female slave followed, holding the hand of a child. The ragged clothes they wore barely covered the essentials. The stark white of the man's eyes was prominent against his coffee face and his breath came in shallow gasps. Sam could smell the sweat trickling off his lean body.

The Quaker announced, "Friends, this is Erik and his family. We'll need to keep them safe."

The spell ended and with it reality returned. Sam was back in the old carriage house. He could tell by the house's musty odor mingled with the scent of stale food. Someone was pounding at his door. That someone was most probably the woman who brought him his meals. He eased off the lounge chair, his bones making a click-clacking sound. He navigated the furniture and made his way to the door.

The moment he eased the door open, a familiar crotchety voice bellowed, "Took you long enough."

Ned Lewis, his friend, a man almost as old as he, entered. "So how you doing?" Ned asked.

Sam swiped a hand across his sweating face and felt for the old armchair. "Not good. I just finished having one ah ma spells. Leaves a man weary."

"Them spells seem to be happening more and more, my friend," Ned said, creaking into the seat opposite him. "You eat lately?"

Sam made a wry face. His meals were usually delivered by a church lady. Miss Maisie was reliable but her no-good nephew wasn't. So Sam had learned to hoard his food.

He heard the crinkle of a paper bag and the delicious aroma of fried chicken assaulted his nostrils. Ned had brought him something from the diner. *Thank God.*

"Place is a mess," Ned grumbled. "I thought Maisie was supposed to send that niece of hers to help you straighten up."

The niece had come but Sam had sent her away. He hated people touching his things and he'd heard the teenager was nosey. As far as he was concerned, she and her brother were cut from the same cloth. He didn't like strange people. He was far more comfortable with his ghosts. He'd lived with them forever.

Ned was up again. Sam could hear his tapping cane as he wandered into the kitchen. The cupboard doors banged open and there was a rustling sound as he searched for something.

"Thank God I thought to bring paper plates and plastic cutlery," Ned muttered. "Your sink's full of dirty stuff. It's a wonder you don't have rodents."

He did, but wasn't about to tell Ned that. At night he heard them scurrying around, munching on his leftovers. The spirits he lived with had adopted them as pets.

Ned returned and plopped down a plate on his lap. Sam's mouth watered when the scrumptious aroma hit him full blast. Much as he carried on, he was grateful to the elderly black man who'd been his friend for over sixty years. Theirs had been an unlikely friendship in the 1940s when it wasn't acceptable for black and white youth to fraternize. But their friendship had survived. Adversity had made them tough.

Sam had first come across Ned hanging out in the churchyard. When Ned didn't think anyone was watching, he'd enter the church and sit quietly in the pew staring straight ahead. Sam, whose job it was to clean up and repair anything that needed repairing, enlisted Ned to help with his chores. He threw him a dollar or two when he could spare it. He soon learned that Ned, who'd been left in the care of his grandmother, was sadly neglected. And even after both men married they'd remained friends.

The men ate in silence until Ned said, "Malcolm left his place to his outside son, a fine boy from what I can tell. Big-time artist he is, but he's having troubles living in that house."

"Did you tell him?" Sam asked, laying a chicken bone down and feeling around for another piece of succulent flesh.

"Course I didn't tell him. He would think I was an old fool."

"That you are," Sam said wryly, wiping a greasy hand in his almost platinum hair.

"There you go again, being a pig," Ned yelled. "There's a napkin in your lap. You could at least use it, you fool."

"Takes one to know one," Sam grumbled. "No need to yell. Nothing wrong with my hearing."

"What was that?"

"You heard me clearly. So tell me about this boy of Malcolm's," Sam said, through a mouthful of food.

"Looks like the old man. Big, yellow skin, handsome. Knows how to handle the girls."

"Sounds like Malcolm's son, all right."

"He's pleasant enough. Picked something to do that isn't manly, but I hear he makes a good living at it. Imagine sitting all day swirling paint and tossing it onto one of them things that sits on an easel."

"Canvas," Sam supplied.

"Whatever."

"So why do you think Malcolm left the boy his house? He had Sara, plus three other children by his last wife."

Ned shuffled to his feet and practically snatched the plate from Sam's hand. "How the hell am I supposed to know? You done eating. Nothing left now except Styrofoam."

Ned tapped his way into the kitchen. Sam heard the refrigerator squeak open, then slam shut.

"I put away the remainder of the food," Ned said, "You can chow down on it later."

"Thanks."

His friend, much as he wouldn't admit it, always cared.

"Anyway," Ned said, resuming his seat, "none of them three children wanted that old Victorian house. Cost too much to maintain and Malcolm never forgave Elizabeth for leaving him. Hell, he wouldn't even acknowledge Sara as his. The little bit of money he had left he squandered."

"What happened to the profits he got from selling his land?" Sam asked.

"That's something only his attorney knows."

"You think he left that Erik some?" Sam asked. "Not that he needs money. That boy makes big bucks."

"You know the boy's name?" Sam heard the slap of an open palm as Ned's hand connected with flesh. "Of course. I keep forgetting you have the gift."

Sam grunted. "The boy's been around a lifetime or two. Has a penchant for helping people."

"Not another do-gooder, just what we need."

Even as he grumbled, Sam heard Ned settling in, preparing to listen. He didn't know whether his friend believed him or not, but he made it seem like he did. Ned was a good listener, and it was comfortable speaking with someone who knew he'd been blessed. His gift of prediction now helped him survive, and the money the townsfolk handed him for foretelling their future kept him alive.

"Go on, old fool," Ned urged. "Why was Erik Price sent here?"

Sam nodded sagely. "You'll see, just give it time."

"What's taking you so long with my pie?" Delilah demanded, swiveling back and forth on the stool that Cassie supplied for those customers choosing to eat in.

"You said you wanted it hot, mouthwatering. Just like that man," Cassie yelled, sticking her head out from the kitchen. "I'm waiting for it to cool so I can add fresh cream to the top. You did want fresh cream?" One eyebrow arched, teasingly.

"Yeah, yeah. It's got to look like I made it special. Like it's right out of the oven."

"All this, for a man," Cassie muttered, coming up front and slamming the still-steaming pie on the counter in front of Delilah. The delicious aroma of pecans, and the crisp pastry encasing them, wafted its way up to Delilah's nose, mingling with the scent of freshly baked bread and the chocolate chip cookies laid out on trays to cool.

Delilah helped herself to a large cookie laden with chips. She took a bite. "Honey chile, this is pure heaven."

"And will go directly to your hips," Cassie said, snatching the tray away and placing it on the shelf behind her, well out of her friend's reach.

"What's wrong with my hips?" Delilah said, standing and striking a pose. She'd changed out of the buttercup-yellow capris and into black pants and a pink halter top. Her breasts rose from the plunging neckline and threatened to spill.

"Not a thing." Cassie smoothed her own slim hips. "Not a thing a diet wouldn't fix, except the hound dogs around here like women with meat. It will be a cold day in hell when you go on a diet."

Delilah glared at her. "You're doing so well you can afford to lose my business? Lucky for you."

"I'm holding my own, even though things are slow."

"Wish I could say the same. You know how our people are. We buy flowers for weddings, funerals, and special occasions. God forbid we think about treating ourselves. It's white folks that keep me in business. Things might be bad, but they've got a live arrangement in the foyer, a vase on the dining room table, and a bloom in the toilet. Makes them feel good."

"Flowers used to make me feel good," Cassie said pointedly, "especially if they came from a man."

"I'm hoping that Erik Price is my man. That would make up for me shutting up my place early and losing what little bit of business there is."

"One problem, girlfriend, he's got eyes for Liza."

"Then he's wasting his time. Liza's his stepsister, besides, she's not interested in men. Ever since that scurvy dog of a fiancé walked out on her, she's put all of her energy into that store."

"I don't know," Cassie said sagely. "Seemed to be a lot of chemistry going on."

"Well, I ain't giving up," Delilah said, looking at the pie and licking her lips. "Boyfriend's got money and that old Victorian fixed up could be worth a mint. Boyfriend's also got big feet and you know what they say."

"No, I don't," Cassie answered, adding fresh cream to the pie and smiling like the Cheshire Cat.

Cassie knew she'd pushed buttons. Delilah's insecurities were kicking in. She'd always been jealous of Liza, the proverbial golden child. Liza was still pretty but nothing like the knockout she used to be, before the mugging.

"There ain't a man I know that turns down booty if it's offered," Delilah said, thrusting her breasts forward.

Cassie guessed Delilah's mind was probably racing a mile a minute, planning how she could offer Erik Price some. "You want this boxed?" she asked, already knowing the answer.

"Hell, no. It's supposed to be homemade. Put it on a plate."

Cassie fixed her with a look, and Delilah said, "I swear I'll get it back to you."

"You better."

"You're going to take it up to his house? Or you're going to call first?" Cassie asked, after Delilah had convinced her to lend her a kitchen towel and put the pie in an unmarked bag so that things looked authentic.

"I might call. Then again I might march myself right up to his front door. Do I look okay?" she asked, removing a bottle of Opium from her purse and spritzing it on with flair.

Cassie coughed and fanned her nose. "You look fine, but that stuff's pretty overwhelming. You need to lose it."

Just then Cassie's front door swung open and a mother with twins entered and approached the counter.

"I'd like a loaf of pumpernickel and a couple of those yummy-smelling chocolate chip cookies for the kids."

"Mama, can we have a brownie as well?" the sweeter faced of them said.

"No, honey, you can have one or the other. I don't want you ruining your dinner."

Delilah used their arrival as an opportunity to leave. Cassie watched her sashay out. No point in lecturing her—Delilah would do what she would do. Plenty of men had ridden side-saddle on those hips. She'd used her Opium to lure them in, and there still wasn't a man in town, married or single, who didn't do a double take when she stepped out. That fresh cream she'd conned her into adding would possibly be used in a very creative manner this evening.

If Cassie knew Delilah, she'd pull out all the stops.

3

After Delilah left, Cassie served the customer and her twins. She wrapped the loaf of pumpernickel and handed it over. The children, munching happily on their cookies, chattered excitedly and skipped ahead of their mother out the front door.

With no customers left in the store, Cassie used that opportunity to race for the bathroom. She shoved two fingers down her throat and purged herself of the day's meal and the batter that she'd tasted while preparing the cookies. She felt better after that.

This was her little secret, the reason she stayed thin. It had been almost a decade since she'd been binging and purging. Now it was a daily ritual and something she could control. As she sat hugging the bowl she heard the outside door open and close. Another customer had entered.

"Hey, Cassie, anyone home?" *Not a customer, just Rona.*

She stumbled to her feet, splashed water on her face, gargled, and took a few precious seconds to compose herself before going out to greet Rona.

"Cassie," her friend again called. "Where are you, girlfriend? I'm starting to get worried. It's not like you to leave your store untended."

Cassie bounced out, a ready smile on her face.

"A girl can't even go to the bathroom without inquiring minds wanting to know." She kissed Rona's cheeks and smoothed the frown off her face.

Rona munched on an almond croissant that she'd helped herself to. She ate it with such obvious satisfaction that Cassie couldn't help but smile.

"That's a buck fifty," Cassie said, holding out her hand.

"Add it to my tab. One day I'll get around to paying you."

"Promises, promises. If I ever gave you a bill, UPS would have to deliver it."

"I closed early today," Rona said, doing a little jig. "The last child was picked up at five, thank God. I thought maybe we could stop by Wine and Roses?"

Rona ran the only day-care center in town and during the summer it was converted into a camp. Young mothers, glad for a break, often dropped their kids off, even if only for an hour or two.

Cassie glanced at the wall clock. It was almost six. The bulk of her customers had come and gone, most heading home to cook dinner. "Good idea," she said. "I could use a drink. All that baking's made me thirsty."

She looked forward to spending time with Rona, whose kids were visiting their dad. And she could afford the calories now. Besides, Wine and Roses was the "in" place in town.

"I was thinking of asking Delilah and Liza to join us," Rona said as they headed out.

"Don't waste your time on Delilah, she already has plans," Cassie said. "She picked up a pecan pie and headed off to Erik Price's place."

Rona chuckled. "I smell a seduction in the making."

"I don't think Erik will bite, but you know Delilah, she's willing to give it a try. We'll call Liza on my cell and have her join us—that's if we can pry her out of that shop."

Liza answered on the first ring, and after a little coaxing, agreed to meet them at the bar.

*   *   *

Wine and Roses was a charming watering hole with an old-fashioned décor in keeping with its name. Inside, an after-work crowd sipped cosmos and wine. It was standing room only. Each occupied table bore a bud vase holding one bloom. The roses had come from Delilah's. Those steady orders had kept her in business this summer.

The owner, Mason, a forty-something dark-skinned man with a well-trimmed goatee, approached. "How you doing, ladies? Let me buy you a drink." He signaled to the bartender to provide them with a complimentary round.

Liza watched Cassie check out the place, looking to see if there was anyone there she didn't know. Her friend wanted desperately to meet a man, just to show her philandering ex that she still had what it takes. At thirty-two, her self-confidence had been badly shaken. Her husband, with no previous warning, had simply gotten up one day and left.

Cassie was attractive but still believed she was fat. She'd convinced herself that men her age were looking for svelte young things that made them feel like a real man, and who didn't come encumbered.

A man sitting alone at a table caught Cassie's eye. He smiled at her and she offered a tentative smile back. He had a shaved head and a diamond stud twinkled in one earlobe. He was most definitely different from the usual type around town and Liza wondered if Cassie would bite.

"Dr. Moore," Rona supplied, her eyes following the path Cassie's had taken.

"How do you know him?" Cassie asked.

"His kid comes to camp off and on."

"He's married, then," Liza said, making it sound more like a statement than a question.

"No. Divorced. He's in town every other weekend to see his son."

"Gets more interesting by the moment. I'm surprised Delilah hasn't made a play for him," Liza said, scanning the place for vacant chairs.

"I think she did, but he turned her down flat."

"That never stopped Delilah before," Liza added.

The threesome chuckled and drained their glasses. Delilah definitely went after any man she wanted.

"Ready for a refill?" Cassie asked.

"Sure. In fact, I'll come with you."

"What about you, Rona?"

"Yes, I'll take another."

Cassie wended her way through the milling crowd and slowed down in front of Dr. Moore's table. Liza followed on her heels. The crowd around the bar was three lines deep and it would be a while before the bartender got to them.

"Mind if I set these glasses down?" Cassie asked the doctor.

"Not at all. In fact if you join me the waitress will come over."

"Liza," Cassie said, "the gentleman has asked us to join him." She didn't wait for an answer before sinking into the chair Dr. Moore held out.

"I'm Kalib Moore," he said. "And you're?"

"Cassandra Newell. Cassie. This is my friend Liza Hamilton."

Kalib Moore seemed to have eyes only for Cassie.

"Cassie has a nice ring to it. Hello, Liza. How come I haven't seen either of you ladies around before?" His brown eyes twinkled as he spoke.

"I've never seen you before, either," Cassie answered, returning his smile.

"That's because I'm up from New Jersey, visiting."

"Then you must have friends in town."

Dr. Moore's smile seemed a bit strained. "No, I'm here to see my son."

Cassie raised a playful eyebrow. "You and your wife have a summer place?"

Oh, God, Liza thought to herself. Cassie was definitely fishing. Liza sat back to watch the flirting begin.

"My ex-wife and I share joint custody of our son," Kalib Moore admitted, letting them know he was available.

A willowy waitress undulated over, putting an end to further conversation.

"What can I get you?" she asked.

"I'm fine," Kalib said. "How about you Cassie, Liza? What will you have?"

Cassie ordered three Chardonnays and the brunette weaved her way around customers and headed off to fulfill their order.

"So what does Cassie Newell do?" Kalib asked, his eyes fastening on Cassie's face.

"I own Sweet Eats, a small bakery in town," Cassie answered, blushing slightly.

"Maybe I'll stop by sometime and buy breakfast."

"I'd like that. What do you do?"

"I'm a gynecologist."

Cassie tossed Kalib an amused look. "Any reason you chose that profession?"

He smiled, flirting outrageously. "I happen to like women's bodies and I come from a long line of doctors, most of them gynecologists."

Just then Rona walked by. Cassie beckoned to Rona. Kalib, the perfect gentleman, procured another chair, making it four.

"Add the drinks to my tab," he said to the returning waitress.

Introductions were made and the group settled in. Rona took over the conversation and Liza let her eyes drift. A man standing head and shoulders above the crowd caught her attention and that of every woman in the room. Erik Price, the last person she'd expected to see here.

Liza kept a bland expression on her face as her years of professional modeling kicked in. "Didn't you say Delilah was off to see Erik, bearing a pie?" she whispered to Cassie.

"Ladies, why are we whispering?" Kalib asked, his eyes trained on the man that had garnered their interest. "Oh, our artist-in-residence is here."

"Do you know Erik?" Liza asked, making sure to keep her voice neutral.

"Everyone who knows anyone knows Erik Price. He's been featured in the *New York Times* and the *Star Ledger* as well."

Rona shot up from her seat, obviously impressed. "I'm going to ask him to join us, do you mind?"

Before Liza could answer she was off and running.

"We met Erik recently," Cassie hurriedly explained. "He was quite taken with our Liza. And we were all quite taken by him."

"No, he was not taken with me as you so old-fashionedly put it. I'm his stepsister, for God's sake," Liza hissed.

What in the world was wrong with Cassie? And why did Rona go racing off like a lunatic to chat the man up? Her friend was already gesturing to the table where the three of them sat.

The crowd parted as Erik followed Rona over. Every eye was now trained on him. His hair curled slightly over his collar and his wide shoulders and broad chest were not in keeping with the lean and hungry look one expected of an artist, nor was the bottle of beer from which he chugged. He pretended to ignore the female attention.

Liza was surprised how well Kalib Moore handled the arrival of another man. He and Erik tapped fists, then Erik pulled up a chair and squeezed in. He nodded at Liza. His arrival brought with it the faintly familiar smell of musky cologne and paint. Rona seized that moment to excuse herself and head for the ladies' room, leaving the four of them alone.

Piano keys tinkled and a soothing romantic ballad filled the air. The conversations around became muted in order to accomodate the music.

"Fancy running into you so soon," Erik said softly, so that she was the only one to hear.

Liza forced an enthusiasm into her voice she didn't feel. "Downtown's a pretty busy place, so it was bound to happen."

Lest he get any ideas, the only interest she had in him was in his house.

Erik, ignoring the less than welcoming vibes, chugged down his beer. "Yes, but if I had known this is where you hang out, I would have come by sooner. I'm wondering if you would consider sitting for me."

Openmouthed, she stared at him. For the life of her, she couldn't understand why a world-renowned artist would want to paint a face that was flawed. One hand idly toyed with the scars on her cheek.

A commotion at the door saved her from committing. Delilah swooped in bearing a brown paper bag. She waved at Mason, the owner, and blew kisses to an assortment of males. She still hadn't seen them.

"Uh-uh. Look who's here," Cassie whispered in a loud voice.

Kalib seemed amused. A dimple in his cheek became even more pronounced as he said, "Delilah Kincaid, in the flesh. Is she a friend of yours?" He threw an arm around Cassie's chair and she beamed.

Delilah, spotting them, descended. "So this is where you are and none of you thought to call me."

"You've been busy," Cassie said pointedly.

Delilah plopped the brown paper bag on the table and inched her way closer to Erik. "I stopped by your place. This was for you." She pointed to the paper sack. "It's a pie."

"It's no longer for me?" Erik asked, raising a curved eyebrow. "What have I done to offend you?"

Delilah's laughter rang out. Flirtatious though she was, she was a good sport. "Aren't you going to ask me to sit down?"

Kalib apologized and gestured to the vacant chair. Liza wondered what was taking Rona so long. She spotted her friend talking to a tall stranger and frowned. Another new man in town.

"Who's Rona with?" she asked out loud, angling her head in Rona's direction.

Both Cassie and Delilah followed the path her eyes took. "That's Tim Delaney, the center for the Hoops," Delilah explained. "You'd have to be dead not to know that. The man's almost seven feet tall. He rents a place on Onondaga Lake and comes to Syracuse every summer."

"I haven't seen him before," Liza said, watching Rona throw back her head and laugh in response to something Tim said.

"Then you need to get out more. A professional basketball player would have no reason to come to your consignment store," Delilah said tartly.

What on earth was the matter with her?

"He hasn't been in my bakery either," Cassie shot back. "I couldn't have missed him."

"Ladies," Kalib said, gaining their attention again, "Erik and I are beginning to think you've forgotten about us."

Liza realized from the set of both men's jaws that they were not at all happy about the attention Tim Delaney was getting. Testosterone had kicked in, and the men were eyeing the competition. Delilah's long red nails flicked Erik's muscular arm.

"So, Erik, tell us about your paintings. What are you working on?"

Erik managed an enigmatic smile, one that probably set every female heart in the place aflutter. "Oh, I don't know. I splash on paint and go with the flow. Speaking of which, I need to get home. Buddy, my dog, is locked in the house." He turned to Liza. "Are we still on for tomorrow?"

"You two going some place tomorrow?" Delilah interrupted, her expression undergoing a subtle change.

"As a matter of fact we are. I'm taking Liza to brunch."

"How come I'm not invited?" Delilah pouted.

Erik's lack of response said it all. Delilah, pretending she wasn't insulted, left to work the room.

"Cassie, what about you and me going canoeing?" Liza heard Kalib ask.

Cassie's voice sounded low and uncertain when she replied, "Sure."

Erik's attention returned to Liza. "I'm really looking forward to tomorrow," he said, getting up.

Much as she hated to admit it, so was she.

4

Liza twisted, turned, and grabbed for the covers. A cool night breeze blew through the open window and the room turned ice-cold. She sensed a presence, one she couldn't see. She struggled to pull herself out of the dream, a dream filled with Erik. He was standing at the door of a huge mansion, staring out at the field, directly at her.

Liza bent to the task at hand, continuing to gather the tomatoes. A black Labrador sat off in the distance, its paws crossed. Every now and then it raised its lazy head to snap at a hovering fly. Nearby, the overseer flicked his whip and she heard a harsh cry as a slave stumbled. The whip had sliced through flesh, causing Liza to avert her eyes so as not to see the flow of crimson blood oozing.

The dream changed to a modern-day scene. She was sitting beside Erik at a sidewalk café, their heads close together, laughing and joking. Liza looked deeply into those compassion-filled hazel eyes. She leaned over, stroked his cheek, and he covered her hand with his. They continued to stare into each other's eyes, awed by the wonder of newfound love and oblivious to the patrons around them.

The dream changed again. This time Liza was in Central Park on a dark night, wandering aimlessly. She'd needed fresh air to clear her head, and she was angry and distracted. She wandered down another unlit path, plunging herself in darkness. An arm closed around her neck and she screamed. The arm tightened, cutting off her breath.

"Take off your clothes and give me your money," a man's gruff voice demanded.

She felt cold metal against her neck and knew it was the blade of a knife. She had no money. She'd left without her purse. She slowly began removing her clothes.

"Beautiful body," the man said when she was naked and her clothes were in a pile on the grass. Now the money," he said gruffly.

She'd never been so scared in her life. Liza tried turning, wanting to see her assailant's face. The metal blade sliced her cleavage and she felt the warm liquid soak her flesh.

Liza opened her mouth to scream. Before a sound could come out he used the tip of his knife against her cheek as if commissioned to do a tribal carving. Blood trickled down her face and filled her open mouth with its metallic taste. Summoning every ounce of strength she had left she bit his arm. He screamed and kicked out.

Lucky for her, a couple out for a late-night jog came running. A man walking a dog joined them. Her assailant ran off leaving her to be found naked and wounded. If it hadn't been for those people she would probably be dead.

Liza's eyes flew open. Her heart pounded. She'd just relived the ordeal of her mugging and attempted rape, all in vivid Technicolor. She sensed she was not alone. There was a presence in the room with her, an icy hand had stroked her face, jolting her fully awake. The curtain at the window fluttered and a smoky substance infiltrated the room. Whispered words she couldn't make out filled her ears.

Liza sat up, clutching the covers and willing her breathing to still. The smoky film enveloped the room, changing shape to form a male silhouette. Liza's heart rate accelerated. She rubbed her eyes, telling herself it was just her imagination. The male form was only inches away, arms held out as if to embrace her. She slid out from under the covers and placed a tentative foot on the floor. Mesmerized, she began walking toward the man.

A dog barked outside and tires squealed as the next-door neighbor's son pulled into the driveway. Liza snapped the lamp on and the figure evaporated as rapidly as it had been formed.

Tiny goose bumps had formed on her forearms. Why was she being thrown back in time? Why was Erik featured in her dreams? And why was she reliving the nightmare she'd tried so hard to forget and spent so many hours in therapy to handle? It had to be this house. It must have a history that she didn't know about.

Blanche Lucas, the previous owner, hadn't said a thing about strange goings-on, but she'd badly wanted to sell the house. No wonder she'd unloaded it for what Liza considered a steal. Tomorrow she would try talking to someone in town, making discreet inquiries to see if her experiences were just a figment of her imagination.

A warm, yellow glow now filled the corners of the room. Liza could see clearly that there were no ghouls and goblins hiding, just the familiar furniture that had once adorned her Upper East Side Manhattan apartment.

She thought about her brunch with Erik tomorrow and debated whether to tell him about tonight's experiences. Much as the man fascinated her, she would not be sucked in by a good-looking face. His house would be the focus. By rights it belonged to her mother and sister.

Erik's father, Malcolm Mitchell, and Liza's mother's marriage had been doomed from the beginning. Elizabeth had been divorced and alone for almost ten years when she first met him. She'd been flattered by the attention paid to her by a man almost twenty-five years her senior. Malcolm had wooed her with gifts and elaborate dinners. He'd promised her the world. Any woman with a young daughter, starving for male attention, easily would have been fooled.

Things changed rapidly once they were married. Malcolm's attention quickly switched to another young thing, and Elizabeth became no more than an appliance around the house. She became pregnant with Sara, and though unhappy, wanted to make it work. But Malcolm's philandering made it impossible.

Once Liza turned eighteen, she'd moved out, heading for New York. She'd won a magazine contest and her modeling career was off and running. Sara was only three when Elizabeth met Phillip, a businessman passing through town. It had been love at first sight. Love mixed with desperation. Elizabeth had quickly packed her things, and with young Sara in tow, joined Phillip in Boston.

Malcolm had immediately cut her off, even refusing to pay child support. It was Phillip who had raised the child, making sure that Sara had everything she needed.

What angered Liza was that Elizabeth had worked her fingers to the bone, maintaining a nice home for her cheating husband, and waiting on him hand and foot. The money inherited from Liza's dead father had been used to make repairs around Malcolm's large but crumbling home. Elizabeth had come to Phillip virtually penniless.

If you added up the years of unpaid child support and alimony, Malcolm owed her mother plenty. The least he could have done was leave her mother and Sara that old house. Thinking about the injustice of it made Liza furious. She'd begged Elizabeth to contest Malcolm's will, even told her that she would help pay the legal fees.

Oh, yes, she would have brunch with Erik Price tomorrow, but all the while she would be on her guard. Malcolm might have been guilted into leaving his illegitimate son something, but her mother and sister had been robbed of what was rightfully theirs.

Tim Delaney's house was a monstrously huge place. It overlooked Onondaga Lake and boasted seven bedrooms. Rona couldn't imagine why a man without a family needed all that space to himself. Then she remembered, Tim was rich.

He'd shown Rona each and every one of the seven bedrooms and their accompanying bathrooms. She'd followed him through the library and into the dining room that held a table easily seating twenty. Then they'd gone outside to allegedly admire the moon.

The terrace ran the length of the house and held comfortable lounge chairs. A bar dominated one wall and a speedboat had been tethered to the dock, one that Tim proudly announced was his own. He'd had the boat removed from its storage space on Long Island and transported up here.

Rona had been fed a lavish dinner his cook had prepared and served. The woman had cleaned up, said good night, and departed for parts unknown. Now she and Tim sat facing each other, sipping on after-dinner drinks.

"So what do you think of my house?" Tim asked, waving his hands expansively, to indicate the house he'd rented.

"It's lovely, but it seems an awful waste of space for only one person to live in."

"Would you like to move in?" he asked, winking at her. "I'd love a roommate." Sensing her discomfort he quickly added, "Just kidding. The guys drop by on the weekends with their wives and girlfriends. Living quarters like these ensure that they don't get in my way."

Rona tried to decide whether he was cocky or just painfully blunt. She decided on the latter. So far Tim didn't seem to be full of himself. Except for the size of his house he seemed like an average Joe.

"Will your friends be stopping by tomorrow?" she asked.

Rona didn't know Tim's reputation but had heard that most professional athletes had a string of women after them. While she could use some good loving, she had no intention of becoming one in a long line of Tim's conquests. She didn't plan on making it too easy for him.

"How come you're interested?" he asked, squinting an eye at her. He set down his drink and splayed his long legs, arms dangling between them.

"No reason at all, just making conversation."

"Actually, a couple of my friends said they might drop by."

"What time is that?"

He chuckled, sizing her up. "Are you worried that you

wouldn't be gone by then?" The toe of an oversized Gucci nudged her ankle and she couldn't help but smile.

Tim Delaney was definitely hot. He had that bad-boy look about him. His skin was the color of bitter chocolate and his hair was closely cropped. A mole quivered on the side of his full lips as he pretended to leer at her. Those lips, she would bet, gave women pleasure. Much as she didn't want to be just another notch on his belt, she wouldn't mind kissing Tim Delaney and seeing if he found her desirable.

"Oh, I plan on being long gone by then," Rona said wryly.

"Not if I have anything to do with it."

Tim propelled himself off the lounge chair, tugging her up to stand beside him. All five feet six of her seemed tiny and slight next to him. They stood, staring out at the lake for a long time.

Rona had expected him to make a move, had even asked for it. She'd practically picked the man up and she'd willingly come back to his house. He'd been the perfect gentleman up until now. In the bar he'd made her laugh until her sides ached, regaling her with stories about his teammates and their shenanigans off court.

"We really don't know each other," Rona said, stalling for time.

Tim's cool dark eyes appraised her steadily. "What is it you would like to know?"

"How old you are. Where you grew up. That sort of thing."

Keep him talking. Make him get to know her as a person. That way she would feel she was a human being and not just some female he wanted to screw.

"I'm thirty. Born and bred in Oklahoma," Tim said.

Rona couldn't help laughing out loud. Tim Delaney was the only African-American she knew from Oklahoma. She tried to picture him in cowboy gear. It didn't seem to go with the whole hip, urban package.

"What's so funny?" Tim asked, chucking her with his elbow.

"Oh, nothing."

Then the laughter came. The image was vivid in her mind. She pictured all seven feet of Tim in chaps, a ten-gallon hat on his head, and a silver star pinned to his chest. It was pure fantasy but definitely erotic.

"Nothing, my foot," Tim said, grabbing her around the waist and pulling her up against the long, rangy length of him.

Rona's breath caught in her throat as his woodsy cologne threatened to overwhelm her. She could feel the heat coming off his flesh and felt the beginnings of an erection pressing against her.

"So," he said, tilting her chin up until she was forced to stare into those dark magnetic eyes of his, "what brought on that robust laughter?"

"I had this ridiculous image of you," she said between chuckles.

"Please share. I could use a good laugh myself."

Why not tell him? It couldn't hurt. All he could do was think her silly.

"You're the first black person I've met from Oklahoma," Rona admitted. "When I think of the state, I see cowboys, lassos, that sort of thing."

"And a black man doesn't fit the bill? You've been watching too many old Hollywood movies. I grew up on a ranch that's been in my family for years. We have several black ranchers in Oklahoma, but conviently the media forgets we exist."

There was a lot more to him than met the eye. Rona was intrigued. She'd bought into the unfair stereotype of the arrogant, empty-headed athlete with lots of money but little brain.

"Educate me," Rona said. "My knowledge of the West is somewhat limited."

"Next time. It may take weeks."

Would there be a next time?

"What do you do?" Tim asked, changing the subject abruptly.

In the bar they'd talked about this and that, but the conversation hadn't gotten personal.

"I run a day-care center. In the summer it's a camp."

The mole at the side of Tim's mouth jumped as he spoke. "You have to have lots of patience and high energy to keep up with kids."

"I have two of my own. Patience and stamina come with the territory."

Rona held her breath. What if Tim thought she came with too much baggage? So what if he did? It wasn't as if she planned on marrying him.

"I have twelve nieces and nephews," Tim admitted. "When those kids come visiting I'm just as happy to see them leave. I love children but they are exhausting. Are you raising your kids alone?"

Translation: was there a husband in the picture?

"I'm a single parent," Rona answered, sparing Tim the gory details.

He frowned, clearly puzzled. "Who's minding them tonight?"

"They're with their dad and his wife in North Carolina."

Was it her imagination or did he heave a sigh of relief? He took her hand and led her inside. "Let's listen to some music," he said, starting upstairs.

Rona, though she knew she was playing with fire, followed him into a gigantic bedroom that could easily be an apartment. There was a sitting area with a leather love seat and two wing-back chairs and a coffee table that held stacks of sports magazines. To the far side was a bar stocked with top-shelf liquor and an expensive selection of wine.

He got behind the bar, picked up two brandy snifters and began pouring cognac into them.

Rona sifted through an eclectic selection of CDs running the gamut from jazz to rap. Tim Delaney was definitely different. After some contemplation, she selected Kenny G and waved it at him.

"Good choice, if I say so myself." He walked away to put the CD in the player, came back, and handed her a brandy.

Kenny G's mellow music filled the room. Tim joined her on the love seat, draping a long arm around her.

"What do you do in your off time?" he asked.

Rona thought about making something up. Her life seemed so humdrum next to his. Most of her time was devoted to looking after children, other people's and her own. She shrugged. "I read and I like being outdoors. What about you? What do you do when you're not playing basketball?"

"I buy classic cars and refurbish them."

"Sounds interesting. How many cars do you have?"

"I'm working on my seventh." He ticked them off. "I've got a Mustang, Corvette, Bentley, Porsche, Mercedes, and T-Bird. I'm negotiating a Jaguar XJ6 as we speak."

"Sounds like an expensive hobby."

"It can be, but not if you do most of the work yourself."

Tim's fingers tugged at her earlobe and Rona gulped her brandy down. She ended up in a coughing fit. Tim slapped her back.

"Are you okay?"

Hell, no, she wasn't. She was in way over her head, but the attention felt good. Tim kissed her cheek and she turned, letting her lips graze his.

"How about we get more comfortable?" Tim proposed, pulling her up.

He helped her climb three little steps that led to a huge bed covered with half a dozen throw pillows. The duvet was some type of animal print and the mattress was firm against her rear end.

Tim skipped the steps and flung himself on the mattress next to her. His hands stroked her bare arms, igniting a burning sensation that traveled down into her fingertips. Kenny G's horns provided beautiful background music. Tim kissed her again, and this time his tongue swept the recesses of her mouth, then dipped and explored.

Rona felt a tingle begin in her toes and make its way up her body. Her center pulsated and pounded. It had been way too long since she'd been with a man. Her ex had been one of those guys that thought foreplay was a waste of time. His lovemaking had left her aching and unfulfilled.

Tim's shirt was off. His lips nipped at her neck and his hands circled her breasts, fingers plucking at the nipples, making them taut. She couldn't go through with this, wouldn't.

"Get out of your blouse," he ordered, his voice a husky whisper.

"No," Rona said, "this is all happening too soon."

Tim's knee nudged her thighs, parting them. Rona's arms slid around his back. Her fingers kneaded his muscles and her breath came in tiny gasps as Tim's hands began to wander. They slid under her waistband, popping the button of her Ralph Lauren jeans, then pushed them down her hips. He cupped her buttocks.

Tim blew a hot breath into her belly button. His tongue circled and dipped, hinting at promises. Rona scrambled up to a sitting position. "I said no."

"Baby, I won't hurt you," Tim whispered, warm fingers trailing up and down her legs, massaging her calf muscles, and molding her thighs.

The pulsing at her center took on a rhythmic beat. Blood roared in Rona's ears, drowning out the music. She ran a hand up and down the sinewy length of his back. It would be so easy to go with the flow, close her eyes, and just let go.

"Come on, baby," Tim cajoled.

Rona began straightening her clothes. Tim huffed out an exasperated breath and rolled onto his side.

She needed to get back in control, to stop the madness before it continued.

Tim was up on his elbows, staring at her. "Can I ask you a question? Why did you agree to come home with me?"

Rona fumbled for something to say and came up with, "Because I enjoyed talking with you and I wanted to see your house."

That wasn't a total lie. Would he buy it?

With supreme effort, Tim catapulted off the bed and gathered his shirt. "You're a groupie, huh? I'll take you home."

She'd made him angry and just like that the evening had ended. Tim no longer wanted any part of her now that she'd said no. She'd asked for it by leading him on and hadn't played fair. But if she slept with him she would be just another in a long succession of women.

Rona didn't want to be just another notch on someone's belt. And Tim Delaney had been a nice surprise. He'd had more substance than he'd initially let on. And yes, she was taking a chance by walking away. But if he was really interested, he would be back. At least she hoped so.

5

Erik was looking forward to seeing Liza Hamilton again. There was something about the woman that intrigued him. Aside from the fact that she was his stepsister, a stepsister that he hadn't known even existed, he liked that she was comfortable with herself and wasn't aware of her looks. He'd heard the talk that she'd been a supermodel, but she certainly didn't act like a diva.

Why would a woman who'd once been the "it" girl now run a consignment shop? he wondered. He wanted to ask Liza about the attack, guessing that it must have been a traumatic experience, and one that had changed her life. But it was probably best not to bring it up until he knew her better. He'd keep the conversation focused on the dreams they had in common. Even last night he'd had a humdinger of one, transporting him back in time. Liza's face had been prominent in that dream. And even after he'd awakened, he'd still felt her presence.

Erik had never been one to pay much attention to his appearance, but today was different. He searched through his closet, looking for something appropriate to wear, clothes that weren't paint-stained and could be considered presentable.

In the back of his closet he found a pair of chinos that he'd forgotten about. Erik snipped off the tag of a monogrammed shirt his mother had given him at Christmas and thanked God it fit. Searching his drawers, he looked for a belt and came up short. Oh, well, he would have to go without. A quick glance in the mirror confirmed that his hair was still damp and curled in an unruly manner over his collar. Someday he would get around to cutting it.

Erik had phoned Ned seeking his advice on a place that served a plentiful brunch. True to form, the old curmudgeon suggested Ned's, but Erik had politely declined, explaining that he needed a place that was more private. Ned had taken it all in stride and then suggested Top of the Hill, a bed-and-breakfast property owned by an English couple. It was ten miles from town and sounded like the perfect place to have Sunday brunch.

For a brief instance, Erik regretted leaving his BMW back home in New York. He put Buddy in the backyard, then got into the black pickup truck he'd bought expressly for country driving. He'd thought the Beemer was way too flashy for the upstate town, but was quickly realizing that downtown Syracuse was a metropolis and the car would have fit right in.

Erik parked the truck in front of Liza's attractive Victorian home. He admired the striped awnings in front of her shop before sprinting up a geranium-lined walkway and onto a circular veranda. He rang the bell at the side door and waited.

"Be right there," Liza called.

Feeling like a schoolboy, he fidgeted with the monogram on his shirt.

The door was thrown open and Liza stood before him, wearing black walking shorts and a red linen shirt tied at the waist. Her hair had been pulled back in a ponytail. Gold earrings dangled from her ears and red sneakers adorned her feet. Erik noticed her faint scars. They made her look beautiful and vulnerable.

"Hi," she said, breaking the charged silence between them. "Come in for a moment. I have to get my purse." She moved aside and he walked in.

He entered a tiny foyer that held hanging plants and a garden bench. He proceeded to a sitting room that was cotton-candy pink with a divan, a couple of overstuffed chairs, and pastoral scenes hanging on the walls. An old harp occupied one corner.

"Sit," Liza said. "Would you like something to drink?"

"No, thank you. Do you play?" he asked, jutting his jaw to indicate the harp.

"Not a note. But isn't it pretty? I bought it at an estate sale. The price was so right I couldn't resist."

With that she left him, mounting a steep flight of stairs.

Erik stared at the back of legs that seemed to go on forever. He watched her cute little tush until it disappeared. He needed to get control of himself. Liza was his stepsister after all, not exactly a blood relation, but there was something incestuous about thinking your stepsister was sexy.

She returned carrying a black summer purse trimmed in red, looking very much the fashion model. "Ready?"

Erik unfolded his limbs and stood up. He watched Liza lock up and followed her down the same flower-strewn path.

"You've got a pickup truck," Liza said with awe, circling his vehicle. "I've always thought they were sexy."

Her comment surprised him. Liza didn't seem the type that would go for a truck. It made him wonder what other kinds of surprises she kept hidden. Gotta get his mind back on the business at hand. Brunch.

"I bought it when I decided to move up here," he answered. "It seemed more appropriate to this type of living."

"And what did you have before?" Liza asked as he unlocked the truck and held the passenger door open for her.

"I still have a BMW," he confirmed.

"Hmmm?"

What did hmmm mean? He tossed her a wry grin, wondering what she would say if she knew that it was a 700 series he owned, that plus a huge loft in trendy Soho. His concentration turned to navigating the streets. Following Ned's directions, he swung off the main roads and climbed the mountainous terrain.

"Where are we heading?" Liza asked as they passed vehicles packed with children and boating and fishing gear.

"I'm told Top of the Mountain serves a good brunch."

Liza smiled. "It sounds wonderful. I'm starving."

Her admission made him smile. An ex-model that ate? He made another right, taking them deep into the country. He slowed, pointing out deer grazing at the side of the road, then hit the brakes suddenly as a flock of gobbling turkeys darted in front of the truck.

A sign announced that he was close to the restaurant. Erik steered the truck up a narrow, steep road. A clapboard house stood at the top. He parked and went around to the passenger side, helping Liza out. She stared at the house, a delighted expression on her face.

"This is perfect, Erik. A great choice."

A middle-aged blonde came out onto the veranda, shading her eyes.

"Hello," she called in clipped British tones, "are you looking for a room?"

"No, we're here to have brunch." Erik's hand cupped Liza's elbow and they mounted steep stairs, their hostess leading the way in.

"Would you like to sit inside or out?" the blonde asked.

Erik looked to Liza. "It's totally your decision."

"Outside is quite lovely," the proprietor prompted. "It's a nice day. Better enjoy the good weather while it lasts."

"Then outside it is," Liza said, following the slender woman through a cozy lobby and toward the back of the house.

A wooden deck ran the length of the property. On it sat an eclectic group of people.

"How's this?" their hostess asked, stopping in front of a table shaded by a sunny yellow umbrella.

"Perfect," Liza pronounced. "Is this okay with you, Erik?"

It was fine by him. The table was tucked away from the others, situated in a cozy corner overlooking a garden. A fountain trickled at the center, and butterflies and assorted birds dipped down to sip the nectar of tantalizing flowers.

"Your waitress will be right over to take your order," their hostess said, leaving them.

Erik looked at Liza sitting across from him. In the clear light of day, she looked lovelier than ever. He slipped on dark glasses, afraid that his open admiration would show and most likely scare her. He didn't want her to think he'd lured her here under false pretenses.

"So tell me about these dreams of yours," he said as they waited.

"I had another one last night. I'm thrown back in time to the days of slavery. I'm toiling outdoors. An overseer shouts orders. Then one of the slaves escapes and dogs take off after him. You're in these dreams, except you're not out in the field. You're standing at the door of a house looking out at me."

Erik couldn't be more shocked. Liza's dreams mirrored his own. In some bizarre way they were connected. While he'd never entertained thoughts of reincarnation before, it merited consideration.

"I'm fascinated. Tell me more," Erik prompted.

Liza shifted uneasily in her seat. "When the dreams first started occurring I thought maybe I was losing it, going crazy, you know. I would wake up with my heart pounding, and sense there was someone or something in my bedroom."

"Yes, I know."

"How could you know?"

"Because I have similar experiences."

A hand worried the necklace at Liza's throat.

"Are you ready to order?" a freckle-faced redhead interrupted.

"Liza?"

"Bottled water, please. Fruit, toast, and scrambled egg whites."

Erik grinned. "God, that sounds healthy. I'll have grits, pancakes, orange juice, and a side order of bacon to start."

"Sounds like you're feeding an army."

Erik laughed. He'd always eaten a lot. A big guy needed sustenance, food to fuel his creativity.

After the waitress left to place their order, he asked, "When you're awake are there strange things happening in your house?"

"Like what?" Liza asked carefully.

"Items showing up that you don't own, maybe from another period. You leave something in one place and it shows up in another, that sort of thing."

"I can't say that I've had that experience . . ." Liza broke off, wrinkling her nose. "Well, last night I had an awful experience. It was as if someone were calling to me. I felt this presence but knew I was fully awake."

"I've had similar experiences," Erik confirmed. "From the moment I took over the house, I felt as if someone were living there with me."

"You, too," she whispered, staring at him in disbelief.

He nodded. The waitress chose that time to return with their coffee and tea. They sipped in silence, staring out at the garden and listening to the tinkling fountain.

"Did it come as a big surprise when Malcolm left you the house?" Liza asked when the waitress set down their food.

"Actually it did. My father had never acknowledged me."

Liza kept her eyes steadfastly on the plate in front of her. He realized he'd made her uncomfortable.

"So what do you think brought about this generosity and why did you choose to accept it?"

He paused in the middle of chewing his eggs, surprised by her directness. "Because, why look a gift horse in the mouth? It was the perfect opportunity to get out of the city. In Manhattan I sometimes found myself doing everything except painting. And my mother thought I should accept my father's gift. She figured it was his way of assuaging his conscience."

"I wish Malcolm's conscience had extended to my mother and little sister," Liza said dryly. "He left them nothing."

Erik frowned, remembering what Ned had told him. "Why would he do that? I thought your mother had run off with another man. Rumor has it my father was heartbroken."

"Heartbroken? I think not." Liza set down her knife and fork and stared at him for what seemed an eternity. "I don't condone what my mother did, but when you become an appliance in your own house, and a stranger showers attention on you, something like that inevitably happens."

"Please don't misunderstand. I'm not judging your mother. Hell, I didn't even know you existed until Ned told me."

Liza raised a sculptured eyebrow but stayed silent. He couldn't tell whether she believed him or not. "So what do you think is really going on with these dreams of ours?" she said after a while. "Frankly the whole thing scares me."

"Maybe there's a history to the houses. Someone in town should be able to fill us in."

"There's always old Sam," Liza said.

"Who's Sam?"

"He's a blind man. Close to a hundred if he's a day. It's said that he can see the past and predict the future. The locals go to him and for a small price he tells them what they need to know."

Erik listened intently while Liza talked. She was so down-to-earth, far from the vain, stuck-up types he often rubbed elbows with. In her heyday she must have had men strewing flowers at her feet, yet she'd remained totally unaffected.

"Shall we pay a visit to Sam?" he asked, polishing off his meal.

Before Liza could answer, a couple interrupted. "Aren't you Erik Price?" the heavyset woman boomed, causing every head to swivel.

"I am," Erik said reluctantly.

The woman elbowed her still-silent spouse. "See, John, I told you I was right. We saw your photo in the paper and read an article about you. John and I couldn't imagine what you would be doing up here. We were lucky enough to acquire two of your paintings." The woman turned to Liza. "You look familiar. Are you somebody?"

"She certainly is," Erik said, turning up his smile a watt. "Liza is my wife. We're on our honeymoon."

Liza made a noise as if she were choking. Erik slid his chair next to hers and patted her back.

"Are you okay? Congratulations," the woman gushed. "We're so sorry for interrupting you." She waddled off, her silent spouse following.

"I hope I didn't embarrass you," Erik said when the couple had taken their seats again. "I said the first thing that popped into my head. Hopefully we won't be interrupted again."

Liza quickly regained her composure. She finished her tea. "When should we go see Sam?"

"I was thinking maybe later this afternoon?"

"You don't waste time. Tell me, do you like your house?"

What was it with her and his house? Was she making idle conversation or was there an ulterior motive he didn't quite grasp?

"Love it. I'm starting renovations slowly. I'd like to restore it to its former glory."

He'd gotten Liza's full attention now. She sat up, a peculiar expression on her face.

"If you're spending that kind of money, you must be considering settling here."

"I'm thinking about it," Erik said, setting his napkin down.

"But isn't that house rather large for one person? What about New York? Your beautiful friends? What happens when winter comes and you get snowed in? How will you get back and forth?"

Erik stroked his chin. Liza made it sound as if it were an awful thing that he had chosen to do. "You've adjusted to Syracuse and you were once a major celebrity," he pointed out. "It's not like I have an office to go to and it can't snow forever. Syracuse has an airport and I can drive into the city. Telephones and e-mail make life easy these days."

"Yes, I suppose," Liza said, but she didn't sound pleased.

Erik signaled for the check. The conversation had taken a strange turn. His companion no longer seemed at ease and he couldn't help wondering what had brought about her sudden change of mood. He paid the bill and stood, offering her his arm.

"Let's walk around the grounds. We'll make our way to the lake eventually."

"Why not?" Liza said, placing her hand in the crook of his arm and forcing a smile.

They headed down a sloping lawn and toward the water. Erik had the strangest feeling that they'd walked this path dozens of times before. It was as if he and Liza Hamilton weren't strangers. Never had been.

6

Kalib pulled the canoe alongside the dock, secured it, and then helped Cassie out. He balanced the picnic basket he'd carefully packed in one hand and together they walked along the shore.

Kalib was easy to be with. They'd laughed and joked, staying away from topics that were too heavy.

"Hungry?" he asked after a while.

"Starving." And she was surprisingly so. The morning had been spent paddling about the lake. The combination of hot sun and rippling water made her incredibly relaxed—relaxed and hungry.

Kalib spread a blanket on the grass and began setting out food. Cassie sat cross-legged watching him remove paper plates and cutlery. Truly it was an incredible spread: assorted salads, a copious amount of cold cuts, rolls, and chicken. There was iced tea and lemonade, with cherries and melon for dessert.

"You've got food for an army," she said.

"Not an army, just two hungry people."

While they were eating Cassie asked him about his son. "How old is your boy?"

"Four and a real demon child. What about you? Do you have children?"

For a brief moment she contemplated not answering. Her ex

had custody of her two little girls and she'd been declared an unfit mother.

"Yes, I have kids," Cassie said carefully, "but they don't live with me. They live with their dad."

"How come? Sorry, no need to answer. That was a very personal question."

She wanted to answer him, wanted to explain that her lack of willpower had gotten her here. But he didn't need to hear all the gory details, at least not yet. Kalib didn't need to know that her bulimia had caused her to be hospitalized one too many times, and when she'd come home, she no longer had her children.

Jim, her ex, had petitioned the court, and successfully won custody of them. A woman with an emotional disorder couldn't be trusted to raise two rambunctious girls. He'd since remarried and he and his wife lived in San Diego, in a house that could easily put hers to shame. At least that's what the twins told her. It was roomy enough to accommodate them, plus the baby Jim's wife was carrying.

Cassie decided a nice time shouldn't be spoiled by doom and gloom. She would put a positive spin on things.

"My ex-husband was in a better position to give the girls a home," she said, biting into a sandwich that tasted like cardboard.

"That was big of you to give in without a fight. Normally the woman gets the kids. If I were you I'd be screaming bloody murder."

She'd screamed plenty but it hadn't done any good. Cassie changed the topic abruptly. "Tell me about your son. Don't you miss him when he's not with you?"

"Of course I do."

Kalib told her that little Mico was the joy of his life, that he'd tried hard to work things out with his ex-wife but she didn't seem to want to. As he spoke his face became animated and Cassie wondered if he was still in love with the wife he referred to as Scarlet. No longer hungry, she tossed her sandwich aside.

"If you're done, help me pack up." Leaning over, Kalib picked up the leftover food, plates, and napkins.

Cassie helped him gather the items. With the basket packed, he covered her hand with his. A tremor ran through Cassie's entire body, an utterly ridiculous reaction considering she'd just met the man.

"Feel like taking a hike in the woods and walking off this food?" Kalib asked, offering her his hand.

Cassie took it, liking the way his calloused palm felt in hers. He was so comfortable to be with, so completely nonthreatening. He must love women. As they trudged through the woods, Kalib carefully pointed out where there might be poison ivy and helped her through the difficult spots. After a while he sank onto a log and brought her to sit beside him.

"Whew, I'm exhausted."

"Me too. How long will you be in town?"

"I'm heading home to Long Island tomorrow. My practice is closed on Mondays but I'll be back, maybe next weekend," he said.

Cassie hoped so, and hoped that he planned on seeing her again. She wasn't about to take any chances. "Can we get together when you return?"

He smiled, apparently liking her boldness. "Plan on it. I've enjoyed your company, and I could use a friend when I'm in town." Leaning over, he kissed her.

It was a chaste kiss, one Cassie was afraid to misinterpret. Trying to cover up her jittery feelings, she jumped to her feet and hurried off. "We need to get back."

Kalib followed close behind, calling softly, "Hey, it was just a kiss and a very nice one at that. Why are you acting like a scared little rabbit?"

"Because I am scared," Cassie confessed.

"No need to be. I'm not going to hurt you. Promise."

When they reached the lake Cassie got back into the canoe without Kalib's help. He seemed hurt and looked off into the distance. "Those two people look familiar," he said, gesturing toward a tall man and his companion on the far side of the shore.

Cassie looked in the direction he pointed, her eyes bugging out of her head. "It's Liza and some guy. Come on, we'll paddle over and say hello."

"Only if you insist."

Kalib began paddling toward the opposite shore. When they got closer Cassie recognized the man with Liza. Erik Price, who would have thought? She waved at her friend, hoping to get her attention. But Liza and Erik were deep in conversation and Cassie's efforts were wasted.

"I'm going to tie up over there," Kalib said, using his paddle to point out a spot.

He brought the canoe alongside shore and helped Cassie out. Once the boat was secured they started off in the direction of Liza and Erik.

"Want to go to the street fair next week with me if I come up?" Kalib asked.

Cassie couldn't believe he was firming up a date with her. It must mean he enjoyed her company as much as she enjoyed his.

"I'd like that," Cassie said, giving his hand a little squeeze.

Liza and Erik were still in conversation when they approached.

"Fancy running into you," Cassie called when they were within shouting distance.

Liza turned, her eyes growing round. "This is a surprise. What are you two up to?"

Erik was all white teeth and bronze skin. "Such a coincidence we would choose the same locale."

"Great minds think alike," Kalib said smoothly. "Cassie and I spent the morning canoeing."

"And Liza and I decided to have brunch and then take a walk," Erik said equally as smoothly.

The conversation turned to more mundane things as the men chatted about an upcoming basketball game. While they were at it, Cassie used that opportunity to do a bit of probing. "What's with you and Picasso? Incest has never been your thing."

Liza pretended to sputter. "Erik and I aren't blood relations, so no need to get your knickers in a twist. What's with you and the gynecologist?"

"We're getting to know each other."

"Some might call that dating. Have you heard from Rona or Delilah?"

"No. Not a word since we last saw them."

"Hmmm, seems strange. Usually they're in touch. I heard Rona left the bar with that basketball player. As for Delilah, that's anyone's guess."

"Ladies," Kalib said, interrupting, "we thought we might join forces and tour the rest of the property." He placed an arm around Cassie's waist. "What do you say?"

"I'd like that," Cassie promptly answered and accepted the hand he offered.

The foursome skirted the lake, talking about this and that. About midafternoon, they decided to call it quits.

And not too soon. Cassie needed to get home to purge.

Sam held on to the woman's hands seated before him. Juanita Sanchez visited him infrequently but just by the sound of her heavy breathing he could tell that she was heavyset. She wept noisily now.

Juanita's life was a mess. She was middle-aged and her husband was dead. Two of her offspring were in jail and her only daughter had taken up with slime. Without the benefit of marriage her daughter now had four kids. All of them resided in Juanita's home. She had a leaky roof, and no prospect of having it fixed any time soon. On top of that, she'd just been to see the doctor and had received the scare of her life.

"Dr. Rabinowitz thinks I might have breast cancer," Juanita sobbed loudly.

Sam concentrated really hard, absorbing her aura and letting the heat from Juanita's hand encompass him. He called on the spirits to help him see what was in store for this poor, sad woman. It wasn't good. For a moment he debated lying to her.

That wasn't fair. She was paying him with what little money she'd saved.

"Juanita, I think you need one of them mam . . . uhh . . . mam, X ray things."

"Mammograms, you mean?"

"Yes. Mam whatever."

"Dr. Rabinowitz already set me up at the clinic. Sam, you need to tell me what I'll find. I need to prepare myself. Prepare the family."

"Cancer ain't the death sentence it used to be," Sam said, stalling.

"But the lump's big, very big. Here, you feel it."

Juanita rustled around for a while, then thrust a limp piece of flesh into his hand. While Sam couldn't see her large breast, he sure as hell could feel it. It wasn't proper, him sitting here with Juanita's breast in his hand, squeezing it.

"I'm not a doctor," he said, hedging, and handing the droopy flesh back to her. Damn his dead libido. In his youth he would have taken advantage of the gift she'd just given him. Juanita needed comforting.

"You gotta tell me, Sam," Juanita cried. "Do I have cancer or not? I need to know so as I can put things in order."

"I don't know, Juanita," he said. But he did know.

"Sam, I need the truth."

"It ain't good," he answered, realizing he could no longer read her. It was as if she were no longer there in physical form and he could see no future ahead for her.

"I'm dying, ain't I, Sam?"

"You need to get this thing taken care of. Go get that X ray soon."

"I'm scheduled for next week," Juanita said.

"Good. After they done with you, you come back and see me. I'll read you for free."

Juanita sniveled and blew her nose. He heard her fumbling through her pocketbook, searching for money, he would guess. She thrust some bills into his hand, shifted her bulk, and stood.

"I'll come back to see you soon as I get it done. You'll tell me how long I have."

"You do that, Juanita," Sam said, as a feeling of sadness descended over him. Poor old Juanita was on borrowed time.

Sam heard a tapping at his front door. He frowned. He wasn't expecting anyone and his food had already come.

"Want me to get that?" Juanita asked, her heavy footsteps already heading toward the door.

"Sure."

He heard her open the door and her wheezing inquiry, "You here to see Sam?"

"Yes, is he in?" a man asked.

Sam didn't recognize the voice. It didn't have the usual Syracuse twang. He concentrated and it came to him. It was that new man in town, Malcolm's son. He hadn't come alone. He'd brought the beautiful Hamilton woman with him. She was beautiful but haunted and had seen tragedy in her life. That Erik Price was drawn to her because their lives were interconnected.

"Come in," Juanita said. "I was just leaving."

Two sets of footsteps headed his way.

"See you next week, Sam," Juanita called, slamming the front door behind her.

Sam pulled himself out of his funk and concentrated on the new arrivals, wondering what had brought them here.

Malcolm's son was supposed to be a big-time artist and the Hamilton girl had been a famous model. Why had they chosen to come to his humble abode? Sam remembered his manners and gestured to where he thought the chairs might be.

"I'm Sam O'Reilly. Find yourself a seat," he said, hoping that somewhere in the cluttered room two chairs might be debris-free.

"I'm Erik Price and this is Liza Hamilton."

He heard rubbish shift and bodies settle. Good, they'd found places to sit.

"What brings you to me?" Sam asked.

"We're hoping that you could provide us with information about our respective homes," Erik answered in a deep baritone.

"You inherited Malcolm Mitchell's house and Miss Hamilton bought Blanche Lucas's property. Am I right?"

"You're right and very well informed."

Sam rubbed his forehead. "What is it you would like me to tell you?"

Liza spoke up. "I'd like to hear about Blanche's experiences when she lived in my house. I'd also like to hear about the previous occupants. Did any of them die there?"

Sam thought long and hard before saying, "Blanche owned that house for approximately thirty years. She and her late husband seemed to be very happy in it."

"I don't doubt that. What I want to know is, did they ever experience strange happenings in my house?"

"Strange happenings like what?" Sam asked.

"Like a presence living there with them? Like peculiar dreams?"

Sam hesitated for a moment, reluctant to say what he knew. Should he tell this eager young woman about the house's real history? He'd liked her mother, Elizabeth, who'd come to him upon several occasions asking for guidance. He made up his mind. She deserved to know.

"Your house is said to be haunted by the ghosts who once used it as a safe house. Several of the slaves never made it to Canada. And yes, some did die there."

"Are you saying Liza's house was a stop on the Underground Railroad?" Erik asked, cutting to the chase.

"Yes, and so was your current home and that nursery school a few feet from my door. It used to be an old church."

"That would explain why our dreams overlap," Erik said, sounding excited.

"It's more complicated than that. You were lovers in another life," Sam said with such certainty that he heard their collective gasps.

"Lovers?" Liza sputtered. "We're stepsister and stepbrother."

"In this life, maybe. But you're old souls forever bound together. Those reincarnated come back to earth to work out issues that were unresolved in a previous life."

Sam figured they must think him crazy. But he was one of the few people still alive that could verify that their experiences weren't unusual. Isn't that why they had come to him?

Erik Price rose and the chair squeaked. His companion also got up, joining him.

"How much do we owe you?" Erik asked, standing so close he could smell the turpentine still clinging to his hands.

"Whatever you can give me."

A purse opened and snapped shut.

"I'll take care of it," Erik said.

"No, no, I insist." A crisp bill rustled as Liza extracted it.

Cash was slapped into Sam's palm. Judging by the size of the wad, Sam had the feeling that money wouldn't be a problem this month. He could pay his electric bill and phone, buy some groceries, and not feel poor.

"Thank you," Erik said. "You've been most helpful. We'll be in touch."

Sam knew they would be back. He had answers they needed.

7

Delilah slammed down the phone for what seemed the ump-teenth time. Where were all her friends when she needed them? Liza could always be relied on to be home, and Cassie, well, Cassie was another story. That girl had problems.

Girlfriend thought no one knew about her bulimia, when in fact everyone did. No one stayed that thin simply by watching what they ate. Cassie never counted a single calorie, at least out loud, but they all knew she was in therapy and how many times she'd been hospitalized.

Rona, on the other hand, was one of those sociable creatures that never stayed home. She had more friends than anyone Delilah knew, except for herself. On Sundays she visited around town. But this Sunday that wasn't the case. Delilah had driven through the neighborhood and knocked on a few doors but no one had seen Rona. Mrs. Wilkins next door had said that Rona's car hadn't been in the driveway for quite some time. That worried Delilah.

With no one to play with, Delilah sulked. She had all this time on her hands and her friends had deserted her. Saturday night at Wine and Roses had been a major disappointment. She'd drifted from one man to the other, but most had set their sights on other women, and for the first time in a long time she'd ended up going home alone.

Delilah decided it was time to snap out of her dreary mood, keep busy, and take control. No point in staying at home. She'd drive over to Liza's and see if that bitch was simply ignoring her ringing phone.

Ten minutes later, Delilah had the top down on her fire-red Cabriolet and the music cranked up. She'd squeezed into a brand-new sundress that she'd been saving for when she lost weight. It hugged every curve and she felt vibrant and sexy.

Liza's Camry was parked in the driveway, which meant she was home. Delilah strode purposefully up the walkway and pressed a thumb firmly on the doorbell. She planned on giving her friend an earful when she answered.

Several moments went by, then several moments more. Still no Liza. Delilah depressed the button again, holding it down for at least thirty seconds.

"Liza," she called. "Open up. It's Delilah."

Liza might be moody but it didn't seem right that she would intentionally ignore a friend. Delilah stomped off, circling the house, and stopping to peer into the kitchen window where the curtains were open.

Inside was spotless, all gleaming tile counters and glass-front cabinets, but no sign of Liza. Puzzled, Delilah retraced her steps. Liza didn't have much of a life outside of her consignment shop, up until a couple of days ago when she'd appeared interested in Erik. That had pissed Delilah off. Liza was supposedly over men. And Erik Price was her stepbrother.

The temptation to drive over to Erik's was too much to resist. Delilah aimed the Cabriolet in that direction. She would never admit it but she'd always been jealous of Liza. Success had come to the bitch at an early age. Liza had lived a life of privilege, hobnobbing with beautiful people, while Delilah's life had always been a struggle and one filled with stress.

It was Liza whose face had adorned the cover of every magazine. She'd been drooled over by rich and poor men of every conceivable age and ethnicity. She'd acquired a large sum of money in a relatively short time and she'd invested well. The ex-supermodel knew anyone worth knowing. What Delilah couldn't figure out was why she was hiding out in Syracuse, playing at the shop.

Erik's pickup truck was noticeably absent from the driveway. Delilah sighed out her relief. She'd set her sights on Erik Price and if Liza was interested in him, things weren't going to be pretty.

What to do now. The entire Sunday afternoon stretched ahead. She could go see if Rona was home yet, she supposed. But Rona was dull; the only thing she talked about were her children.

"That Rona's a sly dog," Delilah said out loud, stepping on the accelerator. Rona had been last seen leaving the bar with Tim Delaney, that pro basketball player. Tim could have virtually any woman he wanted, so why he'd picked Rona was beyond her.

Delilah hurried up the walkway leading to Rona's apartment. She sidestepped children riding bikes and playing ball. She trudged up two flights of stairs, then down a dim hallway, and came to apartment 2J. She rang the bell and waited.

After a while, a muffled query came. "Who is it?"

"It's Delilah," she answered, feeling an amazing sense of relief that one of her friends was home.

The door was thrown open and Rona regarded her warily. She looked rumpled and tired as if she hadn't had much sleep.

"Hey, girl. What brings you over?" Rona smothered a yawn.

"I was worried about you. I tried reaching Liza and Cassie but no one's home. Can I come in?"

"Sure." Rona stepped aside, allowing Delilah to enter. Her tiny living room wasn't as neat as it normally was, and judging by the sheet and pillow on the couch, she'd been napping.

"So where is everyone?" Delilah asked, taking a seat on a comfortable chair.

Rona shrugged and yawned again. "Damn if I know. Last I saw of Cassie and Liza they were with us at Wine and Roses." She sank onto the couch.

"You mean you haven't heard or seen them since?"

"Nope."

This was getting stranger and stranger. Cassie and Liza had virtually disappeared. Delilah wondered if Kalib Moore had to do with Cassie being missing.

"You look beat," Delilah said, giving Rona the once-over.

"I am. I haven't had much sleep."

Delilah, never one to beat around the bush, asked, "How come?"

Was it her imagination or was Rona having a difficult time looking her in the eye?

"I'm overworked, stressed," Rona said, sinking onto the couch.

"Yeah, right," Delilah said. "You work five days a week taking care of kids. It's exhausting but you have the weekends to rest. Spill it, girl."

"I got in late," Rona admitted.

"And why's that?"

Rona yawned again, adjusting her body into a more comfortable position on the couch. "It's a long story."

Delilah narrowed her eyes. "I've got all afternoon. Your lack of sleep have anything to do with Tim Delaney?"

Rona's eyes were already half closed. "Maybe. If you want something to drink there's soda and juice in the fridge."

"I'm okay. Now tell me what's going on."

While waiting for an answer, Delilah got out of the chair and made her way to the stereo. She fumbled with the dials, found a station she could stomach, and waited.

"You sleep with Tim Delaney?" she asked when Rona was still quiet.

"What?"

"All's I know is that my three best girlfriends deserted me this weekend. One may be with Erik Price, the other with the Moore man. You can barely move, and I, the one who never has problems getting men, have a barren weekend. Go figure."

Rona burst out laughing. "Oh, Delilah, stop sounding like such a victim. You and I both know that if you set your sights on a man, he's yours. You're alone because you want to be alone."

Not true. Not this time. "My efforts don't seem to be working with Erik Price."

"So he should be a challenge."

"Not if I'm competing with his stepsister."

"You're competing with Liza?" Rona jolted into an upright position. "Liza hasn't been interested in a man since that no-good fiancé of hers up and left her. You can't be serious."

"Serious as hell. Where is she today? She's not home."

"The woman is entitled to go out, you know. That doesn't mean she's with Erik Price

"I bet you she is, and I'm going to prove it to you."

"How?"

Delilah thought for a moment. "You and I are going to take a drive over to Liza's place. We're going to sit on her verandah and wait until she comes home."

"We're not," Rona said, sounding truly appalled.

"Oh, yes, we are. Grab your purse, girlfriend. We're on our way over."

Liza wanted to hate Erik, but instead she found herself liking him more and more. She sat next to him in the pickup truck, painfully aware of his masculinity. His shoulders touched hers and the heat coming from his skin seared her. She had to keep reminding herself that he'd stolen her mother and Sara's inheritance.

Running into Cassie and Kalib had been a big surprise. They seemed to be getting along well and Liza was happy for Cassie. God knew her life hadn't been easy. She'd been crazy about her husband and devoted to those girls. But Cassie had always been insecure, and that illness of hers had taken over, ruining everything. Liza wondered if she was still seeing her therapist and trying to master her bulimia, or if she had simply given up and allowed it to control her life.

"What's got you looking so down?" Erik asked, breaking into her musings.

Liza smiled at him. He was so in tune. No man with the remnants of morning shadow should look that good. "I was just thinking what a coincidence it was to run into Cassie and Kalib."

"Small world," Erik said dryly, making a right and turning down a narrow road.

Liza focused on his hands, long fingers loosely holding the steering wheel. Hands that she bet would feel right at home on her body.

"That was quite a story the old man had to tell," Erik said abruptly, with skepticism in his voice.

She felt the need to defend Sam. "He would have no reason to lie."

"It's strange that you and I would choose places to live that were depots on the Underground Railroad. Maybe he made it up."

Had they chosen those homes or had the homes chosen them? She didn't want to go there. She already felt guilty that her motivation for going out with Erik wasn't entirely pure.

When they pulled into her driveway, Liza spotted Rona and Delilah sitting on the porch. She huffed in a breath and hurried from the pickup truck before Erik could come around to the passenger door.

"Thanks for a nice day. Stay in touch," she said, waving to him and making her way up the walkway.

"You do that as well," he said, backing out of the driveway.

Delilah and Rona stopped talking as she approached. Delilah looked as if she had swallowed something sour. Liza wondered what had brought that about. Then Liza surmised that because Delilah had set her sights on Erik, she was not happy to see that Erik had spent the day with her.

"Hey," Liza said, forcing joy into her voice. "Nice of you to visit."

Rona shaded her eyes with one hand and stood. "We came over because we were worried about you. Delilah thought something might have happened."

"Nice of you to be concerned. Want a glass of wine or something?"

Delilah shook her head. "Nah. Now that we know you're all right, we'll be heading home."

"Oh, come on," Liza said, walking by them. "Come inside and we'll have a drink."

Reluctantly the women followed her. They took seats around the kitchen table and Liza got a bottle of Chardonnay from the refrigerator and poured three glasses.

An uneasy silence prevailed, broken only by Delilah's nails drumming against the mahogany table. After a while Rona spoke up.

"So what's the real deal with you and Erik?"

"There is no deal," Liza answered, sipping her drink. She wasn't ready to admit that she was using him.

"Bullshit," Delilah spat out. "You and Erik were pretty cozy last night. He just dropped you off at your front door, which must mean you spent the day together."

"That's hardly a crime. And it's none of your business." Liza eyed Delilah warily over the rim of her glass.

Rona, ever the peacemaker, shifted uneasily. "Maybe we should leave. Let's give Liza her space. I've got stuff to do to get ready for the little monsters tomorrow."

"I'm not ready to leave," Delilah huffed, settling in more comfortably. "I want to know why a friend of mind would deliberately go after a man I'm interested in."

Liza slammed down her wineglass and stood. She glared at Delilah. "This isn't just ridiculous, it's utterly insane. If you want the man, then take him, he's yours."

Delilah splayed her hands on the table. "If it were that easy I would. But I don't think he would give me the time of day. You have managed to get in the way."

Liza threw her hands in the air. "This is ridiculous. Rona's right. You better leave. I've had a long day and I'm going to take a shower."

Snapping her ponytail she stalked off.

*   *   *

From the moment Erik entered his house he sensed that something wasn't right. Buddy was restless and the hair on his back stood up. Erik walked through each room unable to shake the uncanny feeling that someone had been in his house. Nothing was touched but his gut told him that someone had been wandering around, snooping.

His bedroom was in the same state he'd left it, the huge bed unmade and the rumpled bedclothes piled at the bottom. Erik stripped off his clothes, stepped into the same pair of shorts he'd left on the floor, and entered the huge walk-in closet. He found a clean T-shirt and put it on. Buddy whimpered.

"What's the matter boy?"

The Labrador looked at him adoringly.

It had been an enlightening day overall, one that he had thoroughly enjoyed. Spending time with Liza Hamilton had been both titillating and relaxing, until she'd started quizzing him about his house. Her questions weren't prompted by idle curiosity and he'd gone instantly on alert. After visiting Sam, he'd squelched his suspicions, figuring that her interest must have something to do with the shared experience they were having.

Enough of Liza Hamilton. He would put her out of his head. He'd moved to Syracuse to get away from busy city life and concentrate on painting. Determined to do just that, he started up the attic stairs.

A sweet, cloying scent filled his nostrils. Lilies. It brought back memories of the grandmother he had loved so much. She'd always smelled faintly like the flower. The odor prevailed, intermingling with the more pungent smell of turpentine, oils, and paints. Grabbing a brush and rag, Erik stepped up to his easel. The canvas he'd been working on was no longer there. It had been replaced by the expressive, pained face of the turbaned woman.

Erik could almost feel her hurt. He stepped back as a searing pain ricocheted through his chest, causing his vision to blur. He tried steadying himself, even shook his head, hoping to clear it.

When he was able to focus again, the painting he'd been working on was back on the easel and the turbaned woman had disappeared.

He had not imagined it. His chest was still tight and his breathing restricted. The smell of lilies hung in the air, and in the distance the labored strains of "Swing Low, Sweet Chariot" were loud and clear. Maybe he was losing his mind.

Sam O'Reilly's words echoed. His house was haunted. The old man had said it was a station on the Underground Railroad, a safe haven for slaves. Could the spirits of his ancestors still be alive in this house? It was a bizarre thought and one that made his skin crawl.

Erik turned his attention back to the canvas and let his creativity go to work. Better to chronicle the sad, contemporary lives of those still living.

One hour later he was still at it until his fingers began to cramp and his head hurt from concentrating. Mercifully, the doorbell rang and although he was not expecting visitors, answering it was a welcome distraction.

"I'm coming down," he shouted to his visitor, taking a brief moment to wipe his hands on a soiled rag. He took the rag with him.

Erik's mind was still on his portrait as he bounded down the stairs, Buddy following. The bell pealed again. This time more insistently.

"Hold on. I'm coming," he shouted.

The silhouette of a woman was seen through the smoked-glass panes of the door. Liza had returned. He threw the door open and Delilah Kincaid came clearly into view. He hoped his disappointment didn't show as she stood, hands on her hips, regarding him.

"Hi," Delilah said. "I thought you could use company."

Damn, she was persistent. He'd never cared for aggressive types and Delilah was becoming a real pain. Erik managed a smile.

"You caught me just before I hopped in the shower," he said, wiping his hands again on the soiled rag.

"Then I arrived in time. Did you enjoy your pie?"

What on earth was she talking about? *Oh, yeah, the pie.* The bag he'd forgotten on the table at Wine and Roses. "What did you arrive in time for?" he asked.

"To shower with you. It's been a long miserable day."

Rendered momentarily speechless, he tried gathering his wits and making light of it. "Then a hot bath at home might be just what the doctor ordered."

Delilah's eyes scanned his body and settled on his crotch.

"I'm not interested," Erik said bluntly.

His rudeness didn't seem to bother her. She shrugged, her ample breasts heaving. "Come on now, men never turn down sex."

She was up in his face, so close he could smell her cloying perfume. It made him nauseous. Erik stepped back, placing a safe distance between them. Buddy growled. He didn't like her either.

"I'm sorry, hon. I'm not interested in anything you're offering. And I'm especially not interested in a quick roll in the hay."

"Who says it has to be quick?" Delilah challenged, standing her ground. "If you like we could make this a long-standing arrangement."

"I'm not into arrangements. Go home, Delilah."

Delilah snorted, her hand reaching out to tickle his chest. "You're a challenge, playing hard to get. We would be so good together."

"Go home, Delilah."

She threw him a wink and Erik watched her waddle off. He shut the door and pressed his back against it.

Wheew! He was safe.

8

Mondays were slow and this Monday followed the usual pattern. Liza spent the morning in the back room inventorying stock and calculating the appropriate pricing. She refused to think of Erik Price and how attractive he was. It confused her that she actually liked him.

Her cell phone rang just as she was thinking that coffee would be nice. Empty cup in hand, she depressed the button on the third jingle.

"Hello."

"Hi, honey," her mother cooed. "Haven't heard from you in quite some time. Is everything okay?"

"Everything's fine, Mom. I've been busy."

The predictable reply came. "Too busy for your old mom, I see."

Elizabeth's gentle chastisement reminded Liza of how close they once were. She should keep in touch but somehow time seemed to get away.

Liza prepared herself for the lecture that would inevitably follow. And sure enough it came. She and Elizabeth weren't that close, but she did love her mother, and she was crazy about her problematic teenage sister.

"You'll never guess who I met recently," Liza said after the tirade had ended.

"I'm not good at guessing games; you know that."

"Erik Price, Ma, Malcolm's son."

"Malcolm's illegitimate son? The one he left his house to?"

"You got it."

The doorbell jingled and a group of people entered, quickly dispersing throughout the store. "How did you meet him?" Elizabeth asked.

Liza told her, intentionally omitting that she had gone to brunch with Erik.

"What's he like?"

"He's pleasant enough." *Downplay reality. He is gorgeous.* "Have you given any thought to contesting Malcolm's will?"

Elizabeth groaned. "What would be the point?"

"The point is that my sister would get a property that's rightfully hers. You could sell that house and use the money for college. Maybe you'll even have a little left over. Ma, Malcolm left Sara nothing."

"I know, I know. I already contacted Paul White."

"And what did he say?"

"He thinks I might have a good shot of winning. Malcolm was not of sound mind when he left his property to that boy."

"I'll talk to Paul as well," Liza offered. "I'll let him know you'll be following up."

Paul was an old friend and an attorney she trusted.

The doorbell jingled again. "I have to run, Ma. The place is getting busy. But I want you to think about this. Phillip should not have to put Sara through college, nor should he be expected to."

"Litigation is such a headache," Elizabeth groaned. "It's tiresome and could drag on for years."

"Nothing ventured, nothing gained," Liza said firmly. "Erik Price isn't broke."

"Did I hear my name?" a gravelly voice behind her said.

Liza spun around to find Erik browsing through a rack of fatigue jackets. Her cheeks did a slow burn. She didn't know when Erik had entered, and she wasn't sure how much he'd heard. His attention was now focused on the jacket he was holding. He held it up to check its size.

"Hey, do you think this will fit?"

To cover her embarrassment, Liza gestured to a standing mirror. "If you like it, try it on."

"Liza, are you there?" her mother called

"Sorry, Ma, I was talking to a customer." She ended the conversation, promising to call in a few days.

Erik's morning shadow had deepened. It looked like he might be growing a beard. For the twentieth time or so, Liza realized how incredibly good looking he was. He shrugged on the army jacket and with an imperious raise of his eyebrows, examined himself in the full-length mirror.

Liza tried not to gape when he buttoned the faded fatigue across the breadth of his chest. On Erik, army green and denim were a lethal combination. He looked both regal and bohemian, and very much in command. Liza lowered her eyes, pushing the carnal thoughts away.

"Well?" Erik asked, splaying his arms. "Should I buy it?"

"It fits."

It more than fit. It was made for him.

"Sold then."

Liza came closer, flipping over the price tag. "Don't you want to know how much it costs?"

"Wrap it up," Erik said, stripping off the jacket to reveal a black T-shirt and well-defined pectorals.

Dry-mouthed, Liza rang up the sale. She accepted Erik's credit card, folded up the jacket, and placed it in a bag.

"Do you have plans for next weekend?" Erik asked, giving her that killer grin.

Oh, Gawd, he was asking her out.

"Next weekend is five days away. But no, I don't have plans. I don't make plans that far in advance."

"Then it's settled. We'll go to the street fair together."

What a cocky son of a B. She should turn him down flat.

Things would only get more complicated if they spent any more
time together. Befriending him would be a mistake, especially if
her mother decided to sue the man.

"I'd love to," she heard herself say.

"Pick you up on Sunday then. We'll go to brunch."

All she could do was shake her head. What was wrong with
her? Why hadn't she said no?

Erik retrieved his purchase and made a beeline for the door.
He turned and said, "Almost forgot, I had the strangest thing
happen yesterday after I dropped you off."

A customer carrying an armful of clothing looked exasperated. She really should help her but she was eager to hear what
Erik had to say.

"If I buy three items will you give me a discount?" the woman
whined.

"Sure."

What possessed her to say that? She didn't give discounts.
When Liza looked up again, Erik had left.

Another long, boring day lay ahead. There were times Sam
wished he were dead. He'd had difficulty sleeping. He'd tossed
and turned, and when he'd finally dozed off, Erik Price and
Elizabeth's girl, Liza, had featured in his dreams.

The dream had started off as it usually did, in a time and
place where slavery was an accepted way of life. Liza was toiling in the fields while Erik, who'd earned the right to work in-
doors, tended to the household. The dream had then shifted to
the twenty-first century. The couple was free, prosperous, and
married with children. They lived in the house that Erik currently occupied.

Sam had known from the moment he met them that Liza
and Erik had a shared destiny. Yet he had a strange premonition that there would be difficult times ahead. But, no pain, no
gain, or so the saying went. He concentrated on what he would
do with his day, remembering he'd been invited by Rona to the
nursery school to tell stories to the children, something he peri-
odically did.

Sam loved the babies, loved their innocence, and loved their naiveté. They were so honest. They made him feel young, invigorated, and refreshed, and guilty for wanting to die.

Aided by his walking stick, Sam managed to make his way into the tiny bathroom and into the shower. He propped his body against the cool tile wall and thought about Juanita. She'd never gotten back to him and he was worried about her. Something cold slithered across his foot and Sam kicked out, almost losing his footing. One day he would slip, crack his head open, and lie on the cold bathroom floor bleeding to death.

Sam had come close to falling several times. Now he stepped cautiously from the stall, navigated his way down a cluttered hallway, and into the bedroom. He felt around the room for some freshly laundered clothing that Maisie's worthless niece had brought him the day before.

Searching his bed yielded nothing but the rumpled sheets he'd slept on last evening. Sam cursed under his breath.

"Damn you. You're at it again."

Here he was standing, an old towel wrapped around his flabby middle, looking for clothes to put on. He would try the dresser drawers but normally Vanessa did not put his items away. He was lucky if she showed up, shoved food and clothing at him, and grunted that she would be back in a day or two.

The first drawer held odds and ends he'd collected over the years but no clothes. The second held socks, ties and underwear he'd forgotten about. The third drawer held what he was looking for.

"One of you must have been a mother," Sam muttered, stepping into his underwear and balancing himself so that the legs of his denims did not tangle him up. He slipped on a starched oxford shirt, had trouble finding a belt, and then decided to use a tie to hold his pants up.

He was ready at last.

Outside he could hear the children yelling as they played tag and raced for the woods. He wished he had their energy and zest. As he approached the door of the nursery school, now serving as a summer camp, he felt light-headed again. Sam leaned against the wall, hoping the spell would pass.

A feeling of sadness and foreboding settled around Sam. He sensed that the couple he'd just seen as clear as day would go through a series of tests. Before the month was over with, one if not both would face danger. Goose bumps popped up on his arms and cold sweat beaded his forehead. Someone should guide those two. Maybe he would enlist Ned's help.

Needing fresh air, and the sounds of living, active people, he grabbed his cane and exited the house.

Outside, the sun felt good against his face and the late August breeze was invigorating. Sam tapped his way across the yard, following the sound of excited high-pitched voices. There was a time when crossing that yard was as routine as breathing. He'd cleaned and cared for that old church for years; now life had changed and he could barely clean himself.

He was an old man now, whiling away time, waiting to die. His days no longer held purpose. He lived for his visitors and the trips back and forth to the nursery school where he played resident storyteller. He only kept up with the community because of Ned, his best friend, and his ever-present visions.

"Hey, Sam," Rona greeted him when he entered the building. She took his arm and pulled him inside the cool interior. Raised, high-pitched voices and the smell of hot, sweaty bodies assaulted his senses. For a brief moment he felt young and alive.

A small body flung itself against him, grasping him around the knees and almost knocking him off balance.

"Sam, Sam. I missed you. Tell me a story, Sam. Tell us about when you were a young man and worked in the church."

Sam stroked a curly mop of hair and tried to place the child.

He felt another set of hands hugging his thighs and a young girl's voice say, "I love you, Sam. Will you stay and have lunch with us?"

"Of course I will, sweetheart."

It felt good to have someone say they loved him. It had been a while since he'd basked in anyone's worship.

"Children, children," Rona admonished. "Settle down. Let Sam find a seat."

Rona's hand remained on his elbow, leading him through a maze of children and fingers tugging at him. She settled him in a chair, clapped her hands to get the kids' attention, and announced, "Story time, everyone. Gather around."

Sam heard the delighted squeals of the children as they pushed and shoved, jostling each other to find seats. The room had heated up with their warm bodies and Sam loved the attention they heaped on him. He felt invigorated and energized by the life they pumped into him.

"Tell us about the time the minister forgot his sermon," a voice Sam recognized as six-year-old Jeremiah's pleaded.

"No, I want to hear about the time when Sam first met Ned," another of the young girls begged.

"How about a new story, one we haven't heard before?" a hoarse voice called, garnering the attention of the others.

"Yes, please. We'd like a new one."

Sam was transported to another time when he was young, able, and his body didn't betray him. He'd just gotten done cleaning the altar and had taken a moment to sink into a pew, close his eyes, and say a word of prayer. He'd been married at that time, and his son, the joy of his existence, had been running a fever. He and his wife had taken the child to the emergency room, but because they did not have insurance they had been turned away.

Young James remained at home tended by his mother. Overnight the fever had shot up and the boy was close to hallucinating. Desperate, Sam was ready to do anything for money. He knew where the minister kept his Sunday collection and he was tempted to run off with the entire stash. Providence had intervened. That was the story he would tell.

Sam slowly began his tale. The children listened raptly, every now and again interrupting with questions. He told them all about how temptation had taken over and how he had been prepared to rob the minister and congregation that had been so good to him. As he'd sat with his head bowed, the minister came up to him and handed him an envelope with the money he so desperately needed. He'd found out about James's illness, and a small group had collected the funds so that his child could see a doctor and get the necessary medication. He'd been so ashamed.

"The moral of the story is never give in to temptation," Sam said, finishing up. "The Lord will provide for you. He always comes through."

The children were quiet, contemplating what he had said. Sam wasn't a particularly religious man, but the Lord had indeed looked out for him. His had been a relatively good life and now he was close to passing over. He still missed his wife and son and couldn't wait to be reunited with them.

"Sam, I have a new friend," one of the children said, wrapping sticky hands around his neck.

"Good. It's nice to make new friends."

Sam had envisioned the child's friend the minute he entered the classroom. The boy had been bedraggled and didn't wear shoes.

"Lela has a healthy imagination," Rona said, coming between them. "She keeps going on about this friend. It's natural at her age to have imaginary friends."

The spirits were at it again, befriending a child they thought worthy. Lela might not know it yet but she'd been carefully chosen. Time would tell if she had the gift.

"Lunch is ready," Rona interjected. "Can you stay?"

"Sure. If it ain't too much trouble."

He was starving. The cook at the nursery school made meals that he liked, things like macaroni and cheese, peanut butter and grape jelly sandwiches, and hamburgers and French fries as a special treat. It beat the stuff Maisie or her niece delivered.

Lela clapped her hands, announcing to anyone who would listen, "Sam's staying for lunch. Maybe he'll tell us another story."

"Yes, Sam, please," one of the children pleaded.

"Only if you're good," Sam said, feeling wanted. He loved his young fans even if many were only five years old.

Rona led him to the table and helped him find a seat. He

heard the clang of a plate being set down and the tinny sound of cutlery. A heavenly aroma that smelled like meat loaf filled the room. Sam ate the portion placed before him and stifled a belch. He definitely should come by more often.

"Sam, Sam," Lela said, tugging on his shirtsleeve. "My friend, Thaddeus, told me he likes your stories. Meat loaf's his favorite, too."

"Where is Thaddeus now?" Sam asked, wiping his lips.

The child shrugged. "I guess he disappeared."

Sam focused and saw the dark-skinned boy with the nappy hair clearly. He was dressed in tattered clothing, wore no shoes, and had a brand on him usually reserved for chattel. He remembered hearing of a young boy who'd died at the minister's home. Supposedly a young slave couple and their child had made it to the station. The couple died in a fire and the child was lost to pneumonia shortly thereafter.

"I don't see any little boy," Sam lied, concerned that the other children might be alarmed.

"Then Thaddeus is playing hide-and-seek with you. He does that sometimes," Lela said, sighing. "Thaddeus, you bad boy, show yourself to Sam.

And Thaddeus did.

9

A customer came breezing through the front door just as Delilah was putting together two huge arrangements for the church. Delilah peered at the woman over the top of several red gladiolas and smiled.

"Morning, can I help you?"

The redhead, assessing the bouquets through the refrigerated glass doors, cocked her head to the side. "I'm undecided," she said, shoving a fistful of flaming red hair out of her face. "I'm having a dinner party tomorrow tonight, maybe a dozen or so people. I'd like something that's not too terribly expensive, but also festive and fun."

"I've got just the thing." Delilah stepped from behind the counter and faced the woman. She was sure her customer was new to town. "Peonies are always a nice touch. They'll give your place a summery feel."

Delilah pointed to the pink flowers that were carefully arranged in a bucket. "You can place them in individual vases. They show nicely on their own."

"What a wonderful idea. I thought a dinner party would be a nice way to meet people. Everyone's supposed to bring a single friend. Erik Price, the artist, is coming and the basketball star Tim Delaney. Having a group will take the pressure off."

"Sounds like fun. How do you know Erik?" Delilah asked, her mind going into overdrive figuring how she could wangle an invitation.

"He and I are business acquaintances and the real reason I'm here. By the way, I'm Sunny."

Delilah introduced herself, shaking the woman's hand. What was their true relationship? she wondered.

"I know Erik," Delilah offered.

"Do you now?" Tawny eyes roamed over Delilah. "I'll take the peonies."

After the flowers were wrapped, Sunny held them in the crook of her arm and beamed at Delilah. "You should come to my dinner party."

Delilah flexed a wrist. "Oh, I couldn't do that."

"Yes, you can. You'll make thirteen, a lucky number for me."

"Who else is coming?" Delilah asked, wondering if there might be other names she recognized and opportunities to work it.

"Let's see now. Liza Hamilton, the ex-model who owns the consignment shop. We ran in the same circles in New York before that unfortunate incident." Sunny named another four people that Delilah sort of knew, adding, "And they're all bringing single friends. Hint, hint."

"Hmmmm," Delilah said, "Liza and I are good friends but she never mentioned your party. Maybe I'll come with her."

"She may be bringing someone," Sunny responded, tawny eyes twinkling.

That did it. "Thanks for the invitation. I'll be there."

"I'll look forward to seeing you then," Sunny said, one hand digging through her pocketbook and finding an envelope that looked like an invitation. "My address and phone number are listed on this."

"I'll bring wine," Delilah said, thanking her.

"Make it both red and white," Sunny tossed over her shoulder, letting herself out.

*   *   *

Cassie had just taken a pie out of the oven when the phone rang. She set down the dish and wiped her hands on a towel, then lifted the receiver.

"Sweet Eats," she said breathlessly, one eye on the outer room where the student she'd hired waited on a couple who couldn't make up their mind.

"Hey," a deep male voice said. "You sound busy."

Cassie's heart thudded in her chest. She hadn't expected to hear from Kalib so soon.

"I am. Today's my baking day."

"What are you cooking up? Anything good?"

"Lots of good stuff. Primarily cakes and pies."

"Sounds heavenly," Kalib said, smacking his lips loudly. "I won't keep you long. Are we on for next weekend?"

How sweet of Dr. Kalib Moore to secure a date before someone else stepped in. Not that there was anyone else, mind you, but he didn't need to know that. Kalib was the catch of the season and Cassie was flattered and delighted that he'd called, but she didn't want to sound too excited.

"Next weekend, let's see." Like she had anything to do.

"Yes, it's the street fair, remember?"

"That's right, I almost forgot." Cassie kept an eye on the shop, which was now quite busy.

"Well, don't sound so excited."

"I am. I'm looking forward to seeing you again."

"Likewise. Wear something comfortable."

Cassie's stomach began to rumble. Things were happening much too fast. She welcomed Kalib's attention but would he really like her once he got to know her?

"You'll pick me up?" she asked, her stomach roiling and the cereal she'd eaten for breakfast threatening to expel itself.

"I absolutely will," Kalib answered. "And I'll call you the moment I get into town and we'll discuss what time."

He blew her a kiss through the earpiece. Cassie quickly hung up as her stomach did another roll. Ignoring the patrons that were now almost two lines deep, she raced for the bathroom and relief.

*   *   *

Rona checked the knob on the front door to make sure she'd locked up and the building was secure. The last child had been picked up early and it felt good to be heading home while the sun was still up. A sporty red number was parked next to her Mazda, a Corvette, she would guess. She thought nothing about the flashy automobile, simply depressed the button on the re- mote key ring, opened her car door, and got in.

A horn blasted loudly, causing her to jump. For the first time Rona noticed a man hunkered down behind the Corvette's steering wheel. She lowered her window and stuck her head out, squinting to see who was behind the tinted glass.

The Corvette's driver lowered his window and smiled at her. That smile almost caused Rona's heart to stop. What was Tim Delaney doing parked next to her?

"Evening," he said in his deep Oakie drawl.

"Evening," she grunted, barely getting the words out.

"Got a minute?"

Of course she had a minute for him, a minute and an hour if that was what it took. She was curious to find out why he was here. And yes, she had hoped to see him again, but she'd been realistic too—men like Tim weren't looking for relationships with depth, not when they could have any woman they chose.

Rona watched Tim slide his long body out of the low vehi- cle. His smooth dark skin had a velvet sheen to it. She refused to think about his body or get all quivery inside. She faced him, summoning a smile. The mole at the edge of his mouth jumped when he smiled back. Her whole body tingled as an expensive cologne and body musk engulfed her.

"I've been waiting for you to get off," Tim said, giving her another heartbreaking smile.

Rona didn't know what to say. She just kept staring at him. The man was just too fine. Casually attired in jeans and a linen shirt, with a thick gold chain lying against his ebony skin, he put any *GQ* model to shame.

"You left without giving me your number," he said. "Lucky

for me I remembered you ran that nursery school, or camp, whatever it is, so I hightailed it over here."

More like lucky for her.

"It was nice of you to come by," Rona managed to get out.

Tim tilted her chin back, forcing her to look him in the face. His gray eyes sparkled and tiny laugh lines fanned out around the edges. She couldn't help trembling under his touch.

"I wanted to see if you'd come to a dinner party with me tomorrow night."

Rona schooled her expression to remain neutral but one eyebrow tilted upward. "Who's throwing this dinner party?"

"Sunny Hirschbaum. She owns an art gallery in Soho."

"What's she doing this far north?"

Tim shrugged. "Beats me. I think she rented a house. She throws good parties, want to go?"

"Sure, why not?"

Tim gave her the details. Pleased with himself, he hopped back into his vehicle and took off, burning rubber out of the parking lot.

"Well, who would have thought?" Rona said, getting back into the Mazda.

Ten minutes later and a lot more composed, she put her car in gear and headed home.

"Oh, God. What on earth possessed me to agree to go?" Liza said, stroking one of the faded scars on her cheek while scanning her reflection in the full-length mirror. "Why am I even getting dressed up?"

She'd resurrected a sexy black dress from her modeling days, added silver jewelry and too-high heels. In her estimation she looked like an Amazon, and an unattractive one at that.

If her appearance put Paul White off it would be worth it. Whatever had prompted her to ask him to Sunny Hirschbaum's dinner party anyway? She'd considered him safe, had gone to high school with him, and he was an eligible man.

Liza had invited Paul on impulse. She'd gone to see him yesterday to find out what her mother's chances were of contesting Malcolm's will. He'd advised her accordingly, and she'd been so grateful she'd extended the invitation.

Paul had one of those rigid personalities that didn't loosen up with drink. It would be an ordeal to have to entertain him all night, but it might be worth it. Sunny had insisted she bring a single professional and Paul, as an attorney, fit the bill. Hopefully he would meet someone at the party, freeing her of further obligation.

Liza permitted herself one final glance in the mirror. She gasped aloud at the image in the mirror. The reflection most definitely wasn't hers. It was that of a café au lait woman wearing an outdated dress. The woman's hair hung to her shoulders and she carried a dark-skinned young boy on her hip. In a blink of an eye she was gone.

Liza covered her mouth and willed her heart to stop thumping. It was merely her imagination playing tricks on her. Could all the weird stuff that had been happening be her imagination or was it posttraumatic stress because of the mugging?

She stared at her reflection in a dress that once fit perfectly but now hugged all the wrong places. She needed to lose a few pounds and needed to see a doctor. She was going crazy, unless of course Sam O'Reilly was right and her house was haunted.

A car door slammed outside, signaling that her escort had arrived. Shaking her head, Liza grabbed her evening purse and the box of petits fours purchased at Sweet Eats that would be her contribution. She opened the door to find Paul handsomely attired in a tan linen jacket and beige slacks. He held a red rose in one hand and awkwardly thrust it at her.

"You look nice. This is for you."

Liza thanked him, wondering why he seemed nervous. This wasn't a date and she would make sure he knew it.

"You'll like Sunny," she said, sliding into Paul's Jaguar and handing him the directions.

"How do you know her?" Paul asked, putting the car in gear.

Liza hated talking about that part of her life. It was long over with, but she owed Paul an explanation.

"Sunny was one of the beautiful people I rubbed elbows with in New York. She's a socialite, moonlighting as a gallery owner, and a widow who inherited the place from her husband, a man considerably older than she."

"What's she doing in Syracuse?"

"I don't know. It seems a long ways away from the bright lights of the big city but I suppose you could ask me the same question."

Paul turned slightly, then fixed his eyes on the road again. "I've often wondered about that. You've had a marvelous life. Success came at an early age. I thought for sure once you left town you'd never come back."

"I thought the same myself, but life has a funny way of taking twists and turns. You learn to twist with it," Liza said, remembering how she'd left the upstate town swearing never to return. But after the mugging she'd wanted a place that she could call home, somewhere she could be herself, and where people remembered her as a too-thin teenager who was not particularly pretty.

Paul made a right turn, approaching a part of town where the houses were more like mansions and sat on a minimum of one acre of land. They turned down a tree-lined street and he slowed, looking at numbers that were painted on posts on the road.

"I think you'll need to go another block or so," Liza said, remembering the description of the house that Sunny had given her. She'd said it was a Tudor that sat back from the road with a winding driveway leading to the house.

Paul proceeded on, slowing the car in front of a home with high hedges and several cars parked out front.

"This might be it," he said, aiming the vehicle up the driveway and coming to a stop when a young man bearing a flashlight waved them over.

Liza was helped out of the Jaguar and Paul turned his keys over to the hired valet. Paul took her elbow, leading her toward an intricately carved front door.

Another smiling hired helper let them into a home that

looked as if it were out of *House and Garden*. The walls were white and the furniture even whiter. Framed black-and-white photos hung on the walls and French doors led to an outdoor patio with potted plants where several guests mingled. Sunny was there holding court.

Spotting Paul and Liza, she waved to them to come out.

His hand still at her elbow, Paul steered her through the French doors and onto the patio. She was still holding the rose. Sunny greeted Liza with a kiss on the cheek, then shook Paul's hand.

"Who do we have here?" she asked, giving Paul the once-over.

Liza handed over the pastry box to one of the hired help, then quickly made introductions. A waiter bearing glasses of red and white wine sidled up to them and held out a tray.

"You're an attorney?" Sunny asked. "What kind of law do you practice?"

"Probate."

"I'm not sure I know what that means."

Paul began to explain and Liza found her attention wandering. For the first time she looked around to see who the other guests were.

She spotted an attractive brunette who sometimes came into her shop and spent a fortune. She'd brought a girlfriend with her, a woman who chattered nonstop. Liza recognized Mason, the owner of Wine and Roses, and nodded to him. He acknowledged her greeting and returned to conversing with a tall, dark-skinned man who was very attractive. Next to him was Rona, who'd not mentioned a word about coming, and Tim Delaney. Liza had ignored the message Delilah left on her answering machine and wondered if she would show up.

Leaving Paul and Sunny chatting, she headed over to where Rona and Tim Delaney stood sipping cocktails.

"Fancy seeing you here," she said to her friend.

"And you."

They exchanged kisses.

Rona wore a stylish white cocktail suit with rhinestone buttons. Her vampy shoes even had rhinestones on the tips. Her eyebrows arched as she looked Liza up and down.

"Great dress. It's good to see you getting out."

"Aren't you going to introduce me?" Tim asked, making himself known.

Rona looked like she would rather do anything but. Liza realized her friend's insecurities had kicked in. Surely Rona should know that Liza had no designs on any man a friend had chosen.

"I'm Liza Hamilton," Liza said, extending a hand.

"*The* Liza Hamilton? Ex-model?"

He'd made the connection even though she was no longer *the* Liza Hamilton. Her modeling days had ended, and not a minute too soon. Liza had loved being in the spotlight and she'd loved the money, but there had been a price to pay, lack of privacy being one part of it.

"Uhh, yes, I am," Liza said rather abruptly. "Nice meeting you, Tim. I'd better go rescue Paul."

Liza made a U-turn and ran smack into Erik Price, who had an Afro-Asian woman hanging on his arm.

"Liza," he said, reaching out a muscular arm to steady her. "This is a nice surprise."

"Yes, yes, it is." She flashed him her supermodel smile.

Why did the sight of a woman she didn't know irritate her, as irrational as it seemed? Erik's date was beautiful. She had a flawless almond complexion, slightly upturned hazel eyes, and full red lips. The entire package made Liza want to spit. The woman's jet-black waist-length hair had a slight wave to it, and she tossed it back frequently as she flirted.

"This is Vivica, my agent," Erik said, pushing the woman forward.

Surely he could come up with a better lie than that. No agent Liza knew was that stunning.

Vivica's French-manicured nails dug into Liza's as she clasped her hand.

"Liza Hamilton, I wondered what had become of you."

Liza blinked. She was conscious of Erik hovering. The smell of soap and cologne made for a heady combination. She smiled brightly at Vivica and tried to block out Erik's presence.

"Have we met before?"

Vivica shook her head, her hair swaying with the movement. "Never in person, but I did see your face on every major magazine cover. I wanted so much to look like you."

"Thank you."

Vivica seemed sincere enough. It was incomprehensible that a compliment was coming from a woman most modeling agencies would be fighting over to sign. As Liza sensed Erik's scrutiny and his intense interest, heat flooded her face.

A hand rested on her shoulder and she turned to see who it was. Paul had come up behind her unannounced. "Sunny went to answer the door," he said. "Let's mingle."

Erik stepping forward, a glint of steel in his eyes. He stretched out a hand. "I'm Erik Price."

"Paul White."

The two men sized each other up, testosterone pumping. Liza scrutinized Erik since she was seeing him dressed up for the first time. He wore one of those collarless shirts with a mother-of-pearl button at the neck. Instead of formal dress pants, he'd settled on navy Dockers and leather loafers, minus socks. Even amongst the more formally dressed men he still stood out.

The customary banalities were exchanged. Liza and Paul headed off, stopping to chat with a woman and man that sometimes shopped at her store. She finished her glass of wine and accepted another from a passing waiter.

Sunny's voice boomed behind them. "Ladies and gentlemen, dinner will be served in exactly fifteen minutes. Has everyone met each other?"

Before anyone could answer, the doorbell chimed. Sunny was off and running. She returned to the patio with Delilah in tow.

Delilah had chosen a strapless lime-green dress. She'd draped a chiffon shawl casually over one shoulder. Spotting Liza she tottered over in heels more suited to sitting than walking.

"How come you didn't return my call?" She demanded, gracing Paul with a catlike grin. "No one gets Paul White away from his work. What gives?"

"Liza has the magic touch," Paul answered, taking a step back and putting a safe distance between them.

"Sure, blame me," Liza said gamely, her thoughts still on Erik and the attractive package he made.

Paul and Delilah began jousting in earnest, the two attempting to outwit each other. Liza used that opportunity to move on. She hadn't gotten very far before two long legs planted themselves in front of her and she looked up into Erik's face.

"You look beautiful," he said, "but the more casually attired Liza is more my style."

Liza sought refuge in her wine. She felt guilty even being this close to him. He'd been the topic of her and Paul's conversation most of yesterday, and she planned on encouraging her mother to contest the will.

"Dinner's on," Sunny called, clapping her hands.

"Good, I'm starving," Erik muttered. He offered Liza the crook of his arm. "In case you're thinking of wandering away, Ms. Hamilton, think twice. You're sitting right next to me."

10

The long oak table comfortably sat the thirteen people that Sunny had invited. Liza sat on Erik's right, and Delilah, pushy woman that she was, had managed to secure a seat to his left. Paul White, looking none too pleased, sat directly opposite them, next to Vivica.

Down the table a bit was Rona and Tim Delaney, and next to Tim was the attractive brunette who'd introduced herself as Keala. Sunny was seated at the head of the table, and Mason, the owner of Wine and Roses, at the foot. The other five people were strategically positioned, boy, girl, boy, girl.

Two of the hired help roamed around pouring wine before a shrimp cocktail was served. Delilah kept chattering at Erik, going on and on about the upcoming street fair. He wasn't sure whether or not she was hinting for an invitation. He answered her questions as politely as he could but wished she would shut up. He was only interested in the woman to his right and wondered if she and Paul White were an item.

"You must have had a busy day," Erik said. "You seem a bit distracted."

Liza smiled wanly and rubbed her forehead. "Does it show? Plus I had another rather unsettling incident happen at my house. I've been trying to convince myself it was my imagination."

"Tell me about it after dinner," Erik whispered.

"What was that?" Delilah asked, leaning over him and giving him an eyeful of cleavage. "What happened at your house that's so unsettling?"

Liza's finger traced a path along a faded scar on her cheek. Her voice was amazingly even when she answered, "Nothing major. My eyes seem to be playing tricks on me these days."

"Hmmm," Delilah said, apparently not buying it.

When the time was right, Erik meant to ask Liza about the mugging and how she'd coped with having a less than perfect face. He also wanted to talk to her in more detail about what was going on at their respective homes. And maybe he could even convince her to sit for a painting. While she might not know it, he planned on getting to know her a whole lot better. He'd grown up an only child deprived of any real family. He had a half sister he'd never met and was intrigued by Liza's mother as well.

Any woman who could walk out on Malcolm Mitchell had guts. His own mother had been unable to sever ties with him after she'd had his child, and watched him take wife after wife. His father was not a man he admired and Erik had only accepted his inheritance because he'd been looking for a quiet, charming place to paint. The Victorian home fit the bill but had come with some major strings attached in the form of some very unexpected occurrences.

Salads arrived and were set down before them. Delilah's manicured fingers stroked his arm as she chattered on about one insignificant thing after another. He wished she would focus her attention on some other single male. Erik finally decided to take matters into his own hands.

"Delilah," he said, loud enough for the people seated around them to hear, "Quinn James tells me he's a freelance journalist. He's looking for a local business owner to interview and your flower shop could use the exposure. You did meet Quinn?"

Quinn, seated across from Delilah, looked up from his salad

and smiled gratefully. He was a bespectacled man in his late thirties who seemed like he needed a push to get a conversation going. A woman like Delilah would definitely intimidate him but at the same time he would be flattered by her attention.

True to form, Delilah batted her tawny eyes at Quinn. "I'd love to be interviewed by you," she said. "I know almost everyone there is to know in this town and I can pretty much tell you how any of the new businesses got started. Where I fall short, Sam O'Reilly can fill in."

"Sam O'Reilly, the old man?" Quinn inquired. "The one who's supposed to be psychic?"

"That would be him."

Erik left them talking and surreptitiously surveyed the remaining guests at the table. Tim Delaney and Rona seemed to be getting along, and Mason and Keala seemed to have hit it off. Sunny and Paul were chatting away, and Vivica, his agent, was occupied with some guy who claimed to be a professor at Syracuse University.

"Sam O'Reilly's name keeps coming up," Erik said to Liza. "Maybe we need to take what he said to us seriously. I'm going to talk to Ned when I get a chance and see if he'll tell me what really went on in my house. Why don't you contact the person who sold you yours and see if she'll talk to you? We'll compare notes when we get together this weekend."

"Did I hear something about a get-together?" Delilah asked, breaking away from her own conversation.

Erik inwardly groaned. He'd never quite met anyone like this woman. She was determined not to be ignored.

Liza, sensing his frustration, interrupted. "It's not the kind of get-together you think it is. Erik and I are going to the street fair."

"I'll be there," Delilah said, sounding delighted. "The Gilded Lily's reserved a booth at the fair. I've hired a couple of college kids to man it so I'm available for whatever."

"Oh, good, then you're free to spend the day with me," Quinn chimed in, and at an opportune time at that. "I'd love it if you'd fill me in on the town and its goings-on."

The shy journalist wasn't so shy after all. Erik owed him a drink. He'd gotten Delilah Kincaid off his back, at least temporarily.

"I'd loved to be interviewed," Delilah said, practically gushing.

The main course arrived, putting an end to further conversation. For as long as it took to eat, they devoured their entrées in silence.

Afterward, Liza said, "And Vivica is up from where?"

"New York. She's my agent."

"I see."

Erik couldn't tell whether she was jealous or not, but the fact that she'd mentioned Vivica indicated that he had gotten her attention.

"She's a business acquaintance and nothing more," he hastened to reassure her.

"But of course," was all that she could find to say.

Tim was ready to leave. The party had been mildly entertaining but now it was time to go. That Rona still held his interest surprised him. He was used to glamour girls, groupies, women who hung on to his every word, those who dropped their drawers if he batted an eyelash. What he liked about Rona was that she seemed to enjoy his company and wasn't overly impressed by him. It intrigued him that she didn't fawn.

Tim wasn't necessarily looking for a relationship, and in fact didn't need one. Not with his lifestyle. He'd meant Rona Fraser to be a quick pickup, a woman to sleep with and quickly discard, as he'd done with so many of the others. But Rona hadn't gone along with the program. To her his star status didn't mean a thing, and that made him want her more.

"Let's get out of here," he whispered to Rona.

"Okay, let's," she whispered back.

"We'll wait until after dessert."

"Why wait until then?" Rona challenged. "Tell Sunny you have to leave for New York or something."

Rona seemed as anxious as he was for them to be alone. It

excited him. And why should they wait? He wasn't that concerned about offending their hostess; an art gallery owner didn't have a whole lot of influence in his world.

Besides, she'd only invited him because of who he was. He finished his entrée and slid his chair back, making a huge production of rising and helping Rona up. Approaching Sunny, Tim piled on the charm.

"Thank you for your hospitality. I apologize that we have to call it a night, but I have an early flight to catch," he lied.

"Oh, Tim, must you leave us so soon?"

Sunny seemed disappointed. She'd been conversing with the stuffy attorney and looked like she could use a break. Excusing herself, she walked them to the door and thanked them profusely for coming, adding that she intended to be at Madison Square Garden for one of his games.

"I'd like that," Tim said, kissing her cheek. "Call me with the date and I'll have tickets waiting at the box office."

A valet pulled Tim's Porsche up to the curb. He patted its hood gently as if reluctant to give the car up, then held the passenger door open and waited for Rona to get in. Tim put the car in gear and took off.

"Where are we going to in such a rush?" Rona asked, fingers playing with the twists that framed her attractive face.

"My house."

She looked at him but said nothing. *Good.* She hadn't made a fuss. He wasn't planning a seduction, just wanted to get her alone.

Rona settled more comfortably in the passenger seat as the speedometer climbed to eighty. In less than fifteen minutes they were parked in his circular driveway.

Inside, his house was neat as a pin and smelled like lavender. Tim headed upstairs to turn on the stereo and called to Rona to follow.

"Come on up. I'll be a good boy, Scout's honor." And he even saluted.

"Promise?"

"I promise."

Upstairs, he flopped down on the leather sofa and kicked off his Gucci loafers.

"Sit next to me," he ordered, patting the spot next to him.

Rona obediently sat. She shrugged out of her jacket and took off her strappy sandals before stretching her legs out on the coffee table. Closing her eyes she listened to a soothing Kenny G tune on the stereo.

"What are you thinking about?" Tim asked, his fingers drawing patterns against the silk camisole Rona had worn underneath her jacket. She shifted, moving away from him.

"Oh, I don't know. I was thinking about how strange the dinner party was. I mean there were Erik and Liza, looking like they wanted to jump each other's bones, and they're brother and sister. Then Delilah shows up, and the last we see of her she's chatting up some bookish type. I'm not sure love connections were made, but it sure looked like the scene had possibilities."

"Yes, I suppose," Tim answered, his hands kneading her arms. "That was the point of the party, to meet and mingle. The artist and ex-model are brother and sister? Sure didn't look like that to me."

"Stepbrother and sister. Erik's father married Liza's mother."

"Come again?"

Rona explained.

"Well, that man's intentions certainly aren't brotherly. He wanted that woman and that's my expert opinion. And the reporter couldn't believe his luck when Delilah turned her attention on him."

Rona chuckled. "You're very perceptive. Who said jocks were totally self-absorbed, interested in things that benefited only them?"

Tim chuckled and nuzzled her neck, enjoying Rona's wry sense of humor. "Oh, I'm definitely interested in what benefits me." He glanced at his watch. "Sure you won't join me in bed?"

"Not a chance. Tempting as your offer is, I have to decline."

The phone rang. Tim muttered a foul oath. "Let the machine pick up."

A taped message came on, then a woman's voice. Shanté. Damn her timing.

"Honey, if you're there pick up."

Rona's posture grew rigid and her light, playful mood disappeared.

"You were supposed to phone me the minute you settled in the boonies," Shanté said. "I waited and waited. Luckily I ran into one of your teammates and he gave me this number. Call me."

Tim rolled his eyes. When would Shanté get the message that they were over?

"One of your groupies?" Rona said wryly.

"An ex-girlfriend that doesn't want to be an ex."

"Sounds like you have your hands full," Rona said, standing up and gathering her sandals.

Damn Shanté. "Where are you going?"

"Home."

"Already?" Tim was up, his hand on her arm.

"It's late."

"Don't be like that." He placed an arm around Rona's shoulders and drew her close.

Rona's audible intake of breath indicated she wasn't as cool and collected as she appeared to be. Tim decided it was now or never. He swooped in for a kiss.

Rona wound her arms around his neck and kissed him back fiercely. Tim deepened the kiss and attempted to lower her back into a seated position. She resisted. He began unbuttoning her blouse. One hand covered her breast. *Nice tits,* he thought, as she squirmed under his touch.

Instead he said, "Baby, we're consenting adults. Relax and have fun."

"Fun's not what I'm looking for," Rona said in a prim little voice.

He had to wonder why she'd agreed to come home with

him. He nipped the sides of her neck, his hands clutching her shoulders. The scent of a bewitching perfume made him long to have her naked and spread-eagled under him. Rona's signals were confusing but he sensed she wasn't the type of woman looking for a one-night stand. She wanted conversation and romance. He wasn't ready for that.

Reluctantly, Tim released Rona. "Fine, since you insist, I'll take you home."

She preceded him downstairs. Tim couldn't take his eyes off her slightly rounded butt.

Delilah glanced at the rearview mirror and saw the headlights of Quinn's car following. The vehicle was about two car lengths behind her. She smiled triumphantly to herself. Quinn had insisted on seeing her safely home, and though she had put up a fuss, he'd refused to back off. Good, she liked that in a man—persistence. He was a gentleman. There weren't too many of those around and she was flattered and touched that he was so thoughtful.

She pulled into her driveway and contemplated asking him in. While he wasn't the type she usually went for, maybe it was time to change her type. God knows she wasn't getting anyplace with Erik Price.

Delilah hopped out of her convertible and approached the driver's side of Quinn's Intrepid.

"Come in for coffee," she said, in her most sultry voice.

His car door popped open before the invitation could settle. He pushed up his glasses, which had slid down the bridge of his nose.

"Thanks, I'd like that."

Delilah wondered what he would look like if he lost the awful spectacles. One thing at a time. First coffee and then she'd see how it went.

Inside the condominium, Quinn took a seat at the bar and gazed around. Delilah poured him the brew, making sure to lean forward so that he would get a view of her assets.

"Interesting décor," Quinn commented, taking in her Chinese-red upholstery and leopard-skin toss pillows. Cream-colored walls were covered with paintings of lesser-known black artists—artists that she'd convinced herself would come into their own some day. If he saw her bedroom his head would be spinning.

"I wanted a place that fully expressed who I was," Delilah said, answering his silent question while sipping on amaretto.

"It does have style." He cocked his head to the side, slowly examining her. "You're a lot different from what I expected."

Delilah took a sip of her drink and studied him back boldly. "How so?"

"You're like no one I've met in Syracuse."

"I'm like no one you've ever met. Period. I'm not middle America and certainly not homespun." She arched an eyebrow in what she considered to be a coquettish manner.

He chuckled. "You said it, I didn't."

"Where are you from originally?"

"Detroit."

"Big city. Lots of black folk."

"That it is, and has."

Delilah crossed one ample leg over the other, letting him see plenty of thigh. Quinn seemed nervous all of a sudden. Ready to bolt. Time to settle him down. The man was as jittery as a trussed-up Christmas hog.

"So what is it you wanted to talk to me about?" she asked, stirring her drink with her index finger, then placing that same finger in her mouth.

"I'd like to know what inspired you to open your own business."

Delilah shrugged. "That's easy. I've always wanted to be my own boss. Can you see someone like me fitting in with corporate America?" She laughed a gutsy laugh. "Besides, I like pretty things and flowers are pretty. So one day I drew up a business plan and got a minority loan. A flower shop won't ever make me rich but there was a need here, and presto, the Gilded Lily came along." She snapped her fingers.

Quinn raised his mug. "To the Gilded Lily and you."

They toasted. Delilah rose and topped off Quinn's drink. She felt his eyes on her and made sure her hands brushed his when she handed him the mug. Let him want her. It was good for her ego and would take her mind off Erik until she could develop another strategy.

"I'm wiped," she said, yawning and making sure her bosom heaved with the motion. Quinn's eyes practically bulged out of his head. He loosened the collar of his buttoned-down shirt.

"I should get going then. It's been a long day. Where should we meet on Sunday?"

"Pick me up here," Delilah said, sliding from behind the bar and undulating toward him. She kissed his cheek, making sure to brush up against him. He was trapped in his chair, her body in the way.

Quinn nervously set down his mug. Coffee sloshed over the sides and onto the front of Delilah's lime-green dress. His Adam's apple bobbed up and down as he grabbed for a napkin.

"Look what I've done. I've ruined your beautiful dress." He dabbed at the bodice front, growing more embarrassed when he accidentally touched her breasts. "I better leave."

He practically sprang from the chair and Delilah was forced to step back.

"See you Sunday at eleven, or is that too early?"

"Eleven's fine."

He backed toward the door, almost tripping over one of her Persian ottomans.

"Drive safely," Delilah said, her hand playing with the stain on her dress, making little circles.

"Yes, yes, of course." He practically raced out the door.

Delilah threw herself on the sofa and indulged in a gut-wrenching laugh.

11

Erik flung his paintbrush down and grabbed a rag to wipe his hands. Who the hell was that banging on his front door? He muttered an obscenity and raced down the attic stairs. Buddy whimpered at the door and Erik patted the dog's head.

"Quiet, boy."

He'd gotten up early to catch the morning light and had worked nonstop for over three hours. He planned on working several more. This disturbance did not sit well with him. Whoever it was had better be prepared to deal with his unkempt appearance and his grouchiness.

"Stay, Buddy," Erik said, ignoring the peephole and yanking the door open wide. A stranger held an official-looking envelope in his hand. Buddy growled.

"Shush," Erik said.

"You Erik Price?" the man demanded.

"Depends on who's asking."

Please, God, let this not be a fan. Not this early.

Buddy yowled and Erik snapped at the dog to be quiet.

"You Erik Price or not?" the man repeated, waving the envelope at him.

The guy had to be an idiot. Erik's paint-speckled appearance alone should be a clear indicator that he was the artist, unless the man was clueless.

"What do you want?" Erik asked rudely.

"I want Erik Price. I have a delivery for him."

"Give it to me." Erik held out his hand.

The man paused for a moment, eyeing him curiously. "If you're Erik Price you'll need to sign before I hand this over to you." He fished into his pocket, retrieved a pen, and thrust it at Erik.

Better sign for the damn thing and get it over with. Erik scribbled his name, accepted the envelope, and without glancing at it, shoved it into the pocket of his sweatpants. Time and light waited for no one.

Duty done, the man quickly slid behind the wheel of an ancient Chevrolet and roared off, leaving a cloud of fumes behind.

"Strange," Erik mumbled, retracing his steps, Buddy at his heels. He climbed the attic stairs still mumbling. "I wonder if Delilah Kincaid is behind this."

The mention of Delilah's name produced another vivid image, that of a willowy cinnamon beauty, perfect in her imperfection. It would be three whole days before he saw Liza again, and the thought of spending time with her excited him. He wondered if she'd had more dreams.

Erik's latest had come to him in vivid Technicolor with a definite erotic element to it. He'd been making love to a woman that looked like Liza. They'd been in an old shack, lying on a cot that barely held their long frames. He could still smell the smoke in the chimney from the mansion on the hill, and see silhouettes of the white people occupying the house through a fluttering curtain.

What he remembered most was the feel and smell of the woman as she moved in perfect rhythm with him. He still felt the press of her hand against his back and her full breasts jutting against his chest as he drove into her repeatedly. What did these strange dreams mean? Sam had told him and Liza that they were lovers in a previous life. But Sam was old and his thoughts confused. Maybe he should have lunch at Ned's. Ned was always a good source of information.

Erik reentered the studio and found the window wide open. Buddy began growling again. He didn't remember leaving the window open. Papers that he'd been sketching on were strewn all over the floor. He bent to gather them and noticed a drawing that he had not seen before. He had a strange sense of déjà vu as he held the sketch up to the light and examined it.

The same shack that he'd dreamt about had been replicated exactly. He lay on a cot making love to a woman who looked like Liza. And the mansion was there, set back from the fields on the top of a hill. Behind the curtained window was the silhouette of the two people. Erik rubbed his eyes. He must be going crazy. First the turbaned woman, now this.

Bracing himself against the windowsill, he stared out on the greenery and let the morning breeze cool his face. He willed his thumping pulse to settle down. Going back to painting would be futile now, not until he processed this information.

He remembered the envelope in his pocket and pulled it out, scanned the return address, and frowned. What could Paul White want with him? The first and only time he'd laid eyes on the attorney was at Sunny Hirschbaum's dinner party. Could Paul be hitting him up for a donation? Erik didn't mind contributing to a worthy cause but the attorney could have at least called before soliciting him.

Erik ripped open the envelope and began reading the contents. *What?* He tossed the letter aside feeling as if he'd been punched in the gut. He'd been conned. He should have known that Liza Hamilton's interest in him had nothing to do with finding him attractive. She'd wanted something from him. She, her mother, and her sister wanted his house. Paul White was representing them in a suit against him.

He'd just accepted a summons from a process server to appear in court. He had a good mind to stop by Paul White's office and give him a piece of his mind. The man had just broken bread with him, they'd even exchanged a word or two, and Liza, well, Liza was another story altogether. He felt betrayed.

How could she do this to him without forewarning? He remembered her strange behavior at the restaurant where they'd had brunch. And they had plans for this weekend. Plans that most likely she would cancel.

Consumed by anger, Erik stomped down the stairs. He entered his bedroom, grabbed a robe, and headed for the shower. Inside he turned the water on full blast. Needles of water hit him squarely in the face. He submerged his head and let ice-cold water stream down his body until he could no longer feel. The numbness was welcome. His mind went blank.

Erik emerged fifteen minutes later, threw on a pair of jeans and a clean denim shirt, and headed out. He would have lunch at Ned's and see if the old man would talk to him. Perhaps Ned could tell him what sort of person Elizabeth Tanner was. But before going to Ned's he had another stop to make. Paul White, attorney at law, was in for a surprise.

It wasn't often that Sam ventured far from his home. But he'd been wooed by Ned's promise of a hearty meal; plus Kelli, Ned's younger granddaughter, had been sent to pick him up. That made it hard to say no.

He sat in the banquette across from Ned making small talk and wishing his meal would come soon.

"Rumor has it," Ned said in his too-loud voice, "Elizabeth's girl's being squired around town by her stepbrother."

"No crime in that," Sam said, sipping on a cup of steaming hot coffee. "What if she is? It's not like the two ah dem are blood relatives."

"Yeah, but people will talk. Things get complicated when a man and woman spend too much time together."

Sam grunted. "Besides, ain't none of our business. Nothing's going to keep those two apart anyway. Not if they're meant to be together."

"There you go again," Ned grumbled, "talking your nonsense."

"Not nonsense, simple fact."

A jingle at the front door announced a new arrival. Sam could tell by Ned's fidgeting that he recognized the newcomer.

"Afternoon," a female said, walking by them.

"Afternoon," they both answered in unison.

"Cassie Newell," Ned supplied, his voice still booming.

"The woman who owns the bakery? The one who's been going out with that doctor?"

"For someone who doesn't get out much, you know a lot," Ned said grumpily, probably because he hadn't heard the gossip.

"I make it my business to."

A clip-clop of heels followed shortly thereafter, and the strong scent of perfume almost made him gag.

"Delilah Kincaid," Ned whispered in a considerably lower voice that was still too loud.

"The woman who gets around."

"Quiet, she'll hear you."

"Good afternoon, gentlemen," Delilah sang, clomping by them. "Talking about me again?" She hurried by. "Hey, girlfriend, sorry I'm late."

Sam deduced that Delilah was meeting her friend Cassie. She didn't seem overly concerned that she'd been the topic of conversation.

A tantalizing aroma filled the air—pot roast, another of Sam's favorite dishes, as he could tell by the smell. He heard the clank of plates and cutlery as the dishes were set before them. Hopefully there was enough to satisfy him and fill up a bag with leftovers.

"Uh-oh," Ned muttered. "Mercy me, something's got Erik pissed off."

"What's that?"

"Erik Price just walked in looking like he wants to kill someone."

Sam heard heavy footsteps come to a sudden stop before them. He could feel Erik's fury.

"Hey, Erik," Sam said. "Haven't seen you around for a while."

"I've been busy. Hello, Sam."

"Morning, Erik."

Erik was coiled tight as a spring. It wouldn't take much for that spring to snap. What had brought this on?

"Join us," Ned said. "Sit down." Ned's hands made a thumping motion against the vinyl banquette seats.

"Long as you don't mind."

"I invited you."

Erik slid in beside Sam. Sam could feel heat and rage pouring out of every pore.

"You okay, boy?" Ned asked. "Want some coffee? Pot roast?"

A fist thumped against the Formica table. "I'm not okay. In fact I'm pissed. Pot roast? Yeah, fine."

"Want to talk about it?" Ned prompted.

Seconds ticked by while Sam attacked his own pot roast, savoring every bite. Some things took time.

"Liza Hamilton's mother's suing me," Erik said, his tone containing barely concealed outrage.

"You don't say. What for?" Ned asked.

"She feels my house belongs to my half sister. I stopped by Paul White's place to give him a piece of my mind. He's the attorney representing them."

"And Paul spoke with you?" Ned asked.

"No, his secretary said he was detained in court. I waited but he never showed up."

Click-clacking heels approached, followed by the seductive fragrance of a strong perfume.

"Erik, fancy running into you," a female voice said, putting an end to the current conversation. "Cassie and I are having lunch. We'd like it if you joined us for dessert."

Sam felt the tension in the air. He couldn't imagine why Erik wouldn't take Delilah up on her offer. In his day a man didn't turn down two attractive women.

"Some other time," Erik grunted.

Delilah sighed. "You know where we are if you change your mind." She stomped away.

"Did you want pot roast, Mr. Price?" Tiffani asked.

"Yes, and a great big glass of water."

"Lunch is on me," Ned said, his voice not brooking any nonsense. "Order anything you want."

Erik stuck with pot roast and Ned's granddaughter departed to fulfill the order.

"I'm glad you're both here," Erik said. "I'd like to hear more about my house and its being a stop on the Underground Railroad. The strangest damn things have happened to me since I got to town."

Ned cleared his throat. His hearing aid beeped loudly but he seemed unaware of it. He turned to Sam. "Tell him what you know."

Sam set down his knife and fork with a clatter. He would tell the boy as much as he needed to know.

"Syracuse received the largest number of fugitive slaves in New York State," he began.

"Is that so?"

"Yup. It was fairly close to Canada and two major terminals were located here."

"And my father's house was one of those depots?"

"Yup. But your home ain't the original house. The old house burned down and was later rebuilt by some of the free slaves sheltered there."

Sam heard Erik shift in his seat. For a long time he said nothing. "Were there people in the house when it burned?"

"Yeah, several lost their lives. An arsonist set fire to any home that was suspected to be a station. The man knew fully well slaves were in hiding on their way to Canada. He didn't care. One couple had been split up because your house was busting to the seams with people. The male died on your property, saving his child. His common-law wife died in another house. Their child was taken in by the minister. Shortly after, he succumbed to pneumonia."

"Was the other house Liza's?" Erik asked.

Smart man. "Yes, but Liza's house only partially burned

down. It was too late though, the man's wife and a couple of men were already dead. They died of smoke inhalation before they could be hauled out."

Erik seemed to be digesting all of it. He remained quiet as if contemplating. "That would explain why that canvas with a portrait of the woman with the turban keeps appearing. She's an old slave woman. I've heard it said that Harriet Tubman helped slaves to freedom using this route."

Sam wasn't surprised. After ninety-three years of living, nothing surprised him. "Yup, could be Moses, savior of the people," Sam confirmed. "Her real name was Araminta Ross. She was barely five feet tall and said to be of dark complexion. She knew all the secret routes north to south and all of the safe houses. Her parents were Harriett Green and Benjamin Ross, both were African."

"What about Liza's house?" Erik asked. "What's the real story there?"

"Like I told you before, hers was another station. As far as I know a minister owned the house."

"If the man's wife was killed in that house, and your reincarnation theory is correct, that could explain why we're having similar experiences, don't you think?"

"Most likely," Ned said, interjecting for the first time since the story had begun.

Tiffani returned carrying steaming pot roast. Sam smelled buttery mashed potatoes and a pungent vegetable that had to be broccoli.

"Eat up," Ned urged, his voice way too loud. "I want to know what you're going to do about that lawsuit."

Erik answered with his mouth full. "Haven't had time to come up with a plan. That house was no gift. It cost me a bundle to move in."

"Yeah, I heard it was mortgaged to the hilt," Ned said. "Typical of Malcolm to live on the edge."

Tapping heels and the powerful smell of perfume announced that Delilah and Cassie were leaving.

"I'll probably see you this weekend at the street fair," Delilah said to Erik. "Take care of yourself, Ned, Sam."

"Take care," they both called to her.

"Yes, Delilah, I suppose I'll see you. Bye, Cassie," Erik added, although he didn't seem at all enthused.

Cassie's farewell was barely audible. She followed her friend's clomping footsteps out.

Sam decided now was as good a time as any for coffee. He'd saved enough room to have a great big piece of Kelli's apple pie and some of Tiffani's homemade ice cream. It wasn't often that he ate food that tasted this good.

12

"Hey, Cass, if I didn't know any better I would think you were pregnant," Rona said, watching Cassie scarf down a huge pork chop on her plate.

Cassie shot her a look of surprise. She'd been eating non-stop for what seemed hours. The basket of bread before them was empty as was the plate that had contained two pork chops, black-eyed peas and a big helping of mashed potatoes. Cassie normally didn't like anything greasy, which made her conspicuous consumption even more questionable.

"I guess I was hungry," she said, picking up her menu and scanning it for dessert possibilities. "I still am."

"What is it you wanted to talk to me about?" Rona asked, pushing her plate with almost half of her Caesar salad away, and regarded Cassie through narrowed eyes.

Instead of looking her square in the face, Cassie beckoned the waitress over. "I'll have the brownie with a scoop of vanilla ice cream. Rona, do you want anything?"

"Cappuccino if you have it," Rona said to the smiling teenager, who couldn't be more than a size four soaking wet.

When the girl left, Rona persisted. "What's happened that's got you so hot and bothered?"

Cassie's eyes darted back and forth and she still didn't look at Rona. It had been her idea to have dinner and she'd been adamant that Delilah and Liza not be included.

"Kalib keeps calling me," she eventually said. "He says he's checking to see if I'm okay. He's driving up tomorrow and wants to take me to the street fair."

"Sounds like he's very caring. You need someone like that in your life after Jim," Rona said pointedly. "Plus I gather he's good company."

"He *is* a nice guy," Cassie admitted. "But it's all happening too fast. I don't know what he wants or even expects. What if I can't measure up?"

"There goes your insecurity kicking in again. Why does he have to want something? Why not just see where it goes?"

Cassie twisted her napkin between unsteady fingers. "There's a lot about me that he doesn't know. He may not even like me when he finds out."

"You told him you have kids, right?"

Rona's eyes never left Cassie's face as she waited.

"Yes, I did."

"He knows you've been married and your ex has custody?"

"Yes," Cassie muttered.

"Then that's all he needs to know. What's there left to tell?" As if she didn't know.

"What if Kalib starts asking me a bunch of personal questions and the whole ugly truth about my divorce comes out?"

"I'm sure his situation is equally as ugly," Rona said sagely. "The man's divorced for crying out loud. He comes to Syracuse a couple of times a month to see his kid and now he's seeing you. It isn't as if you're serious, at least not yet."

The waitress returned with Cassie's brownie and ice cream. She set Rona's cappuccino in front of her. "Enjoy."

After she'd left, Rona turned her attention back to her friend. "If you're worried about your eating disorder, all you have to do is open any newspaper and you can read the story of one celebrity or another facing that challenge. Besides, you overcame it. Didn't you?"

Cassie's bottom lip quivered. "Yes, but I don't recall any celebrity losing their children because they were bulimic."

"You know what I think?" Rona said, making sure her tone sounded chipper. "You agonize too much. You've worked hard to master this problem. You're on an upward climb. Kalib's a doctor. He should understand."

Cassie toyed with the napkin in her lap and still avoided making eye contact. "And if he doesn't?"

"Then he doesn't deserve you."

Rona wasn't that convinced that Cassie had a handle on her illness but it sounded like a good thing to say. Her friend needed support.

"I'm worried that if Kalib gets to know the real me he's not going to want to be bothered. I can't go through more heartache again. I had the shit kicked out of me when Jim walked out."

"And you're in a better place for it. The man was having an affair right under your nose. It was a stressful time. You're human, girlfriend, none of us is perfect."

Cassie wanted to hug Rona in gratitude. Rona was a lifesaver and didn't even know it. Casie's self-esteem had been badly shaken when her snake of a husband had left her. Everyone had known Jim was playing around but no one had wanted to tell Cassie that. She'd adored him and thought he was perfect.

Cassie had been a stay-at-home mom. The perfect wife who kept house, baked goodies, and took good care of her man. It had shown enormous strength on her part to survive a bitter divorce and turn a hobby into a successful business. Cassie underestimated herself.

Rona noticed Cassie had eaten up every last morsel of the brownie and was finishing up the last of the ice cream. She sipped her cappuccino and decided to change the subject.

"I've been seeing some of Tim Delaney," she admitted.

"Yes, I've heard. What's it like to be with a famous basketball player?"

Rona smiled. Cassie was obviously starstruck. "Tim's actually pretty down-to-earth. I'm taking it a day at a time. I don't expect it will develop into anything more than it is. We have fun."

"Hmmm," Cassie said. "I suppose that's how I should treat this thing with me and Kalib and not put pressure on myself."

"Exactly."

A couple walked by them. The man's height was hard to miss. Tim Delaney had a skimpily clad blonde on his arm who clung to him. He followed the hostess to a table off to the side and didn't pay attention to the patrons around. Rona's stomach roiled. So much for taking things a day at a time. She needed to get out of there and she needed to do so quickly, without Tim seeing her. She signaled the waitress for the check.

"Wasn't that Tim who just went by?" Cassie asked carefully.

"Yes, that was him."

"I wonder who the woman is. I bet you anything she's not from these parts."

Rona shrugged and bit back the bile. "Could be anybody. Someone like Tim tends to attract women. I knew that before I got involved with him."

She fought Cassie for the check, slapped down a credit card, and signed the slip. "Come on, hon, let's get out of here."

Unfortunately, Tim chose that moment to look their way. He smiled and waved. Rona couldn't quite make herself smile back. She managed a nod and hustled Cassie out. She'd known what she was getting into when she began flirting with Tim Delaney, but seeing him with another woman still hurt.

"Ma, that's great. Labor Day weekend is perfect. I'll be closing the shop on Monday."

Liza cradled the phone between her ear and shoulder. Elizabeth had said she would come to visit and she planned on bringing Sara with her. Liza missed her little sister even though theirs was less than the perfect relationship. It had been months since she'd seen her family. Moving and setting up the shop had kept her busy.

"Will you drive up?" Liza asked.

"I plan to. Phillip's going fishing with his buddies so he won't mind. It will be just us three girls."

Liza hung up thinking how much she was looking forward to her family's visit. She was surprised she hadn't heard from Erik since they were supposed to be going to the street fair tomorrow and he should have called by now to firm up.

Perhaps she should call him. Liza dialed directory assistance and asked for Erik Price's number. An automated voice repeated the numbered, then offered to put her through for a nominal amount. The phone rang for what seemed an eternity, then Erik's urban baritone came on the line.

"Yo."

She was taken aback by his casual greeting, then rallied. "Uh, Erik, this is Liza."

There was a pause. "I'm surprised to hear from you." His tone sounded gruff and far from warm and welcoming.

Had he found out what she'd been up to? Syracuse was still like a small town and word could have gotten out that she'd consulted Paul White. Erik, having seen her and Paul at Sunny's dinner party, could also have put two and two together.

"Are we on for tomorrow?" Liza inquired, her tone tentative.

Another pause followed. "Sure, if you're still up to it." Erik didn't sound at all enthused.

Something was wrong. Liza sensed his ambivalence, and guilt rushed in.

"We can cancel if you like," she said, giving him an opening.

"No. If you still want to, we can go."

She forced a brightness into her voice she didn't feel. "I was looking forward to the fair and brunch."

"All right then, I'll pick you up at eleven. We need to talk anyway."

Talk? Must mean he'd found out about her inquiries to Paul, then of course she could be overreacting. Maybe something had happened at his house since they'd last seen each other. Things had been quiet at hers for a while.

Liza hung up the phone. She walked out of the back room, surprised to find Sunny Hirschbaum searching through the racks.

"Hi, Sunny," Liza said, "I've been meaning to call and thank you for a lovely evening. Dinner was delicious."

"Yes, it was a lovely time, wasn't it?" Sunny selected a handful of clothing. Liza had never considered her the vintage type but you never know. "Is there some place I can try these on?"

Liza unlocked one of the fitting rooms and motioned Sunny in. She was surprised when the socialite stopped her as she was about to retreat.

"Are you dating Paul White?" she asked, flicking a mane of red hair off her face. "I wouldn't want to move in if you are."

Liza was so taken aback by the question she stammered. "P—Paul and I are just good friends."

Sunny seemed delighted by her answer. "Fantastic, darling. He looks like someone I'd like to get to know better. I'm fascinated by attorneys. All that black-and-white thinking is a big turn-on. If you have his number I'll give him a call."

Liza left Sunny to find her Palm Pilot. When she returned, the woman was wearing an ankle-length peasant skirt from the seventies, and a buttoned-down cardigan that looked like it had been worn to a sock hop. They seemed strange choices for the sleek sophisticate. Was Sunny's appearance at the shop just an excuse to quiz her about Paul and get his number? She decided to turn the tables.

"Does Erik Price show his work at your gallery?" Liza asked.

"Not currently, though it's something I'm working on. I'm putting pressure on that agent of his, Vivica, to convince him to be my featured artist. His name alone brings in a crowd."

"And does Erik seem amenable so far?"

Sunny slipped out of the skirt. "Erik can be prickly at times. Money isn't a primary motivator for him."

"You sound like you know him well. Have you been friends for a while?"

Sunny tugged off the pink sweater. She wore no bra underneath and Liza averted her eyes, but not before noticing that her breasts thrust forward and had no tilt to them. She was in magnificent shape for a woman in her forties and Liza wondered if she'd had help.

Sunny chuckled throatily. "I've known Erik for a while, ever since he was a struggling artist living in the Village." She waggled her melonlike breasts that didn't quite move. "I first met him at a local dive. God, was he gorgeous! He had that lean and hungry look, doe eyes, and marvelous caramel skin. And he was all male, no mistaking that. I wanted to take him home forever but it didn't work out. A relationship with Erik never works out. A number of women tried; some were even willing to buy his affection."

Was Sunny one of those women?

"And did he take any of them up on their offer?" Liza asked, wondering what Sunny was not saying.

"Not that I know of. Erik was totally into his art, and money was immaterial. Most of the woman he dated lasted less than a month. When he became big it got even worse; women were practically throwing soiled underwear at him but he kept none of them."

"Erik's never been married or even had a live-in?" Liza asked, curious as to why a man with Erik's looks and fame had never had a life partner.

"He was married briefly a couple of years back. She was a high-powered businesswoman constantly on the go. Someone he met at a showing."

"What went wrong?" Liza asked, knowing that she was prying, but Sunny seemed willing to talk and she was willing to listen.

Sunny stepped into a pair of sailor pants and asked Liza to help with the laces at the back. "Who knows? Erik is very tight-lipped."

That he was. In the time they'd spent together he'd shared very few personal details. Liza made a mental note to bring up the topic of his once being married tomorrow. She had reservations about Erik but at the same time she was curious. Curious, and a little bit jealous of the faceless wife who'd known him intimately, even if just for a short time.

Sunny stepped back into her clothes.

"What have you decided?" Liza asked.

"I'm taking the lot," she said airily. "Tell me you take American Express."

"I do." Liza held out her hand.

"Good, then wrap them up and don't forget to give me Paul's number."

"Not a problem."

Liza was happy to pass Paul on to Sunny. She had no interest in Paul White. Now Erik was another story. She'd grown increasingly more intrigued as Sunny spoke. Her stepbrother was someone she liked more than she was willing to admit, but pursuing a relationship seemed impossible.

Sunday turned out to be one of those picture-perfect sunny days without a cloud in the sky. Liza had awakened early, gone jogging, and was now heading for the shower. She stepped into her walk-in closet and debated what to put on. She chose at least a half dozen possibilities and dismissed them all as not being suitable. She needed something casual and comfortable. Overalls might be appropriate.

Liza found a pair of baby-blue overalls at the back of the closet. She shook the wrinkles out of a cream-colored T-shirt and headed for the shower. Ten minutes later she emerged, lotioned her body, and got dressed. The outfit would be perfect with sneakers. She found a cream-colored pair of socks, shoved them on her feet and laced up her sneakers. Her hair hung in damp ringlets and needed attention. She ran a brush through it in an attempt to get out the knots, gave up, and scooped it into a ponytail, then shoved on a cap. An hour to go before Erik showed up but she was ready.

What to do now. It was only ten o'clock but surely one of her friends must be up. It seemed like ages since they'd spent any time together. Delilah, though she owned the neighboring shop, had maintained her distance. Liza didn't quite know what to make of it. The few times she'd seen Delilah she'd claimed to be busy and didn't have time to talk.

No, Delilah would not be her first choice to call. She'd phone Cassie and if Cassie didn't answer, then Rona would be next. Liza picked up the telephone and dialed. Cassie answered on the second ring.

"Hey," she said when she heard Liza's voice. "I wondered what had happened to you. I thought maybe Erik was keeping you busy."

"What's that supposed to mean?" Liza asked. Cassie wasn't usually that snide.

"Rumor has it you've been spending a lot of time with your brother."

"And where would you have heard such a thing?" Liza asked.

"Delilah mentioned you were at the dinner party."

"I went to the party with Paul White. Erik was there with another woman."

"Yeah, but I heard that you sat next to Erik and he didn't really give the woman the time of day. She was his agent or something."

"Delilah talks too much," Liza said, irked with Delilah for even mentioning it. "What are your plans today?"

"I'm waiting for Kalib to show up. We're going to the street fair."

"So am I. Maybe I'll see you there."

Liza hung up thinking that it was good that Cassie's attention was being diverted. For too long all her energy had been focused on her ex. It was good to see her getting out and enjoying life.

For something to do Liza flopped down on the couch and began leafing through a fashion magazine. At one time she would have been one of the models featured on the pages. Now her old career seemed shallow and a waste of time. What was the point of beautiful women being photographed in outfits that were so expensive that the average Jane couldn't afford them? She snapped the magazine shut.

That life had been left behind. She wasn't doing too badly.

At twenty-eight she owned her own business, a house, and an apartment that she rented out in Manhattan. The only thing missing was someone special in her life.

She'd had someone special once, at least she'd thought she had. She'd loved Wade with a fierceness she didn't think possible. She'd met him at one of those glitzy parties that anyone who was anyone attended. Wade wasn't a total stranger, but a well-respected fashion photographer that made his models look like dreams. When Wade sought her out, Liza had been flattered. Wade Dafoe could have his pick of any model in town.

Theirs had been a whirlwind romance. Wade had wined and dined her and made her feel like a million bucks. Then he'd convinced her to let him shoot her. The photographs he'd taken had brought her more fame, and Liza's already successful career veered off in another direction. Cosmetic companies came beating down her door. The money they'd offered had her tongue hanging to the floor. Quickly she'd signed a lucrative contract with one of the bigger names, La Femme, and had become the darling of the world.

When Wade proposed, Liza had enthusiastically said yes. In so many ways he'd made her, plus he understood the business and would not feel threatened by her travel schedule.

Who could have predicted that her cosmetic career would be short-lived? After the mugging and attempted rape, she'd been a mess. La Femme had been glad to exercise the out clause of their contract and no one could blame them. Her face was disfigured. It had taken several bouts of plastic surgery to get her to the point she was at today. Her mental state was fragile and Wade had not been much support, not that she hadn't known he was shallow. He'd promptly packed his bags and taken off, claiming he'd gotten an assignment in Europe. It was the last she'd seen of the bastard.

Liza's doorbell rang and reality returned. She glanced at her watch. If that was Erik he was fifteen minutes early. She hurried to the door with some trepidation but hoped it was him.

Erik was the type of man who made your limbs weak and your mouth go dry. He was dangerous.

13

"Coffee?" a perky waitress asked, balancing a tray in one hand and a coffeepot in the other.

"Yes, please." Erik pushed his cup forward but Liza declined, opting for tea.

From the moment he'd picked her up he'd been tense and noncommunicative. Erik had answered Liza's questions politely but had not initiated a conversation. She was beginning to think it was a mistake to have agreed to come out with him. But perhaps she was being paranoid. His aloofness could have little to do with her and more to do with artistic temperament.

"How's your painting coming along?" Liza asked to break the uneasy silence between them.

"Coming slowly."

"Anything strange happen at your house since we last spoke?"

A muscle in Erik's strong jaw twitched. "Nothing stranger than a man ringing my doorbell and handing me this." He stared at her for a moment before removing an envelope from his pocket and slamming it down on the table.

Liza glanced at the official-looking envelope, puzzled.

"Go on," Erik urged. "Read it."

She extracted the letter inside, read it, and frowned.

"Oh," she said, "that was quick."

"Is that all you have to say?" Erik snarled between clenched teeth.

"I didn't expect Paul to act so prematurely. I went to him for advice, and then I asked my mother to call him."

Erik's hazel eyes flashed fire. She could feel his rage. "I can't believe you'd do this to me. We were just getting to know each other and were becoming friends. You could have spoken to me first."

"Friendship isn't the issue here."

"Like hell it isn't. What about family loyalty? I was just getting to know and like my stepsister and you pull something like this on me."

He said he liked her. She, on the other hand, had been attracted to him from the moment she met him, and it wasn't just his physical appearance that turned her on. It was all that coiled-up creativity that found its outlet on canvas. It was what went on in his head. She'd been drawn to him, determined to find out what made him tick. She'd even been jealous of an ex-wife she'd never met, and she'd wanted to ask him why his marriage had failed.

"Paul acted too quickly," Liza said, not certain he had. She'd been pushing and pushing her mother to pursue a lawsuit. Maybe Elizabeth had decided to move ahead.

"No wonder you were willing to go out with me, my house being the motivating factor," Erik mumbled bitterly.

"That's not totally true."

Erik just looked at her.

The waitress returned, set down Liza's tea, and gave them a wide smile. "Ready to order?"

"I'm no longer hungry," Liza said, her throat closing up on her. Sitting opposite an angry Erik had robbed her of her appetite.

"Neither am I," Erik snapped, glaring at the waitress.

The woman quickly excused herself. "Signal me when you're ready," she said.

"If my house isn't totally the reason you're here," Erik said after a while, "then why?"

Liza thought for a moment, then figured telling him the truth might be best.

"When I met you I didn't expect to like you," she admitted. "I thought that you had buttered up a senile old man and that's why he left you his house. Sara was Malcolm's legitimate child and he left her nothing." She covered her mouth, realizing that she might have hurt him. "Oops, that was awful of me. What I meant was my mother was married to Malcolm and yours wasn't."

What she'd just said was even worse. She'd opened her mouth and inserted her foot even deeper.

Erik's eyes hardened and the muscles in his jaw twitched. She'd made it sound as if his illegitimacy were his fault and was something to be ashamed of.

"I'm sorry, Erik," she said, reaching for his hand. "I didn't think. My sister will be going to college in a few years, at least we hope she will. Tuition and room and board are expensive."

The hand she covered was pulled away as if touching her was repulsive.

"If you'd done your research," Erik answered, tight-lipped, "you would have discovered that Malcolm's house came with a price. He owed plenty on it and was in debt when he died. Is your mother and her husband in a position to pay me back for all the cash I put out?"

"What cash? Malcolm had money. He sold all that land to those big manufacturers. He had investments."

"And as I am sure you are aware, the stock market is in a precarious position. Ned told me your mother spent her last dime fixing up that house. That should have been a sure indicator Malcolm had nothing."

Impossible. Erik had to be lying. "Malcolm was cheap," Liza cried. "He didn't spend a bad penny once he roped a woman in."

"If my father had money," Erik said, smiling grimly, "he kept it a secret. Tell you what, if your mother wants the house so badly we don't have to go to court, she'll just need to hand over a nice fat check. Doubtful she'll recoup any of it even if she sold the house."

Erik slapped some cash down, gave her a disgusted look, and strode out. Liza followed, wishing that things hadn't taken such a bad turn. She'd ruined their day.

Outside, Erik said, "If you still have any interest in the street fair we better go."

It was the last place she wanted to be, but she had no way of getting home.

Delilah had decided to pull out all the stops with Quinn. While he wasn't exactly her type it could be fun to get his engine revving. She chose her wardrobe carefully, wanting something that would make him drool. The truth of the matter was that she hoped to run into Erik Price so that he would see what he was missing.

She climbed into a bright red tube top, knowing that her ample breasts would be prominent against the slinky fabric, then slipped into a pair of black capris. Red slides completed the look. She debated adding beads to her braids but decided to forgo the ingénue look. For a brief moment she contemplated calling Liza and then dismissed the thought no sooner than it had surfaced. She was really annoyed with Liza, sly dog that she was. Liza had known of her interest in Erik yet Liza had not backed off; if anything she seemed determined to flaunt Erik's interest in her face.

Delilah used her cell phone to make a quick call to one of the students she'd hired to run her booth. She wanted to make sure that someone had been assigned to pass out fliers. She was giving out a free red rose to anyone who stopped by her booth. She'd figured that a free rose would attract interest and give the Gilded Lily much needed exposure. With fall coming she was worried about sales. September and October were traditionally slow months. People hoarded their pennies for the upcoming holiday season.

The sound of a car in her driveway got her attention. She peered through the blinds and spotted Quinn's black Intrepid. He was on time. She liked that in a man, must mean he was anxious to see her.

Delilah flung the door open, and hand on hip, struck a pose. Quinn emerged from the car, blinked, and slid his glasses up his nose. Delilah thrust her breasts forward, knowing it would be hard for someone like him to think when size-40 double-Ds were in his face. She held her cheek out for his kiss.

"Quinn, it's so nice to see you again," she said, pressing herself up against him. Quinn grinned from ear to ear and made no attempt to extricate himself from her hold. Delilah gently disentangled herself. "Can I offer you something to drink? Coffee, juice, water?"

Quinn seemed to debate. He stood in the doorway looking uncertain. Delilah realized he was nervous and pressed her advantage. She made sure those size 40s remained close to his face.

"Oh, come on now. We're going to be outside hoofing it for the better part of the day. We don't want to get too dehydrated." She moved aside, letting Quinn slide by.

Delilah waved him to one of her leopard-skin bar stools. "Sit," she ordered and bent over to retrieve a bottle of orange juice, Pellegrino, and a couple of croissants she had in the refrigerator. "Are you hungry or did you have breakfast?"

"I ate," Quinn admitted.

"Sure you don't want to try one of these?" she tempted, holding out the box with the croissants.

Quinn shook his head. "I thought maybe you would let me take you to lunch."

Delilah's grin was Cheshire wide. "Now you're talking." She poured the Pellegrino and slid the glass toward him.

Quinn practically gulped the water down in one quick swallow. He stood, dangling his keys. Delilah grabbed a red purse and followed him out, stopping only to lock the doors.

After circling several blocks they found parking about four streets over. They followed the crowd toward the riverfront where a band played an upbeat song and several people danced.

"Looks like there's already a huge turnout," Quinn said, taking her elbow so that she wouldn't be jostled.

Delilah liked the fact that he was a gentleman. There were

too few of them left. Quinn James could hardly be considered drop-dead gorgeous, but he was attentive, gainfully employed, and had smooth dark brown skin.

As they strolled by, young mothers pushed prams or balanced toddlers on their hips. More ambulatory children held on tightly to balloons and wolfed down cotton candy with their free hands. Couples proudly held dogs on short leashes, and teenagers, dressed in baggy shorts and skimpy tops, sported tattoos and piercings that got a rise out of more conservative adults.

Delilah roamed down one aisle with Quinn close at her side. He still had hold of her elbow. She kept an eye out for the Gilded Lily's booth. She'd paid top dollar for a visible spot and she wanted to make sure the students that had been hired were doing what they were supposed to do and were handing out fliers.

Quinn stopped in front of one of those silly booths where you are challenged to throw tennis balls into a clown's mouth.

"I'll take ten dollars' worth of tickets," he said to the attendant.

Delilah stood back and watched him flex his muscles and take aim. He had a nice body and she was pretty sure he worked out. It took several tries but his aim was good and he proudly suggested she pick out a prize.

"Those are your choices," the young man manning the booth said, pointing out the selection.

Delilah quickly dismissed a gross-looking snake, opting for an overstuffed red teddy bear with a black ribbon around its neck. The toy matched her outfit. She hugged the stuffed animal close and they continued on their way.

Outside one of the food booths several empty chairs and tables were shaded by umbrellas.

"Let's sit," Quinn said, holding out one of the plastic chairs. "I'll grab us drinks and chips."

"This isn't lunch, is it?" Delilah said, sinking gratefully into the chair he held out.

"No, it's not. I promised you lunch and you'll definitely get it." He departed to fetch them drinks and munchies, then returned to sit in the chair opposite her.

"Let's get the interview over with and enjoy our day," Quinn said, removing a notepad from his shirt pocket and flipping to an empty page. He found a pen. "Did you go to college?"

"Sure did. I attended Syracuse University."

"And did you graduate?"

She laughed. "Yes with a 3.5. But I got married shortly after and the degree I earned wasn't put to use."

"What did you major in?" Quinn asked, scribbling away.

"Finance. Can you believe it?" She guffawed even louder.

"I believe it," Quinn said with a straight face.

Delilah had been expecting a sarcastic remark and when none was forthcoming she regarded him with renewed wonder. Her college major had always been a source of amusement to most men who expected her to have majored in basket weaving or some other brainless interest.

"You got married young," Quinn commented, studying her quietly. "How come?"

"I was twenty-one and in looove." Where was this going?

"And how long did the marriage last?"

"Five arduous years. I was never so bored in my life."

"Want to talk about it?"

Delilah shifted in her chair uneasily. Her marriage was not something she wanted to talk about, nor was it relevant to this interview.

"You dumped him?" Quinn asked.

"We dumped each other. We both realized that we weren't happy, so why prolong the pain?"

"There weren't any children?"

"Thank God, no." Delilah took a long, soothing sip of her frappuccino as unhappy memories began to surface. Willard had been a classmate and by far one of the best-looking men she'd ever met, but he wasn't ambitious and preferred to live life in the past, recounting his days as a star football player. She'd done herself a favor getting rid of him.

"So what made you decide to want to open your own business?" Quinn asked, scribbling furiously.

"After my marriage ended I took a course in interior design. I loved being surrounded by beautiful things. What I didn't like was working for a company and being forced to answer to people who made money while I made none."

"And you've always lived in Syracuse?" Quinn asked, his admiration clearly evident by the look on his face.

"I was born and for the most part grew up here. Willard and I left for a brief time after we got married. We moved to Cleveland where his folks were, but the Midwest was not for me."

"Why was that?" Quinn asked, still jotting notes.

Delilah brayed. "Do I strike you as the midwestern type? I stuck out like a sore thumb. I'm not exactly the type to stay home and bake cookies."

"What about Liza Hamilton? She's a friend of yours."

Delilah felt her agitation build. Why were men always fascinated with Liza?

"Yes, she is," she answered uneasily, not that she and Liza could be considered friends anymore. Not since she had taken up with Erik.

"Liza owns her own business, doesn't she?"

"Yes, and so does Cassie Newell. Cassie owns the gourmet bakery."

"What about your other friend, the one who attended Sunny's party with the basketball player?"

"Rona? She runs the nursery school."

"Four accomplished businesswomen who are friends. That's rare. Speaking of which"—Quinn shaded his eyes and squinted into the distance—"looks like a couple of those friends are heading our way."

Delilah's glance took in two people strolling toward them. Liza and Erik's presence would make for an interesting afternoon. Erik's tall, well-muscled body commanded attention and Liza's willowy height and cool comportment drew several male glances. Something was definitely going on between these two and Delilah planned on finding out exactly what.

She slid from her chair, leaving the teddy bear behind, and walked toward them. Quinn quickly followed, bringing the bear.

"Hi, you two," Delilah said, stepping into their path.

Liza removed dark glasses before kissing her cheek. "Hey, girlfriend, I thought you'd fallen off the face of the earth," she said as she flashed the wide grin that had made her famous.

Delilah wanted to wipe that grin off her face. Sneaky bitch. She'd gone on ad nauseam about not wanting to be involved with a man after what she'd been through.

Erik nodded an acknowledgment but kept his sunglasses on. He looked attractive and mysterious with dark stubble on his chin. His khaki walking shorts covered powerful thighs, and his periwinkle polo shirt opened at the neck revealing a sprinkle of sexy chest hairs.

Lord have mercy, what she wouldn't do to run her fingers through those hairs. A man like Erik would be wasted on Liza. She wouldn't have a clue what to do with him.

The men shook hands and exchanged small talk. Liza and Delilah began a strained conversation.

"Did you just get here?" Delilah asked, hoping to get a handle on what was really happening between Liza and Erik.

"A little while ago," Liza answered. "Quinn seems like a very nice guy."

"He is."

There was something about Liza's forced conversation that seemed off. On closer inspection it appeared as if she and Erik weren't getting along. Never one to miss an opportunity, Delilah issued an invitation. "Why don't you join us? Quinn and I were just talking about you."

Erik took Liza's elbow. "That might not be a bad idea. There's safety in numbers."

The two had had a fight and it hadn't taken much coaxing. Delilah danced ahead of them, shouting over her shoulder,

"We'll find a stand selling Bloody Marys and walk along the river."

They made their way to the river, dodging teenagers selling oversized helium balloons and couples maneuvering strollers. Clowns entertained young kids by painting patterns on their faces but there was still no sign of the students she'd hired to give out fliers. In an hour or so she would check out her booth, but right now she needed to make headway with Erik.

Delilah spotted a kiosk selling Bloody Marys and mimosas. She ordered four drinks and beckoned her friends over. Holding their drinks they continued to walk along the riverbank, side-stepping couples in various stages of making out. Finally they found a bench and sat.

"All that walking's made me thirsty," Delilah said, slugging down her drink.

Quinn clinked his plastic glass against hers. "I hear that." Then he finished his Blood Mary in a neat swallow.

Erik sat, careful not to even touch shoulders with Liza. Delilah concluded there most definitely was a problem. She threw diplomacy to the wind, and asked, "You two have a fight or something?"

Liza's voice wobbled. "What would make you think such a thing?"

Erik said nothing and simply sipped on his drink.

"Your long faces for one," Delilah said. "Chill, peoples. Life's too short. Enjoy the warm weather while we have it. In another month or so we'll see snow."

"Snow in October?" Erik asked, sounding incredulous.

"We've had snow in September," Liza confirmed. "We are pretty close to Canada."

Erik seemed delighted. He spoke mainly to himself. "I'll get to light a fire in one of my fireplaces earlier than expected."

"Don't count on it," Liza said, glaring at him.

What was really going on? Liza had once admitted to being pissed off that Malcolm had left his house to Erik. Could she be trying to get near him because the house was what she wanted?

Quinn shifted uneasily and Delilah realized he must be picking up the tension. They needed a distraction, something to focus attention back on her. As bumblebees swooped down to sip nectar from the flowers she got an idea.

"Oh, my God," Delilah said, springing up and slapping her chest. "I've been stung."

The two men's eyes practically popped out of their heads as she yanked down her tube top and began swatting her breasts.

Liza was up, shielding her from the men's gaping looks, but Delilah sidestepped her. She rubbed her breasts and held them out like offerings. "It hurts."

Both men gaped openmouthed.

14

Kalib's hold on her hand made Cassie feel safe. She wandered through the fair, an unfamiliar feeling of contented happiness surfacing. It had been a long time since she'd had this much male attention.

He made her feel beautiful and for once she wasn't worried about her physical image, or the huge breakfast she'd consumed. She would deal with the extra calories later. One trip to the bathroom would take care of any doubts.

They stopped in front of a booth where a silversmith was busy making jewelry. Kalib bent to examine the merchandise and Cassie admired his shaved head. He wore bald well, and the diamond stud in his ear made him look distinguished and handsome.

Cassie peered around Kalib at the array of silver jewelry on display, noting assorted rings, earrings, chokers, and bracelets. The metal and inlaid gems glittered under the midday sun.

"Look at that piece," Cassie said, pointing out three slender pieces of silver that wrapped around and around. Two leaves served as clasps on the ends. "It's so unique."

Kalib examined the slave bracelet, quickly agreeing. He approached the vendor. "How much is that one?" He pointed out the piece.

The man, glad for a customer, stopped what he was doing and came over, scratching his head. "You have good taste. That's a favorite of mine."

Cassie began to feel uncomfortable. She'd been admiring the bracelet, not hinting for it.

"Uh, Kalib," she said, "we've got quite a bit of ground left to cover. Let's move on."

"This should only take a sec." He tossed her an enchanting smile and his feet remained planted where they were.

The vendor removed the piece from the showcase and Kalib held it up to the light, carefully examining it. Up close it was even prettier and more exquisite than she'd thought. He haggled with the vendor until they came to an agreement, then said, "Wrap it up."

Cassie began to protest but Kalib silenced her with a stare. Money exchanged hands and the bracelet was placed in a velvet pouch, which Kalib pocketed. When they were halfway down another aisle he handed the little bag to her.

"I can't accept this," Cassie said. "It's much too expensive."

"I want you to have it. In fact it would please me if you wore it today. It goes well with your blouse."

Before Cassie could utter another word, he wound the bracelet around her upper arm and stood back to admire it. "There. It was made for you," he said, taking her arm.

It was a sweet thing to do but it made her uneasy. Gifts from a man were not something she was used to. Cassie spotted the river in the distance and couples strolling along the banks. Kites flew high in the sky and children raced by on skateboards. She was overwhelmed with emotion and needed to get away from the milling crowd. Jim had never been this good to her.

"That looks like fun," she said, pointing at a rock-climbing wall that had been erected on the riverbank. Several people monitored the progress of a few adventurous souls.

"Let's go take a look," Kalib said, hustling her in that direction. "Maybe we'll give it a try."

"Uh, let's not."

She wasn't exactly dressed for a sport that required finding toeholds and hauling herself up. She was wearing shorts and a linen halter top and she couldn't risk making an ass of herself or, even worse, falling out of her blouse.

Lucky for her, a long line of people waited their turn. Kalib decided they would take a walk and check back later.

"Aren't those friends of yours heading our way?" Kalib asked, squinting in the distance.

Sure enough, two men and two women were coming toward them. One of the females looked a little like Delilah. As the group came closer, Cassie recognized her friend. Walking with her were Erik, Liza, and a strange man she didn't know.

Delilah, spotting Kalib and Cassie, let out an audible whoop. She began running toward them. The other three followed at a more leisurely pace.

Cassie gaped as she got a good view of Delilah's outfit. The woman was truly outrageous. Her nipples were clearly imprinted against the thin fabric of a tube top and every loose piece of flesh jiggled and bounced.

Delilah huffed to a stop in front of them.

"Girl, I didn't know you were coming," she panted. Her eyes fastened on the newly acquired bracelet. One hand reached out to touch it. "This new?"

Cassie didn't answer right off because she knew whatever she said would initiate a barrage of questions. Kalib, who was standing behind her, came to the rescue.

"As a matter of fact it is. I bought it for Cassie. Doesn't it suit her perfectly?"

Delilah oohed and aahed until the remaining threesome caught up.

"Look," she said, pointing out the bracelet. "Look what Kalib bought for Cassie. Quinn, all you got me was a bear."

The jewelry was suitably admired and the studious-looking man was introduced as "Quinn James." He seemed entranced by Delilah, who was too busy wiggling her hips in Erik's face to pay him much attention.

Liza seemed a bit subdued but she dutifully kissed Cassie. Erik Price didn't look happy at all. In fact he looked like he didn't want to be there. Cassie wondered what had happened to make Erik, who was normally civil, so rude. She was relieved when Kalib suggested that they move on and continue their perusal of the booths.

"Please take me home," she heard Liza say to Erik as they departed. "I hate to be a party pooper but I do have a terrible headache."

Erik made his excuses to the remaining couple, placed a hand on the small of Liza's back, and steered her toward the exit.

The afternoon was still young and Erik did not feel much like painting. He was angry as all hell and the vein at the side of his head throbbed. To keep himself busy he grabbed a sketch pad and headed out to the back verandah.

Liza's deceit still rankled. Why would she do something like this? He was mad at himself for getting sucked in and not realizing she was a user.

Erik had learned not to trust a long time ago. He'd had reason to as he became more famous. Women would say and do anything just to be around him. But it wasn't him they really wanted, just his money and fame.

That's why he'd been relieved to meet Paulette. Truth be known, he'd married her because she'd been supportive, self-sufficient, and crazy about him. She didn't seem to want or need anything besides his company. She earned a good salary, had her own place, and adored his paintings. She'd ended up purchasing two. Erik had convinced himself that at last he'd met someone who didn't view him solely as a meal ticket. Paulette appreciated his art and appreciated him. He'd been wrong.

Erik, pressing hard on his pencil, made a few deft strokes on the notepad. A face quickly emerged. He felt as if his hand was being guided by an unseen force. He sketched features that had exotic slants and angles to them. He added lashes to the almond-shaped eyes, shaded in high cheekbones, and outlined full lips. Damn if the face didn't look like Liza Hamilton's.

Liza was on his mind, blast the conniving witch. He'd inadvertently sketched the face that was the source of his irritation. Disgusted with himself, he tossed down his pad and began slowly pacing the verandah. He was not a hard-drinking man but right now he could use a drink.

He'd liked Liza from the moment he'd met her. She'd seemed warm and open, and despite her mostly faded scars, was by far the most attractive and interesting woman he'd met in a long time. He'd wanted to paint her. Felt compelled too and didn't even know why.

Like Liza? It was more than like. There was something about her that had drawn him like a moth to a flame and it had little to do with her being his stepsister. But all she'd been interested in was his damn house, a house that was not a gift, but a liability. His father had given it to him probably thinking he couldn't afford to accept it and it would have to be sold. He'd shown the old man.

Erik remembered Liza's peculiar behavior when they were at brunch the first time. The questions she'd asked all had to do with his house. It had been the house from the beginning. Always the house.

Paul White had never gotten back to him. He had a good mind to give the attorney another call, but it was Sunday and the law office would be closed. He needed to do something to take his mind off this mess. Confining himself in the attic was not a good idea and painting was out of the question. He couldn't paint when he was this angry. He would call his mother and see if she knew anything about Liza's mother, Elizabeth.

He unsnapped the cell phone he kept clipped to his belt, pushed a button with the programmed number, and sat back to wait. His mother would eventually pick up.

"Hi," Rachel said, sounding out of breath.

Erik thought that she might have been gardening, a favorite pastime since he'd bought her the house. His mother had never married and she spent her days volunteering at a soup kitchen or teaching adults how to read. He was glad that he was finally in a position to take care of her.

For too many years Erik's mother had gone without, sacrificing to send him to art classes and remaining supportive when others weren't. Most of her friends had told her that she was coddling him and that his time would be better spent pursuing professional sports or finding a real job. But Rachel had stood by him and, by God, he would stand by her.

"How have you been?" Erik asked, already knowing the answer.

"Busy. I've assumed you've been too, that's why you haven't called me."

A gentle chastisement was always her style. He didn't doubt that she was busy. His mother was the type of person who needed to have every second of the day occupied or she would feel useless.

"I'm sorry I haven't been in touch," he said, momentarily contrite. "You know how I get when I'm painting."

She sighed. "Yes, I know. When you were a little boy, half the time you didn't remember whether it was day or night. All right, Erik. Tell me what's wrong." He never could fool her. She was in tune with his moods, his voice.

"Liza Hamilton's mother is suing me," he admitted.

"Whatever for?"

Erik explained what little he knew.

"That's ridiculous," Rachel said, sounding irritated. "Didn't you tell me that house cost you more than it's worth? If Elizabeth Tanner remarried and lives in Boston, what would she want with a house in Syracuse?"

"I don't think she wants the house for herself. It's for her daughter."

Rachel made a rude sound. "Sure she does. Sounds like pure greed to me."

"What kind of woman is Elizabeth?" Erik asked.

Rachel remained silent for a moment, thinking. "I only know what I've heard, and I never heard anything negative. Malcolm was the one painted as the villain. It was said he took advantage of her."

It took a lot for Rachel to say that. She'd been in love with his father and probably still was. She'd been patient watching Malcolm go through an assortment of wives, but he'd always come back to her. If anyone had been taken advantage of, it had been she.

Although Erik had never met his father, his opinion of him had never been very high. What kind of man would impregnate a woman and then refuse to assume responsibility? As far as he was concerned, his father had been dead long before his physical death. He'd only accepted his inheritance because he'd been looking for a quiet place to paint and because he wanted to thumb his nose at the father who'd abandoned him.

"So what are you going to do about it?" Elizabeth asked.

What *was* he going to do? "I'm going to try to speak with Paul White. He's the attorney representing Elizabeth. If that fails, I'll attempt to contact Elizabeth directly and reason with her."

"Who would ever have thought it would come to this?" Rachel said, snorting.

He certainly hadn't. With a deadline to meet and paintings to deliver, he needed a lawsuit like he needed a hole in the head. Maybe he would drive over to Liza's and try speaking with her again. She should have had enough time to take a couple of aspirins and get over the headache she'd pretended to have.

Then again his arrival might bring on a full-blown migraine. But maybe not.

Erik chuckled.

"Damn it, Mother, why didn't you tell me you told Paul to deliver a summons?" Liza yelled, her hand clutching the receiver like a vise.

Elizabeth responded in her cool manner, "Please lower your voice, dear. I'm doing what you encouraged me to do. You've been after me for months to go after what's rightfully Sara's, and now that I do you're mad at me."

"I thought you were going to get Paul's advice and then we'd talk. I was really embarrassed when Erik confronted me. I would never have agreed to go out with the man had I known that he'd already been summoned."

Elizabeth was quiet for a moment. "Why don't we talk about it this weekend when I come up?"

"Fine, but you need to know that things have gotten complicated. According to Erik, Malcolm's house was not given to him free and clear; there were expenses that had to be paid. He expects to be reimbursed for the money he laid out."

"He expects what?" Elizabeth gasped.

"You heard me. He expects to be paid back for the liens and mortgages on the house. He claims these costs far exceed the home's worth."

Liza could hear her mother beginning to panic. It came over loud and clear in her voice. "And what would be the point of me going after a house riddled with debt? I'm supposed to be doing this for Sara. We had hoped to sell the house so that we could take care of her college expenses."

"Exactly. I'll try to get hold of Paul and we'll discuss a plan this weekend."

"Dear God," Elizabeth said, "I never expected something like this."

"Don't panic, Mother, we'll think of something," Liza said, hanging up. She pressed her forehead against the cool refrigerator. What a mess she'd made of things. Elizabeth couldn't afford to buy Erik out. It might be cheaper to forget about the house and just pay Sara's tuition.

The sound of a motor revving in her driveway got her attention. Distracted, Liza went to the door. She spotted Erik's black pickup truck. Why was he back? He'd been only too glad to drop her off and hadn't seemed to want to linger.

Liza opened the door and stood, hand on her hip, as he sauntered up her walkway. She could tell by the set of his jaw that he was still angry. But he made an attractive, brooding figure, and she felt self-conscious standing with her hair loose and no shoes on.

"Did you forget something?" she asked when he was closer.

"We've got unfinished business," he said, grabbing her elbow and hustling her into the kitchen. "How's the headache?"

What headache? She stood captive as he balanced a hip on the kitchen counter. A door slammed somewhere upstairs and Liza swore she heard laughter.

Erik must have heard it, too. "Do you have company?" he asked.

"No. It's probably an open window and the neighbors' laughter drifting in."

But there were no open windows that she remembered and certainly no breeze. She was left to assume her ghosts were amused.

Erik continued to stare at her. Liza stared back, standing her ground.

"Well?" she said to break the uncomfortable silence.

"Why did you encourage your mother to go after me? Had we talked, I could have helped."

"Helped with . . . ?"

"Money, if that's what she needed."

"You would help my mother and a sister you never met?"

"Why not? I help plenty of people, most of them strangers. Why wouldn't I help blood?"

Liza stared at him, speechless, wondering if he was pulling her leg. The world of modeling had been filled with shallow people, people who didn't lift a finger unless there was something in it for them. What could be in it for Erik, except maybe a tax deduction?

"I owe you a huge apology then," she said uncertainly, not sure she trusted his motives. "It's just strange that a successful artist would take over an old house that he didn't need."

"Who said I didn't need it?" Erik asked, coming closer, until his breath caressed her cheeks and she could see the earnestness in his face. "That house has helped me keep my sanity. It's kept me real. You of all people should know how easy it is to get carried away with the glitzy life and all the adoring people telling you how wonderful you are."

Liza understood where he was coming from. Fame and fortune weren't all they were cracked up to be. It came with a price, and real friends were few and far between.

She remained standing, anchored in his hold, though a little voice in the back of her head warned her to be cautious. Surely he must know that she was attracted to him. Had he decided to work that angle? Well, he was in for a rude surprise. First thing tomorrow she planned on calling Paul so that he could check out the story behind these alleged liens and mortgages.

"I wish you'd consider sitting for me," Erik said, his finger outlining one of the scars on her face and sending her heart jumping.

Liza opened her mouth to respond, but before she could, Erik leaned in and kissed her. It was merely a brush of the lips but it made her pulse pound and the blood pump in her veins.

"What are you doing?" she asked when she was able to speak.

"What we've both wanted to do for quite some time."

"Why, you cocky—"

A melodic peal of laughter came again from somewhere upstairs.

Liza jumped, and stepped out of Erik's arms, needing to put distance between them.

"Sure you don't have company?" Erik asked.

She ignored him. "I'll think about sitting for you. And I'll talk to my mother when she comes up this weekend and see how she wants to proceed."

"Both would be appreciated," he answered, coming closer again. The back of his hand stroked her cheek and she could feel the heat of his body and smell the musky soap that he wore.

"I hope you'll think about this as well," he said, gathering her into his arms and kissing her again. This time there was nothing gentle about the kiss. It was demanding, probing, and urgent, requiring an answer she couldn't give.

But pursuing anything with Erik would be dangerous. She still didn't trust him.

15

Sam's doorbell rang. His hobbling steps picked up a bit as he trudged the well-worn path to the door. He already knew who was on the other side. Elizabeth Tanner was in town and he'd sensed her presence long before she'd unpacked her first bag. He'd known it would only be a matter of time before she visited.

"That you, Elizabeth?" he asked in his excitement, buttoning up his shirt the wrong way.

A soft chuckle came from outside. He opened the door and stepped out to greet her.

"I'm glad you came."

He remembered Elizabeth's face from a long time ago. She was a real beauty. More importantly, she was kind. He was suddenly filled with embarrassment that his place wasn't the kind into which you could invite a nice woman. If he wanted to visit with her, their time would be spent outside.

Elizabeth touched his face and he smelled her flowery scent. She smelled as if she'd taken a bath in rose petals.

"Good to see you again, Sam," she said, kissing his cheek.

"Good to see you, too. I missed you, Elizabeth. Missed your visits."

He felt all quivery inside, like a young pup that'd been salivating after a woman who finally responded. At his age it wasn't appropriate to have these feelings.

"Aren't you going to ask me in?" she said gently.

A cool breeze brushed his face and he felt for her arm. "My place ain't presentable. Let's take a walk."

"Oh, Sam, as if I care."

Sam was choked up with emotion as they started up the path he'd memorized. He knew it well and remembered how the trees intertwined and the branches merged to create a shady walkway. They were close to the old cemetery when Elizabeth came to a stop.

"There's a bench, Sam. Let's sit," she said. "It's a lovely afternoon and it would be nice to talk."

He sat next to her, feeling happier than he'd felt in a very long time. Elizabeth had always had that effect on him. She made his creaky bones feel young again. She made him smile.

"What brings you to town?" he asked, as if he didn't know. *Malcolm's damn house and her daughter's obsession with it.*

"I came to see Liza. You've met her, I hope. I also have business to tend to."

"You brought your other daughter with you," Sam said. "She's a real live wire and a handful. But with time she'll settle down."

Elizabeth sighed. "I hope so. Right now she's driving me crazy."

Sam covered her hand with his. "It'll work out. I'm glad that you found a man who's good and takes care of you."

Elizabeth gave his hand a little squeeze. "Phillip is wonderful. He is the best thing that happened to me. I worry about Liza all alone though. I wish she would meet someone."

"She'll be all right," Sam said with certainty. "Malcolm's boy will take good care of her."

"You mean her stepbrother? What do you know that I don't know?"

Sam tucked her hand in the crook of his elbow. "Some things are better left to fate. Those two have problems to work out but they'll do great."

Sam heard the confusion in Elizabeth's voice as she said, "What are you talking about, Sam? Liza dislikes her step-brother. She's been encouraging me to go to court and get that house."

"Leave it alone, Elizabeth," Sam urged. "Malcolm left that boy his place for a reason. Guilt, I suspect. He used his mother just like he used you."

Elizabeth's voice sounded uncertain when she said, "So I'm just supposed to let it go? What about Sara? She was Malcolm's child as well."

He sensed her anguish and sought to comfort her. "Your life is good now. Put the bad times behind you and move on. Have the child apply for a scholarship."

"I'm meeting with Paul White," Elizabeth said, rising. "I'll find out the truth about that house and go from there."

"Do that," Sam said, knowing that he could do nothing to dissuade her.

Slowly, Sam propelled his old bones up. He took the hand Elizabeth offered and retraced their steps.

"Take care, old friend," she said, kissing his weathered cheek.

"You take care. And listen to me, no good will come of you going after that property. The spirits will not be kind to anyone other than Erik living in that house."

"Oh, you and your foolishness," Elizabeth said, kissing him again.

He felt himself blushing. "Not foolishness, simply fact."

Sam was about to let himself back into the house when Elizabeth tugged on his sleeve.

"Come to dinner tomorrow. I make a mean casserole."

He was flattered, honored, hungry. "Love to," he answered, thinking how much he'd missed Elizabeth, and how much he would welcome a home-cooked meal.

"What's going on?" Erik asked a group of people gathered in front of Shoppers Express grocery store. A police car was parked out front, sirens still wailing.

A grandmotherly type balancing two bags of groceries answered, "Some teenagers were got caught shoplifting. Where the parents are is what I want to know. Young people should never be left on their own." Her head wagged back and forth, clearly disapproving.

Erik managed to sidestep the crowd and entered the store. Two uniformed policemen were at the entrance interrogating six teenagers, two of them girls. The grocery store manager who'd caught the kids stealing yelled at them, gesticulated wildly, and pointed to a number of items on the floor.

"How dare you come in here and help yourselves to things you can't pay for? You think stuffing magazines down the front of your pants and sticking candy bars in your shirt pockets are what nice kids would do?" He wagged a finger at two sullen-faced teenagers. "You two girls should be ashamed of yourselves." He opened his hand to reveal several lipsticks and numerous eye pencils.

"And you"—he turned to the boys—"how on earth did you think you would get out of here with these six-packs?" He pointed to packs of beer on the floor.

Erik noted the surly faces, the nonchalant attitudes, and the hip-hop attire the teenagers wore. He remembered how difficult life was at that age. You didn't think you were understood. He too had acted out, hoping to get attention. He felt especially sorry for the younger of the two girls who, despite the outward bravado, seemed close to tears.

"Better give me your names and I'll call your parents," the beefier of the policemen said to the girls. "Billy and Roger, you're old pros, shame on you for involving the ladies. Okay, ladies, let's have it."

The teenagers looked at each other but none of them spoke.

"Come on now. I'm counting to ten, then I'm taking you down to the station," the cop said, lining them up.

The girl who'd been close to tears finally broke down. Erik felt sorry for her as her bony little shoulders shook.

"My mother's going to kill me," she wailed. "And my sister,

much as I hate her, is gonna be pissed. She's gonna say I embarrassed her."

And you did.

"You should have thought of that before you acted," the previously silent policeman said, not unkindly. "Now give us your names."

Erik had come to Shoppers Express to do his marketing, passing on the larger Giant supermarket chain where he had more of a chance of being recognized. It was none of his business, but he felt sorry for the wailing girl, because she at least showed remorse. The others were tough. They smirked and challenged the cops to arrest them. Something prompted Erik to intervene.

"I'll take responsibility for the two girls," he said, speaking up and beckoning to the weeping one. "You're in a lot of trouble, young lady."

The beefy policeman eyed him curiously. "Are you a relative, sir?"

Erik didn't know what prompted him to lie, but lie he did. "As a matter of fact I am."

The crying teenager stared at him through mascara-streaked eyes. She would be a beauty one day if she got rid of the hideous makeup, the orange hair, and the outlandish clothes. The other girl stared openmouthed.

"I'm Erik Price," Erik said, fishing in the pocket of his jeans to find his wallet where he kept his driver's license.

"Price, the artist?" the other policeman said with such awe the teenage boys lost their bored looks and gawked at him.

The grocery store manager seemed rattled for a moment. He came to Erik's side and stuck out his hand.

"Mr. Price, my wife is a big fan of yours. She admires your work. Not that we can afford any of it, mind you."

Erik thanked the man as he continued to gush.

"He's my brother," the still-sobbing girl blurted, looking to Erik to back up her story. He gave her credit for going along with his lie.

He'd drive both girls home and talk with their parents. They needed guidance and a firm hand. They should never have been allowed to run wild with these thugs.

"Yes, I'm her brother," he said, not missing a beat, "and like I said, I'll take responsibility for both of the ladies." He turned to the store manager. "How much do they owe you?"

The man began to calculate, ticking off the items on his fingers. "Total comes to thirty-five dollars, give or take a bit."

Erik peeled off several bills and pressed them into the manager's hands. "Consider the merchandise paid for, plus some. You've had to leave your business to take care of this. Do me a favor and let this go. They're kids. Drop the charges."

"I don't know," the store manager muttered. After a few moments of hesitation he declared, "All right, Billy, Roger, and the rest of you lot, get going. I don't ever want to see you back in my store again."

The fat policeman cleared his throat and shifted from one foot to the other. "Ron, you sure you don't want to press charges?" he asked the manager. "Teach Billy, Roger, and their friends a lesson. This isn't the first time they've done something like this and I know it won't be their last."

"I got paid," Ron said, struggling with his conscience. "No harm done, I suppose."

"Yes, Ron, kids will be kids. Give them a break. You were young once. The girls will get punished when they get home. Do this for me and I'll sign a lithograph for your wife and drop it off."

"Only because it's you," Ron said, still sounding dubious, although he beamed from ear to ear.

Erik thanked him and motioned to the girls. "Let's go."

The boys scooted by, not even pausing to thank him for saving them. The cops shook their heads and groaned.

"See what I mean?" the thinner one said. "They'll be at it again."

Erik placed an arm around the frail shoulders of the child who'd claimed to be his sister and led her out to the parking lot. "Come on," he said to the remaining girl, a Lauryn Hill look-alike. "You're going home with me."

Inside the pickup truck, he squeezed his alleged sister's shoulder and said, "That was quick thinking on your part."

She jerked away and turned to face him. "I didn't lie. You are my brother."

Erik squinted at her. "Sure I am. Give me your names and addresses and I'll drop you off at your homes. Don't even try lying to me or you'll be sorry for having ever run into me."

The Lauryn Hill look-alike started jabbering almost immediately. "I don't have parents. They're dead."

"Puhleese," Erik said. "Just give me your name and give me directions."

"Betsey," she finally said.

"And does Betsey have a last name?"

She thought for a moment, rolling her eyes. "Devine."

"Sounds like a porn star. Come on, you can do better than that."

His sister managed a very small smile and for the second time that day he realized how beautiful she was.

"Here are your choices," Erik said, "either give me the correct names and addresses or I'm taking you to the nearest police station."

"You won't do that," Betsey protested

"Try me. What about you?" he asked the other. "Do you have a name?"

The girl bit her knuckles and looked at him. "Uhh."

"Cough it up," Erik snapped. "You're both beginning to try my patience."

"Sara," she said reluctantly.

Erik frowned. He'd heard that name somewhere before, and repeatedly. He regarded her suspiciously. "And what's Sara's last name?"

"Mitchell."

Erik started, wondering if she was pulling his leg. "Sara Mitchell," he repeated. "You wouldn't happen to be Liza Hamilton's sister?"

This time there was a visible reaction. "Yeah, Liza's my sister."

"So you weren't lying. I'm your brother."

"Told you," Sara said, assuming a snotty voice.

"Jesus, kid. Why the hell are you hanging out with thugs? What could you be thinking of, shoplifting? How am I going to explain this to Liza?"

"Not your problem," Sara said in a sulky voice.

"You just made it my problem," Erik snapped. "As for you, young lady," he said to the other one, "better start giving me directions to your house."

Betsey reluctantly gave him her address. She lived in a nice part of town, not too far from Sunny Hirschbaum's house. Erik wondered what her parents were like as he parked his pickup in front of a sprawling house, took her by the elbow and hurried her up the walk. He turned briefly, admonishing Sara, "Don't even think of getting out of the vehicle and running off. You're already in enough trouble."

Erik rang the doorbell and waited. After a while hurried footsteps came toward the door and he was greeted by a rotund, pecan woman with an elegant hairdo. She frowned at the teenager.

"Is Alanna in trouble?" she asked, moving aside to let them both in.

"I'm Erik Price," he said, introducing himself.

The woman looked blankly back while the teenager cringed and attempted to slide by.

"Not so fast, young lady."

Alanna froze.

Erik took in a beautifully appointed living room furnished with what must be expensive antiques. He stood on marble floors gazing up at a winding staircase and mullioned windows on the second floor.

"Alanna was caught stealing," he said, as the teenager pouted and kept her eyes lowered.

"Alanna!" The woman gave the child a steely-eyed look. "I'm the housekeeper, Mrs. Hardy," she explained. "Mr. and Mrs. Jamison are away for the weekend. Alanna left to meet friends at the mall. Wait until her parents find out what she did."

"I'm going to my room," Alanna said, prancing up the staircase. She turned back once to glare at them.

"Thank Mr. Price," Mrs. Hardy ordered sternly.

But the teenager continued on her way.

"Thank you for bringing her home," Mrs. Hardy said. "How can Mr. and Mrs. Jamison reach you when they get back?"

Erik gave her his address and phone number, then retraced his steps. When he got back to his vehicle Sara was gone.

"Damn that child," he muttered. He shouldn't have left her alone. Revving his engine, he took off.

About a quarter mile up the road he spotted a blur of color darting through the woods and suspected it was Sara. Erik parked the pickup truck on the side of the road and raced after her. He dodged brambles and low-lying branches, easily covering the distance between them. Crunching footsteps ahead gave him a clue as to her location. Sure enough, she darted through the underbrush and he heard her labored breathing. Erik quickly closed in. Wait until he got his hands on her.

"Give it up," he called out. "You're really starting to piss me off."

Sara darted behind a tree and he heard a heavy thud as she fell.

"Yeow."

"Are you hurt?" he asked, approaching the place where she sat, hugging her leg.

Sara's orange hair was disheveled, and her makeup streaked, giving her a raccoon-like effect.

"My ankle hurts," she wailed as Erik squatted down to examine the leg she held up. He carefully prodded the area that had begun to swell and bit back the lecture on the tip of his tongue, deciding now was not the time or place. Sara was in obvious distress. He needed to get her home.

Erik scooped the girl up into his arms, surprised at how light she was. She needed to gain weight and put a few pounds on that skinny frame. When he placed her in the truck, she broke down.

"Please don't tell my mother I got caught shoplifting," Sara sobbed. "She'll kill me and I'll be grounded for weeks."

"We'll see how it goes. I'm not making promises I can't keep, especially after what you just pulled."

Erik jerked the vehicle in gear and took off. As luck would have it, he now had the perfect opportunity to meet the infamous Elizabeth Tanner, and talk they would.

16

Liza's shop was still open when Erik pulled up in front of the building. Green and white awnings fluttered in the breeze and two customers with shopping bags that read Visage were coming out.

Erik held on tightly to Sara's arm and steered her through the open door. He felt some trepidation seeing Liza again. It would be the first time they saw each other since that heart-stopping kiss. The intensity of that connection still had him reeling and scared him a bit. Where could it all lead? But he was still mad at her. Not just mad, he felt betrayed.

An attractive woman with salt-and-pepper hair stood behind the register ringing up a purchase. Erik scanned the area looking for Liza but saw no sign of her.

"Sara," the woman said, finishing up with her customer, "I wondered where you'd disappeared to. You're a mess. And you're hurt. Who is this man?"

Erik stepped forward, bringing his limping sister with him. He released Sara's arm and stuck out his hand. "I'm Erik Price. You must be Liza and Sara's mother."

"I'm Elizabeth Tanner," she answered, clasping the hand he offered in a warm grip. "My God, you look just like Malcolm," she said in an awed voice.

Erik's mother had often alluded to his uncanny resemblance to his father. He preferred to think he looked like himself and not like the faceless father that had played no role in his life.

"Mother, have you seen . . ." Liza's head emerged from the back room. Pink flushed her cappuccino skin as her eyes met Erik's.

"Hi," she said, sounding slightly out of breath. "I see you've met Sara." Her expression changed as she noted her sister's tear-stained face and her hobbling gait. "What's she been up to?"

The teenager seemed none too happy at being spoken about as if she didn't exist. She gave Erik a pleading look. Erik's conscience warred with him. Elizabeth and Liza deserved to know about the child's tangle with the law, but he knew it was important not to violate her trust. He would never make headway with Sara if he ratted her out.

"I came to Sara's rescue when she hurt her ankle," he said. "I don't think it's broken, probably just sprained, but she'll need ice and she'll need to elevate it."

Elizabeth shoved a chair Sara's way. "I'm afraid to ask what happened. Thank you, Erik, for bringing her home."

Erik debated for a moment. "How about you and I find a quiet place to talk?"

"I'd like to be included," Liza said, coming to stand beside her mother. "If you'll give me a couple of minutes I'll get some ice for Sara, then close up."

Erik nodded. Liza hadn't given him much choice. As she disappeared into the back room, he admired her well-toned body in her crisp white shirt and straight-legged black pants. The outfit would have appeared conservative on anyone else, but on Liza it looked downright sexy and smart. Two buttons opened to reveal a hint of cleavage and the view from the back left his head spinning.

Sara ungraciously accepted the ice pack Liza offered. Erik kneeled next to the teenager and silently held out his hand. Without a word, Sara turned over the towel with the ice, and Erik placed it on the swollen ankle.

"Oow," the teen said, flinching.

"Must hurt like crazy," Erik muttered. "Maybe we should get you to a doctor."

"No. No doctor. I'll be all right."

With pursed lips Elizabeth surveyed the scene. "We'll see how you feel tomorrow," she said to her daughter, then turned back to Erik. "Should I ask where you found her?"

Sara's eyes sought Erik's, pleading with and challenging him.

"She was attempting to walk home. I picked her up."

Sara came down with a coughing fit and Liza raised an eyebrow slightly. She continued about her business, tallying money in the cash register, and pulling down the blinds.

"Ready?" Liza asked, dangling the shop's keys in her hand.

"Careful," Elizabeth said, ordering Sara up. "Don't put weight on that foot. Take one arm, Erik. I'll take the other."

Together they managed to get the teenager out the door.

"The stairs may be a problem," Liza said, as they made their way to the side entrance of the house and onto the verandah.

Erik slung the protesting teenager over his shoulder. "Where to?"

"Bring Sara up to her bedroom. I'll show you."

Liza started upstairs and the small procession followed behind her. Sara was laid down on her bed and tucked in under a pretty quilt while Elizabeth rushed off to get ibuprofen and water, muttering under her breath about children who didn't mind.

With the teenager settled, they returned to the living room. Liza was bursting with energy all of a sudden. She flitted about, plumping up cushions and picking up imaginary pieces of lint off the rug.

"Come sit," Elizabeth said, taking over. "Erik, can we get you something to drink, or better yet, can you stay for dinner?"

Erik was flattered by the invitation and surprised. He hadn't pictured Elizabeth to be so warm and welcoming. He had thought of her as a cold, hard, calculating bitch. Her sincerity got to him.

"I'd hate to impose," he said hesitantly.

"Mother, I'm sure Erik has plans," Liza said too quickly.

That did it. Liza seemed anxious to have him gone and there was no reason for it. It wasn't like he'd done anything to her, if anything it was the reverse. She'd been the one to betray him.

"I'd love to stay for dinner, if it's not too much trouble," Erik said, speaking up.

He slanted Liza a look and noted that she flushed again. She was hardly immune to him, which was a good thing. He planned on making her squirm.

"You would not be imposing," Elizabeth said firmly. "I made a casserole last evening and there's other company coming. I've invited Sam O'Reilly. He's an old friend."

How could he turn down the opportunity to see Sam again? Better to address the issues of the lawsuit before company arrived.

"Mrs. Tanner, this court business makes me uncomfortable. I'm by no means greedy, but I've had to pay off my father's debts and it would be far less expensive for Sara to get a student loan. If you add attorney fees it's going to be exorbitant."

Elizabeth listened quietly while Liza continued to fume.

"Have you had a chance to speak with your attorney?" Erik asked. "He should be able to get proof of all I've laid out."

"Liza already contacted Paul," Elizabeth answered. "We're waiting to hear back from him."

Paul White still hadn't returned his calls. Why? Erik tried appealing to Elizabeth's reasonable side. "Mrs. Tanner, you appear to be a sensible woman. This entire situation can be easily settled out of court. I have an idea."

The doorbell rang before he could voice his thoughts. Liza rushed to the door, and Elizabeth disappeared into the kitchen, muttering something about needing to heat up her casserole and make a salad.

Clomping footsteps and a tip-tapping cane headed his way. Erik changed seats so that Sam wouldn't have to navigate the entire room. The old man had cleaned up for his outing and wore a freshly pressed shirt and much laundered trousers. Sam entered grinning from ear to ear.

"Knew we'd run into each other again, boy."

"Nice seeing you, too, Sam." Erik slapped the old man's back.

Sam folded himself into a chair. "That was a good thing you did," he said loudly.

"What are you talking about?"

"Helping out your stepsister and her friend."

Erik wondered if the man was really clairvoyant or just up on the happenings in town.

"What did Erik do?" Liza interrupted, her tone taking on a softer note as she quizzed the old man.

Sam chuckled. "Your little sister got caught shoplifting. Erik paid for the merchandise and assumed responsibility for her."

"Tell me she didn't." Liza looked stricken. Her expression slowly changed to confusion.

Erik remained silent. He'd kept his promise but old Sam had inadvertently blurted out the story.

"Child's a handful," Sam mumbled, "embarrassing Elizabeth."

"Did I hear my name?" Elizabeth called from the other room.

A pleading look was exchanged between Liza and Erik.

"It's nothing, Mother."

The conversation quickly changed.

"House giving you problems, eh?" Sam asked Erik.

"House has a life of its own."

The truth was that the house had been surprisingly silent, while Erik's dreams had become increasingly more erotic. They seemed to always feature Liza or a woman that looked like her. He'd awaken to find himself drenched in sweat.

"If the house is such a pain, Erik should consider giving it to Sara," Liza muttered.

So much for being grateful that he'd bailed their sister out.

"You two have a quarrel?" Sam asked, sitting back, his rheumy, unseeing eyes flickering this way and that.

Liza glared at Erik. He returned her glare with a calculating smirk. He had the feeling that Elizabeth liked him and might just go for what he proposed.

"Dinner's ready," his stepmother called from the dining room. "Erik, pour the wine and I'll take Sara's food up on a tray."

Erik helped Sam up and together they entered the formal dining room. No two pieces of furniture matched but the décor was typically Liza. Erik had to admire her style. The pieces, while not quite antiques, were old and well polished. An ivory tablecloth held mismatched china and wineglasses that looked to be Rosenthal.

Once Sam was seated, Elizabeth departed and Liza handed Erik two bottles of wine.

"Pour," she said. "Mom likes red, and I'll take white. What about you, Sam?"

Sam indicated his preference for red. Elizabeth returned with a salad and a delicious eggplant casserole in hand.

"Get the basket with the rolls," she ordered Liza.

The conversation throughout dinner was light and upbeat, centering mostly on local gossip. After the meal was complete and coffee and a mouthwatering crème brûlée served, Erik offered to help Elizabeth clear the table. Liza was left to entertain Sam.

In the kitchen, Erik portioned leftovers into Tupperware containers and sealed the lids.

"I'd hoped we could speak privately," he said, keeping his voice low. "I have a proposal for you."

Elizabeth, busy stuffing dirty dishes into the dishwasher, turned on him with wary eyes. "And what is that?"

"If you'll drop your lawsuit, I'll help with Sara's education."

"Why would you want to do that?" Elizabeth asked carefully, stacking dish after dish into the racks. She straightened up to look him in the eye. "Is Malcolm's house that important to you?"

"I've got a lot invested in it," Erik admitted. "And it's not just the money I'm talking about. I've come to love the place. I like Syracuse and being away from the action. And yes, I could easily buy another house but my father's gift wasn't so much a gift but a test. He left me the house not knowing I had the means to assume his debts. It might sound silly but staying in that house means a lot to me. It's my way of thumbing my nose at him."

"Why is it so important for you to thumb your nose at your father?" Elizabeth asked, a challenging eyebrow raised. "He's dead, and what satisfaction could you possibly get by—"

"Sticking it to him," Liza finished, entering the kitchen unexpectedly. "Plenty. Didn't you say Malcolm never acknowledged Erik as his?"

Erik had no idea how long she'd been standing there listening to the exchange. He wasn't sure if Liza felt sorry for him or was about to say something smart. He was comfortable with his illegitimacy. Thanks to his mother, Rachel, he'd been comfortable with it for a long time.

Liza continued. "Please don't accept a penny from Erik, Mom. And don't let him manipulate you."

So she wasn't feeling compassion for him or taking his side.

"Liza, you're being rude," Elizabeth admonished. "Erik has graciously offered to help with Sara's education."

"And why would he do that?"

Enough was enough. Liza was beginning to piss him off.

"For God's sake, Sara's my sister," he snapped. "I help complete strangers, why not help her?"

"Because we don't need your help."

"Liza, please be civil."

"Mom," Sara wailed from upstairs. "Mom, can you bring me something to drink?"

Elizabeth left to take the child juice, leaving Erik and Liza glaring at each other.

What was it with his stepsister?

Cassie sat across the table from Kalib, toying with a fattening bread pudding covered in rum sauce. She'd had an equally calorie-laden dinner, consisting of ribs, greens, and sautéed potatoes.

Kalib had taken her to a quaint little restaurant up in the mountains. It was nestled on a cliff and was rustic and romantic. After the day she'd had, it was perfect.

The conversation shifted from their respective businesses to their children, a touchy subject for Cassie since she still hadn't adjusted to not having the twins.

"I'm surprised you don't have custody of your kids," Kalib said, his fork spearing his carrot cake.

She felt slightly nauseous and it had nothing to do with the food she'd stuffed down. Inevitably that subject was bound to come up. Kalib had to be curious as to why she didn't have custody of her kids.

"It was a tough decision," Cassie said, keeping the emotion out of her voice. "When my divorce was final, Jim was in a better position than I was to raise two girls. It worked out for the best. With the long hours I put in at the bakery I would have been doing them a disservice."

It wasn't exactly a lie. Jim was in a better position to raise the twins. He didn't have the issues she did.

"You must miss them," Kalib said, finishing off his cake and looking at her with such intensity that she flushed.

"Yes, I do. I miss them terribly."

And she did. Nothing and no one would ever fill that void. For so long her children had been her lifeline. They'd helped her keep her sanity when she realized she'd simply gone through the motions of being a wife and her marriage was over with. They'd kept her strong, helped her survive when Jim's energy was no longer focused on her.

And in the long run it hadn't mattered. Even though Jim was a philanderer, the judge had turned the girls over to him. Jim had painted an ugly picture of her, using her eating disorder to prove her an unfit mother. She'd coped by binging and regurgitating and eventually had to be hospitalized.

"Cassie, I'm sorry. I should never have brought the subject

up," Kalib said, his eyes sympathetic, his fingers intertwined with hers.

Hot tears dripped down her cheeks and she realized she was crying, making an absolute fool of herself in front of Kalib Moore, a man she was just getting to know.

He handed her a napkin. Cassie dabbed at her cheeks and gave him a watery smile. What he must think of her.

"Tell me about your son," she managed.

Kalib's expression changed, softening. "Oh, Mico. He's wonderful. He's real active and getting into sports."

"And your ex-wife? Do you have a good relationship with her?"

"As a matter of fact we do. Divorce is painful but we'd come to realize that we'd outgrown each other. We're good friends now."

She wished she could say the same about her and Jim. Their relationship was cordial but still strained.

Kalib signaled for the check. He produced a credit card, signed the slip, and got up. She'd made a mess of an evening that had started out with such romantic possibilities.

"How about a nightcap?" he surprised her by asking when they were on the road. "There's a nice bar in the lobby of my hotel."

"Oh, all right."

She'd surprised herself by agreeing so readily but she could use a drink and she wanted to spend more time with him. The thought of going home to her empty house suddenly wasn't all that appealing.

An hour later, they were still seated at the dimly lit bar and Cassie had begun to relax. She'd let Kalib talk and he'd filled her in on his life. He'd come from a professional family but he still gave credit to his mother for encouraging him to be the best person he could be. She'd told him life wasn't always about making money but about feeling fulfilled.

"I wish you'd stay with me tonight," he said, his fingers circling her wrists.

Cassie had expected something like this but it was a tremendous step to take, moving their relationship to a more intimate level. Emotionally she was still very frail.

"I'll need to be in the store tomorrow by eight," she answered.

"Is that a yes?"

"Yes."

He sounded elated as if her response was not what he expected. It hadn't been what she'd expected either. She'd surprised herself.

He was up almost instantaneously, wallet in hand, counting out bills. He shoved a wad at the bartender, then took her hand. Together they headed for the elevator.

Cassies's heart thumped as she entered the sterile hotel room with its sofa, king-sized bed, utilitarian lamps, and standard-size TV. What was she getting herself into? She'd had the occasional fling since her divorce but the man she was with seemed to want more than a fling, and it scared her.

"Would you like another Kahlua and cream?" Kalib asked, opening the minibar.

"Sure."

And why not? She'd purposely chosen a drink that wouldn't send her senses reeling. She wanted to be in control, to savor every minute of their time together.

"Cassie, I'm not forcing you to do anything you don't want to," Kalib said, coming to sit down beside her. He placed an arm around her shoulders and began nuzzling her ear.

"I know," she answered in a strangled voice that didn't sound like hers. But she was starving for a man's touch and here was Kalib, whom she possibly liked too much.

He dipped a finger in his drink. With that same wet finger he traced a path across her clavicle and on the exposed flesh where her blouse gaped. Cassie twined her arms around Kalib's neck and laid her head against his chest, inhaling the clean, fresh fragrance that was him. He stroked her hair, made little mewling noises at the back of his throat, and covered her breast with his hand.

Cassie's nipples stiffened, and she felt tiny pinpricks on her flesh. She was coming alive; every nerve ending was raw. Her hands toyed with the buttons on his shirt until one of them popped. She slid a hand into the opening, weaving her fingers through his thick chest hairs.

"Cassie," Kalib said in a hoarse voice, "meeting you has been the best thing that's happened to me."

"It's the best thing that's happened to me, too," she admitted. And it was true but she needed to be cautious, see how this would go. "You're a very nice man," she said, "a caring man."

"I hope I become much more than that to you."

Kalib moved her from the couch and next to the bed before taking off his shoes.

Cassie followed suit. She watched Kalib slide out of his trousers and take off his shirt. Things were happening too quickly. She took several deep breaths hoping to calm down, but Kalib's broad shoulders and muscular legs filled her vision and made breathing hard. A strip of hair curled from his chest to his waist and dipped below his boxers.

Cassie's panic built. Would her less than perfect figure please him? Having twins took a toll on your body, regardless of whether you were considered thin. Would Kalib see her stretch marks in the muted lights of the lamps and still think her beautiful?

"Need some help?" Kalib offered when she still hadn't shed a stitch of clothing.

"With my zipper, yes." She turned her back to him and waited for him to help her.

Cassie felt his breath against her back, his fingers against her skin. He tugged down her zipper and wrapped his hands around her waist, pulling her up against him. He began touching her in places she felt like she'd never been touched before.

Kalib pulled her dress over her head. He stepped back to look at her, making appreciative sounds.

"Beautiful," he announced. "Just like I envisioned.

She wasn't perfect. She was flawed. She'd borne twins. Her stomach had a definite pouch and her breasts sagged slightly, maybe more than slightly. Her thighs reflected every calorie that she'd ever inhaled. And he was saying she was beautiful.

Kalib took a step toward her, gathering her in his arms. "Cassie, you've come to mean a lot to me," he said, bringing her closer until she could feel those dark chest hairs.

Sweet talk. Nonsense. More than she'd expected to hear.

He unclasped her bra and removed her panties, backing her up until her legs hit the bed, and pressed himself up against her. His kiss made her lose her last semblance of control. Cassie kissed him back with fervor, wound her arms around his neck and, pulling him down on top of her, lay back on the bed.

Kalib's knees parted her legs. His tongue caressed her breasts and shoulders. He stopped briefly to kick off his shorts before returning his full focus to her. Cassie felt an erection so huge press against her that she was scared. Could she accommodate him?

"I plan on getting to know every single part of you before this is over," Kalib said, placing her feet firmly on the floor and spreading her thighs.

Getting on his knees he went to work, his tongue and lips taking on a magical quality of their own. She felt an intensity of pleasure she'd never felt before. Then she turned her attention to Kalib, hoping she could make him feel as good as she had.

They were panting, gasping, close to imploding when Kalib reached for his wallet on the nightstand. He removed a foil package and opened it. She should have known he would be responsible. His profession alone dictated it. Here was a man who'd probably seen every imaginable communicable disease there was, and this definitely was a changing world.

Kalib slid the condom on. Cassie arched her back and splayed her legs. He slowly entered her. Cassie's entire body tingled, and her mind went numb. As the rhythm built, she realized she was in over her head, but it was too late to pull back now.

A quivering began in her lower body and heat flushed her chest. Her limbs began to spasm.

"Let go," Kalib ordered. "Let go."

And she did let go, losing touch with the world and tumbling deep into an abyss of pleasure.

When reality returned, it had her racing for the bathroom and her only means of control.

Her belly needed to be empty because her mind was on overload.

17

___

"**Y**ou need to call your brother and thank him for coming to your rescue," Elizabeth ordered, thrusting the portable phone at Sara.

Sara grimaced but made no effort to take the phone. "Maybe later," she said, hobbling away.

"You get back here, young lady, and do as I say."

Elizabeth had received call after call from supposedly well-meaning neighbors filling her in on Sara's brush with the law. Even Liza's friend Delilah had called, but not to speak with Liza, mind you, but to tell Elizabeth about the shoplifting episode. News tends to travel quickly in such a tight-knit community.

In the kitchen, Sara faced her mother and the two stared each other down. The injured ankle had not been broken, but badly sprained, or so the doctor said. Sara now wore an Ace bandage.

"What am I supposed to say to Erik?" she muttered. "I barely know the man."

"Try saying thank you," Elizabeth said, a hand on her hip. "If it hadn't been for him, you would probably have been taken down to the station and booked."

"You wouldn't let that happen," Sara answered cheekily.

Elizabeth wagged a finger. "Don't count on that. Now begin pushing those buttons, young lady."

Liza chose that moment to enter the kitchen, the strap of her purse slung over one shoulder.

"What's going on? Why are you two shouting at each other?"

Elizabeth was the first to respond. "I've asked Sara to call Erik and thank him." She squinted at her older daughter, noticing for the first time that she wore makeup and a cute off-the-shoulder top, plus jeans and heels. Elizabeth raised an eyebrow though she was pleased. This was more like the old Liza. Glamorous Liza. "Are you going somewhere?"

"Yes, to the grocery store. I want to get the food for tomorrow's barbecue. I'm thinking of asking Cassie, Delilah, Rona, and a few others to join us. Want anything special?"

Sara spoke up. "If you're going out, I'm coming too. I'm bored. Can I, Mom?"

Elizabeth nodded.

Cabin fever must be setting in. Even though Sara was grounded she needed to spend time with her sister. They'd always been like oil and water. After what Sara had pulled yesterday, their relationship was even more strained.

"Why would you want to come with me?" Liza challenged. "I'm going to Shoppers Express and most likely Ron, the manager, will be there."

"So?"

"So if I were you I'd want to hide my head in embarrassment. You stole from his store."

"I'm not embarrassed."

Sara hadn't shown the slightest bit of remorse for having been caught stealing at the grocery store. Elizabeth was still taken aback by the teenager's attitude.

"Okay, smart-ass, Shoppers Express is exactly where we're going," Liza said. "You can apologize to Ron and on the way home we'll stop by Erik's and you can pay him the money you owe him."

Elizabeth wanted to applaud but stayed quiet. Good for Liza.

"All of it?" Sara cried in outrage. "Three-quarters of what we stole wasn't even mine."

"That's your problem," Elizabeth said, entering the conversation. "You've got money saved up, and you'll need to use some of it to pay Erik back. Liza, are you planning on inviting him to the barbecue?"

"What?"

Elizabeth had sensed the attraction between the two. Privately she believed that Erik was just what Liza needed. He seemed take-charge and responsible, and he wasn't stuck on himself. He would bring a sense of stability to her daughter's life. God knew she couldn't continue this way, living a solitary life in an upstate town, selling old clothes.

"You heard me," Elizabeth said in a voice that brooked no nonsense. "It's Labor Day tomorrow and the man has no family except for us."

"We aren't family."

"We are the closest thing he has. Sara and Erik share the same blood."

"But I don't," Liza cried.

"Exactly. So why not make him a friend? If anything should happen to you, you'll have someone looking out for you."

"I have plenty of friends," Liza huffed. "I don't need Erik Price to watch over me."

Elizabeth studied her daughter carefully. There was a time when Liza had been bubbling with energy, when her sole mission was to take on the world. But since the time she'd been mugged and almost raped, and then her fiancé left her, her personality had undergone a drastic change. She now took life too seriously and she'd become distrustful of people.

"Where are all these supposed friends?" Elizabeth asked carefully. I've been here almost four days and I haven't seen one of them. Delilah was the only one who called and she wanted to speak with me."

"I'm leaving, Mother," Liza huffed, digging into her purse for her keys. "Coming, Sara?"

Sara was up and hobbling beside her. She called over her shoulder, "I'll invite Erik, Mom, if Liza won't."

"Don't you dare," Liza warned, stalking ahead.

"Try stopping me."

The door closed behind them while they were still squabbling.

Fifteen minutes later a car pulled into the driveway. Elizabeth frowned. They were back too soon. She parted the curtains and looked out. She didn't recognize the automobile.

A tall man got out and started up the driveway. On closer inspection Elizabeth saw it was Paul White. An older Paul White and one more sophisticated than she remembered. He had more salt than pepper in his hair.

She went to the door and opened it with a warm smile. "Hi, Paul."

"I was hoping to catch you at home," he said, giving her a warm embrace. "May I come in?"

"Why certainly."

Elizabeth moved aside to let him enter. He stood awkwardly in the living room, grinning at her. "You look more like Liza's sister than her mother," he said bashfully.

"Thank you. Please have a seat," she said, gesturing toward one of the Queen Anne chairs. Paul sat stiffly.

"Is Liza around?" he asked.

"You just missed her. Is there something you wanted, Paul?"

"Actually I wanted to speak with both of you about the pending lawsuit against Erik Price. Erik's been phoning me. I haven't returned his calls."

"Erik was here for dinner last evening," Elizabeth admitted. "We talked."

"Hmmm," Paul muttered. "You're suing him but he had dinner with you?"

Elizabeth explained what had transpired and what had prompted her to invite Erik for dinner. "Is it true what he tells me about Malcolm's house?" she asked.

"What did he tell you?" Paul asked in typical attorney fashion.

"That the house was mortgaged to the hilt and that there were liens attached. Erik claims he paid them all off and it was a pretty expensive proposition."

"Erik is right," Paul said. "I got hold of the deed. Malcolm apparently used that house as collateral to secure several loans."

Elizabeth frowned. She'd known Malcolm was cheap, in fact stingy with his money, but he'd had land, plenty of it, and he'd sold that land to several manufacturers.

"What happened to Malcolm's money?" she asked.

Paul splayed his hands. "I suppose I could do an asset search and see what turns up. As far as I know your ex-husband died penniless. Ned was the one who paid for his funeral."

"Ned? Why would he do such a thing?"

"They were good friends."

Elizabeth made a mental note to get with Ned before she left. If what Paul said was true, it was useless pursuing a suit that would be costly with no guaranteed outcome. It made better sense to take Erik up on his generous offer. She would talk to Liza when she returned.

"What's your recommendation?" Elizabeth asked Paul.

"Much as I hate to see myself fired, think carefully before you proceed. Forget the emotions and weigh the pluses and minuses. You're on cordial terms with Erik; you might be able to work it out."

Elizabeth nodded, contemplating. "Where are my manners?" she said, remembering that she'd not even offered the man a glass of water. "Would you like something to drink?"

"Thank you, but no. I have to get going. Please have Liza call me when she gets back."

"I will. What are you doing tomorrow?" Elizabeth asked impulsively.

Paul retrieved a pocket organizer, pressed the requisite buttons and squinted at it. "I may have a date."

"May?" Elizabeth knew she sounded perplexed. In her day you either had a date or you didn't. None of this open-ended business with plans firmed up at the last minute.

"I suppose I should give Sunny a call," Paul muttered more to himself than anyone else. "See if we're on."

"Well, whether you're on or not, stop by and join us for a barbecue," Elizabeth said, following him out.

Thanking her, Paul left.

"How's the portrait coming?" Vivica asked. "You're late delivering. The Silversteins are getting anxious."

"I'm almost done, just putting the final touches on," Erik replied, patting Buddy's head absentmindedly. The dog let out a woof. Erik balanced the cordless phone between his shoulder and ear and examined the completed work from another angle. It had taken him an eternity to finish the piece, but it was special and would bring a small fortune.

"Sunny keeps calling," Vivica nagged. "She really likes your stuff and wants you exclusively for her gallery. She claims she's had several requests for your work, and can get you twice what you're currently asking. I think it's worth exploring."

"I suppose. Sunny does have useful connections."

Erik knew he sounded like a grinch but given their history he had to question Sunny's motives.

"What does Madam Hirschbaum know about art?" Erik grumbled. Privately he thought Sunny was a powder puff, a lot of show and a lot of fluff. "She's a socialite who happens to own a gallery."

"A very successful gallery, I might add."

He couldn't tell Vivica that he and Sunny had once had a fling. It was long over with and they were cordial to each other but he still didn't trust that her motives were purely professional.

Vivica chuckled. "You're being a temperamental artist. Sunny's an astute businesswoman with the right contacts. Don't underestimate her, she's pretty shrewd. A word in the right ear and your career could skyrocket."

Erik grunted.

Shrewd Sunny was. Shrewd, pushy, and reluctant to understand he no longer was interested in taking up with her. He'd regretted their brief affair when he was still a struggling artist, hungry for recognition. Sunny had been there at the right time, fulfilling a need that had been building. Her mistake had been trying to buy him. Still, it would be foolish to turn down an opportunity.

Buddy whimpered and began circling. At the same moment the doorbell sounded.

"Gotta go, Vivica. We'll talk about this later."

Erik gave a parting glance at the portrait. He did a double take as the face of the woman with the turban surfaced. The Labrador's nails made a scratching noise on the floor as he bounded down the stairs, and Erik slowly followed.

"Who is it?" he called from the vestibule.

A young, whiny voice answered, "It's Sara and Liza."

Erik lengthened his strides and threw open the door.

"This is a nice surprise," he said to the sullen-faced teenager who bent over to pet Buddy. The dog licked her hand. Liza stood there staring at him. "Please come in," he said, standing aside.

Reluctantly Liza entered with Sara hobbling behind.

"Sara brought you something," Liza said, prodding her sister forward.

Sara thrust a handful of bills at him. "I'm here to pay you back, and my mother wants you to come to a barbecue we're having tomorrow. That is, if you're not doing anything."

"I'm sure Erik is busy," Liza quickly added.

"As a matter of fact I'm not," he said equally as quickly, and watched her flush. "Sara, hold on to your money," he said to his sister. "How's your ankle?"

Sara made a wry face. "Better, but it still hurts and I'm still limping."

"Yes, I can see that. Sit down. Ease the load. Liza, come with me. I want to show you my painting."

"I want to come," Sara sniveled.

Erik wanted Liza alone so he said, "Some other time, short stuff. Stay and play with Buddy. Two flights of stairs are going to be murder on that ankle."

The look on her face showed that she didn't particularly like being called short stuff, especially since she wasn't much shorter than them. "Yeah, I suppose," Sara said begrudgingly.

Before Liza could protest, Erik got hold of her elbow and moved her toward the staircase. He wanted her to see the portrait of the old woman, but more importantly he just wanted her to see his work. Maybe then she'd be willing to sit for him.

Liza opened her mouth and shut it as they walked side by side. He liked the way she looked, casual but elegant, her long frame made even taller by the heels she wore.

"It'll only take a few minutes," he said as they continued to climb.

The click-clacking of her heels made his imagination go wild. A tantalizing perfume wafted its way up to his nostrils. He remembered their kiss, every millisecond of it. He remembered the way she'd felt in his arms.

When they arrived in the studio, Liza stopped at the door and her eyes went round.

"Oh, my," she said, taking in the canvases, paints, oils, and turpentine.

A million smells came at them, smells he'd grown used to. He'd never been able to paint in a tidy room. Much like his mind, the studio reflected a disjointed mishmash of thoughts and ideas.

"I want to show you something," he said, beckoning to her. "Come over here, closer."

Liza stepped into the room and almost tripped over a box holding canvases and sketches. She teetered and for a while he thought she would fall. He grabbed her by the elbow, steadying her, and steered her around the mess to stand in front of his easel. He liked the way his large palm circled her slender arm. It made him feel protective.

"What do you think?" he asked, waving his free arm expansively.

"It's striking. You do beautiful work."

The painting on the easel had changed again. The turbaned lady had disappeared.

Erik smiled grimly, more certain than ever that he was losing his mind.

"That's not what was there when I left," he said.

"It isn't?" She blinked at him, long lashes fanning sculptured cheeks.

Erik rubbed paint-flecked knuckles across his forehead. "You'll think I'm crazy, but a few minutes ago there was another portrait in its place."

She looked at him dubiously. "Your ghosts at work?"

"My whatever."

"Liza," Sara called from the bowels of the house, "are you about ready?"

"I'll be down in a minute."

He didn't want her to leave. Not yet.

"I wish you'd consider sitting for me," he said. "There's a spirit about you I'd like to capture on canvas."

She looked at him warily. "Oh, I don't know. You have plenty of models to choose from."

She was beginning to waver and he pressed his advantage. He took hold of her chin and tilted it up.

"Now don't be coy. You've got a beautiful face. I'd like to paint it."

"Surely there are others who'd be better suited for your kind of work."

"Like? Who are you suggesting?"

"Delilah for one. She'd make a good model."

"I'm not interested in Delilah," he answered, putting his cards on the table. "I'm interested in you. Your face has character. It speaks to me."

"Erik," she said, attempting to step out of his reach.

He tilted her face this way and that. "Your bone structure is unusual. Your eyes are alive with light and your mouth . . . Well, your lips are perfect."

He could tell that he was getting to her. He rested his forehead against hers until he could see his reflection in her eyes. "You're beautiful, Liza, so very beautiful and you don't even know it."

"I'm no longer beautiful," she answered, matter-of-factly. "My face has been reconstructed and I have scars."

"That's what makes you beautiful. And very appealing to me," he said, lowering his lips to cover hers until their tongues danced.

"Liza, how much longer? I'm getting hungry," Sara called in a cranky voice.

"I have to go," Liza said, stepping back and putting a safe distance between them. The back of her hand wiped away evidence of his kiss but her eyes were unusually bright and her breasts heaved.

"What time should I come by tomorrow? And what shall I bring?" Erik asked.

"You're actually coming?"

"Better believe it, I am. I'm not saying no to your mother's good cooking."

"There'll be quite a few people there," Liza warned.

"The more the merrier. I'd like to meet more family."

"You're not my family," she reminded him as if he needed reminding.

Thank God, he wasn't. The evidence of that weighed heavily in his pants. Erik turned away, hoping not to embarrass her and himself.

Liza started down the stairs.

Seconds later, Erik followed.

18

Labor Day turned out to be a beautiful day without even the hint of a cloud in the sky. It was Rona's last day on her own; tomorrow her kids would return. She planned on making the most out of the day. She missed her children but at the same time she'd loved the freedom of coming and going as she pleased.

So far there'd been no word from Tim, so she'd assumed he'd lost interest in her. It was a blow to her ego but to be expected, she supposed. Men like Tim didn't need or want nursery school teachers in their lives.

Liza had called last evening inviting her to a barbecue. There would be people to talk to and little time to reflect on why she'd failed with Tim. From the beginning she'd known that he was passing the time and wasn't looking for someone like her.

The phone rang, bringing her back to earth. It was probably Liza with a request to bring something she'd forgotten.

"Hi, what's up?" Rona answered.

"Hey. How did you know it's me?"

Tim Delaney's sexy Oakie drawl wasn't what she'd been expecting. Rona willed her pounding heart to be still. The last time she'd laid eyes on Tim he'd been with that blonde and she hadn't heard from him since.

"Nice to hear from you, Tim," she said, trying to keep the excitement out of her voice. "It's been a while."

"I've been trying to get in touch with you but your phone rings and rings."

Lying dog. Then she remembered the new answering machine she'd never gotten around to hooking up. Tim could be telling the truth, she supposed. But if he'd really wanted to see her he could have stopped by the nursery school.

"Scout's honor, I called," Tim said. "I even thought about dropping by where you work but I didn't want to be accused of being a stalker."

A likely story. She repressed a chuckle. She couldn't imagine Tim as a Scout but she could clearly picture him in chaps. Chaps, and nothing else. Damn it, these X-rated thoughts had to stop.

"You should have come by," Rona said boldly. "It would have been a nice surprise."

"Except that the camp was closed for the holiday weekend and I didn't think you'd appreciate it if I showed up at your house. I'd like to today if you're available."

Rona didn't want to sound like she didn't have any plans. She hemmed and hawed. "Uh, I may be going out."

"Is that a no? What are your plans?" Tim persisted.

"I've got a barbecue to go to."

"I'd like to come," Tim said, surprising her.

She was so stunned by his request it took her a moment to get herself together. Having him attend a backyard barbecue might be fun. It would give the girls a chance to look him over and give her their opinion.

"What about the blonde?" Rona asked. "I thought you'd want to spend time with her."

The green-eyed monster had surfaced before she could stop it, but better to know what was going on than not.

"Oh, her." Tim chuckled. "She's a friend."

"That's what they all say."

Tim's robust laughter filled her ear. "So what time would you like me to come by?"

"How does five sound?"

"Five is fine. I'll be there."

He hung up, leaving her stunned.

Rona picked up the phone and began punching in numbers. She desperately needed advice on how to play this. In a pinch the girls could be counted on to come through.

Liza made the rounds, making sure drinks were replenished and plates full. Elizabeth kept an eye out as her daughter played the gracious hostess.

The impromptu barbecue was turning out better than she expected. All the neighbors were there, and Liza's friends, with the exception of Rona and Delilah, had come. Still no sign of Erik. Elizabeth thought about calling him.

Liza stopped for a moment to speak with Cassie, Kalib, and another couple who lived across the street. Her laughter carried and it was good to see her having fun. Sara, who was hobbling less and less, was chatting up a storm with a friend she'd introduced as Alanna.

Elizabeth decided to join the laughing group. She hadn't seen Cassie Newell since her divorce but she'd heard about Cassie's troubles. By the looks of her she seemed to be doing well, which might have something to do with the man she was with. Cassie held a heaping plate of food in one hand. Her dark-skinned companion with the bald head had his arm around her and looked like he was in love. Good. Cassie deserved a nice man. Jim, her ex-husband, had been slime.

"Liza," Cassie said, "you look wonderful, just like your modeling days."

"What you're telling me is I've looked like shit," Liza said laughingly, putting her hands on her hips and pretending to glare.

And her daughter did look good. Better than good. Wonderful. There was a glow to her face that hadn't been there in a while. And her outfit, though casual, shouted chic. Liza, in white short shorts and a turquoise halter top, was breathtaking. Fresh. Elizabeth hoped she would settle down soon. Erik would be a good companion. There had to be some way to get the two together.

As Elizabeth came closer she heard Cassie say, "My bet is Erik Price has something to do with the old Liza resurfacing."

"Pleeeease!" Liza swatted her friend's shoulder playfully. "Now what brought that up?"

Cassie gave her a knowing look and slanted her gaze at Erik, who had just arrived. Spotting Elizabeth, she moved aside to include her in their circle.

"Mrs. Tanner, you've met Kalib."

Elizabeth nodded. "Yes, but I haven't been introduced to your other two friends."

Introductions followed. They stood chatting about this and that, at the same time making sure their guests weren't neglected.

"Uh, Liza," Cassie hissed, "Erik is behind you."

Liza spun around and almost bumped into Erik. He steadied her with one hand, the other holding a foil-covered plate. There was a teasing smile on his face.

"Hi," he said, "sorry I'm late." He thrust the dish at Liza. "I brought you dessert."

Liza thanked him but refused to meet his eyes. The chemistry between them was palpable and Cassie smirked. A delicious chocolate scent filled the air as Liza lifted the foil wrapping.

"Ummmmmmm. Smells heavenly," Cassie said as the men shook hands and slapped each other's backs.

Elizabeth noticed a faint tinge of pink coloring her daughter's cheeks. So she was hardly immune to her stepbrother. It should make for an interesting evening.

"I made brownies from scratch," Erik boasted.

Liza's lips twitched as she tried to smile. "I didn't know you were domesticated."

"That's because you haven't made it a point to get to know me."

Erik was flirting outrageously, giving Liza the full effect of his hazel eyes and those sinfully long lashes. Elizabeth would have paid money to see Erik whipping up that bowl of batter. It would be like watching a star linebacker playing Betty Crocker.

Liza, after thanking Erik, pointed to a table laden with food and desserts. "Please put the brownies over there."

Just like that she'd dismissed him. What was wrong with that child? Elizabeth quickly rescued the dish. "Let me take that. Liza, get Erik something to eat. Give him some of my ribs and that delicious chicken Ned brought, and don't forget the corn bread and the gravy you made."

Liza had no choice but to accompany Erik over to the buffet table where several people hovered, one of them Ned. The younger neighborhood kids ran around them, then headed for the woods and a game of tag.

From a distance, Elizabeth kept an eye on the couple. Erik, with Liza's assistance, filled a plate and grabbed a drink. Ned ambled over and began talking with Erik, and Liza moved away. From the rigid set of her daughter's shoulders, Elizabeth deduced that Erik's arrival had made her tense.

The energy picked up when Delilah and a man Elizabeth didn't know put in an appearance. As usual she was wearing something outrageous and totally unsuitable. Leopard-skin bike shorts cupped her wide butt, and a canary-colored shirt was tied at her waist, leaving an inch of skin bare. She tottered toward Elizabeth in three-inch mules. Her bespectacled companion, bearing a blender and what looked to be the fixings for daiquiris, followed.

"Hey, peoples, I'm here," she announced to no one in particular, nor did anyone seemed to care. They nodded at her politely.

Delilah approached Elizabeth. "Mrs. Tanner, you're a sight for sore eyes. How long has it been since we last saw each other?"

"Years," Elizabeth said dryly, accepting the woman's kiss. Delilah had never been one of her favorite people. She was loud, competitive, and out for herself, not that Elizabeth had ever shared that sentiment with Liza. Some things were best kept to oneself.

Delilah's companion, whom she seemed to have forgotten

about, quietly introduced himself as Quinn James. He seemed a nice enough sort and Elizabeth thought them an odd match. She pointed them to the bar and walked over to where Ned and Erik conversed, joining them in time to hear Ned say, "So you've decided to make your home here?"

"If Elizabeth will let me," Erik joked.

"I've been thinking about your offer," Elizabeth answered. "We'll talk later."

Erik's attention was momentarily diverted by some late-arriving guests. Paul White and a woman Elizabeth didn't recognize had arrived. He excused himself and headed over, leaving her alone with Ned.

"Nice boy," Ned said when Erik was out of earshot. "A credit to Rachel, given that Malcolm was never a part of his life."

"Malcolm was never a part of anyone's life," Elizabeth said sourly. "The truth, Ned, did Malcolm die penniless?"

He sipped his drink, then said to her, "I have reason to believe he did."

"But what about the money he got from selling that land?"

"Lost on the horses, probably."

Elizabeth made a sharp intake of breath. "Malcolm gambled? I didn't know that."

"Malcolm had several nasty habits you didn't know about. Loved the horses and placed wagers on anything that moved."

"Oh," she said, "and now I find out."

Ned placed a hand on her shoulder. "At least you're happy now. You're with the right man."

Liza's other friend, Rona, had arrived, bringing with her a man so tall that everyone's interest was diverted. Even Sara seemed spellbound, which was rare for her daughter.

"Tim Delaney," the teenager screamed. "Got to get his autograph." Forgetting about her friend, she grabbed a napkin off the table and took off as fast as her injured foot would carry her.

The man called Tim seemed pleased when Sara, awed but insistent, waved the creased piece of paper at him. He produced a pen from his pocket and with a flourish signed the napkin and handed it back.

Elizabeth approached the couple. Rona she'd known since she was a teenager. She was a nice girl who seemed to have her life together.

"Rona, it's been ages. You look good." Elizabeth offered her cheek for a kiss.

"Mrs. Tanner, how are you?" Rona asked, kissing the proffered cheek. She prodded the tall man forward. "This is my friend Tim Delaney. Tim, this is Elizabeth Tanner, Liza's mother."

"How you doing, Elizabeth?" he said, in an accent that definitely wasn't upstate New York. He held out two bottles. "We brought wine."

"Thanks," Elizabeth said, accepting the bottles.

"Gawd, Mom. I thought this was going to be one of these boring barbecues," Sara gushed, still staring at Tim. "You didn't tell me Tim Delaney was invited. Wait until I tell my friends back in Boston."

"Am I supposed to know you, Tim?"

Rona chuckled. "Tim's a professional basketball player, Mrs. Tanner."

Tim just stood beaming at her.

"Oh."

That explained the height. Elizabeth was never one to be easily impressed but had to admit Rona had done well for herself. "Come with me," Elizabeth said quickly. "Let's get you over to the food before it disappears."

"I'll take them over," Sara offered, still sounding elated. "I want to talk to Erik and see how his dog, Buddy, is doing."

Good, Sara was warming up to Erik. That would make things so much easier. In light of Elizabeth's recent conversation with Paul, she'd decided to accept Erik's offer to help out with his sister's tuition. But it would be a loan. Sara needed to be responsible.

Liza tugged on her arm. "Look who's here, Mother. You didn't tell me that you'd invited Sam."

Elizabeth didn't remember inviting him either, but figured

that Ned might have mentioned it knowing that the lonely old man had nothing to do. She was glad that Ned had made up for her oversight.

Sam was being led to Ned's side by his granddaughter, Kelli. Elizabeth and Liza went over to greet him. Elizabeth enfolded Sam in a tight embrace.

"I'm glad you came," she said. He smelled like mothballs. "Liza, go get Sam a plate of food and something to drink."

"Make it nonalcoholic," Sam answered in a distracted manner. Liza hustled off to fulfill his request, and out of the corner of her eye, Elizabeth saw Erik follow her.

She turned her attention back to Sam. He seemed unfocused. Physically here, but mentally elsewhere. Why?

"Having one of your spells?" Ned asked, in tune with his old buddy.

"Yup. A bad one. Came to warn Elizabeth her child's going to have problems."

Elizabeth's heart almost stopped. Sam's premonitions were usually right on target.

"Which child?" she asked, her stress level building.

"Liza."

"Sam, you're scaring me," Elizabeth said, clutching Ned's arm.

He rubbed her back, hoping to calm her. But she was not to be calmed. How could she be when she was just told one of her children was going to have trouble?

"What kind of problems?" Elizabeth asked.

"Someone's going to break into her house. That girl needs to take precautions," Sam mumbled.

"What kind of precautions?"

"Lock up soundly, though even that might not help. She'll need to call on the spirits to help her." Sam's sightless eyes rolled back in his head. After a moment he snapped out of whatever had overcome him and sniffed the air. "Is my food here?"

"Coming up shortly," Elizabeth said, wanting to take him off to the side and question him. Spirits? What nonsense. It was the break-in that concerned her. Maybe Liza needed to buy an alarm.

Ned kept a firm hold on her arm. "Sam may be wrong, Elizabeth," he said gently.

Elizabeth searched for Liza and spotted her deep in conversation with Erik. Sara hovered, holding on to Sam's plate. She was pleased that all three were at least making an effort with each other.

"You're probably right, Ned," Elizabeth said wearily. He released her, and Sam's words replayed themselves in her head. She started toward her daughters.

Liza was in danger. As her mother she would do anything to protect her, and she would start with asking Erik Price to watch over Liza.

19

A creaking floorboard brought Liza fully awake. She'd been having problems sleeping anyway. Now with her company gone, the old house had become lonely and ominous. Every nighttime noise was questionable. It made her think her ghosts had returned.

These were good ghosts, she reminded herself when the floorboard creaked again. Were those muttered whispers that followed or just her fertile imagination at work?

The window was open and a cool breeze blew in. She didn't remember leaving a window open. Liza lay, eyes tightly shut, listening. Distinct footsteps padded about and there was a muffled oath followed by a thud as a dark form came through the window and made a clumsy landing. Her heart almost stopped. She opened an eye, peering into the semidarkness.

"Careful, you idiot. You're going to wake the bitch up," a male voice muttered.

Forget about ghosts, these were flesh-and-blood people who'd invaded her house.

Think, Liza, think. Examine your options. She could close her eyes and pretend to sleep, and let them take what they wanted, or she could wait until they went downstairs, hide, and use her cell phone to call the cops.

No time to move or hide. They were coming closer. She could make out three bulky forms tiptoeing around the room. Liza felt the panic begin to build. Through squinted eyes, she watched one man sweep everything from the dresser top into a sack. The other made a beeline for her walk-in closet. They'd stopped talking.

She lay still, trying to keep her breathing even, and pretended to be asleep.

"Thought you said she was a model," one of the men whispered, emerging from the closet. "Not a lot of fancy stuff in here."

"She must have jewelry, a safe. You look around, Roger."

One of them approached the bed. "Sure she a model? She don't look so hot with no makeup on. She got scars."

Liza could feel him staring at her. She kept her mouth closed and bit her tongue. Flashbacks of another time and place surfaced when she'd felt helpless, victimized, totally at the mercy of another. Better to lie still, pretend to be asleep, and let them take what they wanted.

"Do what we came for and get the hell out of here," a gruff voice snarled.

"Wonder where she keeps the money from the shop."

The voices sounded young. Rough.

"Probably same place she keeps her jewelry."

It was money and merchandise they were after, thank God. But the figure standing over her still hadn't moved. Suddenly memories of that terrifying evening in Central Park came rushing back. Liza opened her mouth and screamed.

"What the hell?" the boy said, stepping back. "I didn't even touch her."

"Billy, do something. Shut her up. We don't want to be arrested."

A stampede ensued, and then stopped, as they scrambled to get to the open window. An unseen force lifted one of the men off his feet and hurled him against the wall. He let out a bloodcurdling scream, slid down the wall, and hit the floor.

"The place is haunted. Let's get the hell out of here," the boy screamed.

A mad dash followed as they raced toward the door. Everything turned chaotic. A dark shadow hovered above, covering the boys. Their sack was flung across the room and Liza's things spewed everywhere. Gasps and cries were followed by intermittent groans. One of the boys tried taking on the ghostly force but was hurled across the room and ended up on the floor.

Liza watched wide-eyed, her scalp crawling. Gathering every last breath she could muster, she opened her mouth and screamed again.

Erik circled Liza's block for what must be the third time. Elizabeth had told him about Sam's premonition, and Erik had assured her he would look out for Liza. He meant to keep that promise.

He'd taken to dropping by the store when Liza least expected it. Each time he made sure to buy something, so that his appearance wouldn't arouse too much suspicion. Liza seemed pleased to see him and conversation came easily now that the lawsuit had been dropped. With time he might even convince her to sit for him.

It had become a nightly routine to cruise by Liza's block. He'd check out the neighborhood and make sure there were no unsavory characters hanging about. But tonight something was different. Perhaps it was the pitch-black sky and slick roads. Things just didn't feel right.

He brought the vehicle to a slow stop in front of Liza's Victorian home. The house lay in darkness. As he squinted into the blackness, Erik noticed an open window on the second floor. It didn't make sense that Liza would leave a window open, not when it was drizzling and there was the definite threat of a storm in the air.

He spotted a ladder leading up to the open window. Before he could figure out what that meant, a piercing scream catapulted him out of his truck. Erik vaulted over a hedge and scrambled up the ladder. Simultaneously, a man's head emerged from the window.

"Who the hell are you?" Erik demanded.

The head ducked back inside as if someone had pulled it.

"Answer me or I'll shoot."

Erik didn't have a gun, but what did it matter?

It sounded like cattle stampeding inside. Furniture crashed and howls and agonizing screams followed. Lights came on in the surrounding houses. At least people were awake if he needed backup.

"Call the police," Erik shouted, scrambling up the last few rungs and sticking a head in the open window. What he saw inside made his mouth hang open.

Bodies were being hurled across the room by a dark shadow that reached down from the ceiling. Liza sat frozen in bed, clutching the sheets tightly against her. Bloodcurdling yells filled the air. In the distance a siren wailed and neighbors in various stages of undress were out on their lawns staring at him.

"I'm a friend," Erik shouted. "The burglars are in the house."

Inside, the bedlam continued, and then abruptly stopped. Erik shimmied over the window ledge, and waited for his vision to adjust. Something that looked like a lamp was within arm's reach. He fumbled for the switch as Liza, spotting a new arrival, brought her screams to an even more deafening pitch.

"It's me, Erik, sweetheart," he said, gathering her shivering body in his arms and trying to calm her.

She took deep breaths, gulping in air. "Erik? I've never been so happy to see anyone in my life."

Liza twined her arms around his neck, almost choking him. She began crying in earnest, hot tears soaking his shirt. The boys remained on the floor moaning and groaning. Another head popped through the open window.

"Police. Don't anyone move."

Erik spotted a glint of steel. A body followed the head.

"I'm Erik Price," he said, hoping his name would help. "I

was driving by, noticed an open window, and decided to investigate."

"I own the house," Liza said in a shaky voice, teeth still chattering. "Those boys on the floor are the ones you want."

"Show me identification and no sudden moves," the cop said, entering the room, gun still trained on them.

One of the boys on the floor moaned, and the policeman began circling the group.

"Don't try anything funny," he said, "or I'll shoot."

"I'm getting my driver's license," Erik said, reaching for the wallet in his pocket.

The cop nudged one of the moaning young men with his toe. His partner, a man that looked fitter than he, straddled the window ledge and vaulted into the room.

Erik had one arm around Liza's shoulders. She was still shaking and couldn't seem to stop. He used the other to flip his ID at the first cop. The second one circled the moaning boys on the floor.

"Names?" the cop barked. "And make it quick."

"Roger Williams," one of the groaning boys managed.

The name sounded vaguely familiar. Remembrance slowly came back with vivid clarity. A Roger had been caught shoplifting with Sara—this burglar might be one and the same.

"What about you? Do you have names?" the cop asked, squatting down and glaring at the boys.

"Bill Lindsay," one of them grunted while the other continued to groan.

Roger and Billy, the two shoplifters he'd rescued. Thugs. Erik's testosterone kicked in and with it came a desire to pummel them senseless. You'd think that giving them a break would have made them thankful. He cautioned himself to control his temper. This type of thing was better left to the police.

Liza still had her arms wrapped around his neck. He inhaled her clean, sweet fragrance, regretting that he couldn't shield her from the ugliness to come, the unrelenting questions that would make her feel more like the perpetrator than the victim. But he could be there for her.

The second cop was still standing over the boys, gun drawn. The other cuffed them and began searching through their pockets.

After a while they were led downstairs by one of the policemen. The boys were still muttering about the haunted house.

The remaining cop rolled his eyes. "Such B.S. You restrained these boys, right?" He turned to Erik.

"I did." Better to lie than to explain the bizarre story. No one in their right mind would believe them anyway.

The policeman dutifully turned his back, allowing Liza to grab a robe so he could question her.

Erik held Liza's hand as the policeman went through the formalities. She answered his questions calmly, but the tremors ricocheting through her body were sure indicators that she was badly shaken. Who wouldn't be, especially since her rescuer had been a ghostly presence?

By the time the cops were through with them it was almost dawn. They took the boys down to the station, leaving Liza wide-awake and wired.

"Coffee?" she asked, picking up the still-brewing pot.

"Yes, sure."

And although Erik had heard the question answered repeatedly, he needed to know for sure. "Did any of those boys hurt you?" he asked. He took Liza's hand and held it across the table.

Tears welled in her eyes. "No, they didn't. Not in the physical sense. I may have overreacted. One kept standing over my bed, staring at me, and I lost it."

"I'd hardly call that overreacting. You were alone in your house. I can't imagine what it must have been like to awaken and find you were being robbed."

"Horrible, I assure you. And then on top of that I witnessed this . . . dark shadow; I swear it was a supernatural presence taking on those boys. You saw it, too, didn't you? But if I'd supported the boys' story the cops would have thought I was crazy for sure."

Liza started to cry again and Erik crouched down in front of her and held on to both hands.

"Talk to me, baby. Did this break-in cause ugly memories to resurface?"

She nodded, and in staccato words began telling him about the previous mugging and attempted rape, and about the months spent in therapy.

"No wonder you chose to retreat to Syracuse," Erik said. "You're in hiding. Healing. You can't be alone right now. I'm staying with you."

"Would you?" Liza pleaded, holding on to his hands and squeezing. "Will you at least stay until I fall asleep?"

He longed to tell her that if it was left to him, not only would he stay, but he'd make mad, passionate love to her. But now was not the time. Not while she was so vulnerable.

"You make steak like my mother does," Tim said, chomping appreciatively on the porterhouse Rona had set down before him.

Rona had invited him to dinner at the town house and had been surprised when he'd readily accepted

She sipped her merlot and glanced at him coyly over the rim of her wineglass. "And just how is that?" Imagine that, she cooked like his mother?

"You prepared my steak medium, with plenty of seasoning, and you didn't rekill the cow."

Put like that, she couldn't help laughing. Tim joined in. Rona gazed at the mole at the side of his mouth. It quivered. Those full lips were very capable of doing exquisite things to her.

Her children were spending the night with Cassie, thank God. She should take advantage of their absence. Tonight would be a good time to let things take their natural course. Why let some blonde have him when she was here, able and willing?

"You haven't touched your food," Tim said, breaking into her musings.

Rona stared down at her best china, coagulating mushrooms and soggy potato seeping into her meat, wilting salad in a bowl on the side. She took another sip of wine and said, "I ate."

"Very little."

Tim enthusiastically polished off the rest of his meal, wiped his mouth on a napkin, then stood. "I'll do the dishes," he offered, beginning to stack platters.

"Thanks, but you're my guest. I can handle it."

Her response sounded stuffy, formal, and gruff. But it was her good china he was talking about, and she didn't want anything to get ruined or broken.

Tim ignored her, deftly stacked dishes, and took them into the kitchen. Rona's late husband had not lifted a finger and she was surprised that someone like Tim, someone used to having servants, would even make the effort.

"My mama raised me right," he said, answering her silent question.

What was it with this guy and his mama? Still there was something to be said about a well-trained male.

Rona watched Tim fill the sink with warm water, add detergent, and scrape leftovers into the garbage. He placed the soiled dishes in the sink.

"I do have a dishwasher," Rona said, pointing to the built-in appliance under the kitchen counter.

"Good china needs to be hand-washed," Tim lectured, wagging one finger at her, and squirting liquid detergent on a sponge. With his free hand he began soaping the dishes.

Rona's eyes were focused on Tim's large hands with the soapy suds squirting through his splayed fingers. Those hands had touched her body, igniting feelings she'd thought dead. It would be so easy to sleep with him and be done with it. In a few weeks he would be gone from her life anyway, and things would be back to normal. Not normal. Boring.

Determined to banish the X-rated thoughts, Rona grabbed a kitchen towel and joined Tim at the sink. "Scoot," he said, flicking soapy water at her.

She pretended to give him the evil eye. When he scooped up

a handful of suds and threatened her again, Rona stuck a hand into the tepid dishwater and let him have it.

"Okay, you asked for it," Tim threatened, shaking the suds from his cheeks and setting down the dish he'd been washing. Using those same soapy hands he grabbed her around the waist and lifted her off her feet.

"Put me down," Rona cried, pounding on his back, conscious that the short linen dress she'd worn had risen way beyond thigh high. She was wearing thong panties no less, something she usually avoided. Except this evening she'd wanted to feel sexy.

"It'll cost you," Tim answered, still holding her high, his hands sliding down to cup her hips and butt.

Tim's damp hands grasped her behind. The tips of his fingers pressed into her flesh, and his eyes bored into hers, issuing a definite challenge.

"What will it cost me?" Rona asked, her voice raspy, her breathing coming in little spurts.

Tim's tongue rimmed his lips, then settled in one corner near that cute, sexy mole. "Let's see," he drawled, pretending to think. "I'll settle for a kiss."

"What about my dishes?"

"We'll do them later."

"So it's *we* now, is it? Before you didn't need help."

Tim lowered her to eye level and pressed her body up against his. "Wrap your legs around my waist, and kiss me, woman," he ordered.

He was mad, a definite lunatic. But she complied, wrapping her legs around his waist and leaning in to receive his kiss.

Tim deepened the kiss. His tongue circled her mouth and did a swan dive. Rona's head reeled. Tim's expensive cologne intermingled with the scent of warm flesh. Rona's center pulsed. She attributed the heady experience to too much wine.

When Tim set her back on her feet, the floor tilted up, then down again. She needed to cool off and quick. The sound of water dripping got her attention.

"Oh, shit!"

She raced for the sink to shut off the faucet and slipped. She tried to regain her balance but the soapy water spilling onto the floor made it impossible. She landed on her back with a thud.

Tim crouched down and offered her his hand. "You okay, babe?"

She'd had the wind knocked out of her but otherwise was all right. She hung on to his hand.

"Rona, say something, babe."

There was genuine concern in Tim's voice as the back of his hand grazed her cheek. She was lost in his eyes, vaguely aware of the dripping water that continued to spill onto the floor.

"I'm fine, just had the wind knocked out of me. Would you mind turning off the tap?"

He left her briefly to do as she asked, returned, plopped down, and gathered her in his arms.

"You'll ruin your slacks," she mumbled, burying her face in his chest.

"They're not my only pair."

Warm water seeped through the linen material of her dress. Tim's arms around her felt incredibly good. Then the ridiculousness of the situation hit her. Here they were, sitting in at least an inch of warm water on her kitchen floor. She began to laugh and found she couldn't stop.

"What's so funny?" Tim asked after a while.

"This," Rona said, spreading her arms, tears running down her cheeks. She'd carefully selected an outfit, taken time to apply makeup, and for what?

Tim kissed her again and one damp, soapy hand trailed across the front of her dress and cupped a breast. She felt herself responding, felt the nipple go taut. The pulsing in her center took on a life of its own.

Tim lowered her onto the wet floor and Rona was glad she didn't have one of those expensive hairdos that required maintenance. Thank God for twists.

He was definitely a lunatic, and a creative lunatic at that. Her skirt hitched up above her hips as he ground his erection into her. Then he was kissing her again and she felt as if she were floating in that warm soapy water. His knee parted her thighs and he stopped briefly to lower his zipper and free himself.

She thought about the consequences of letting it go further. She was open to sleeping with him now, but he was an athlete and God knew where he'd been. She wasn't stupid.

"Uh, Tim?"

"Yes, sweet thing?"

"Do you have a . . ."

"A rubber? Sure I do."

She should have known he would come prepared.

Tim rolled off her to kick off his slacks and dig through his wallet. Rona sat up and pulled off the ruined linen dress. Then they began making love in earnest—Tim sliding in and out of her, dipping his fingers in the sudsy water and using those same fingers to draw sensual patterns against her skin. Tim rolled over, bringing her to her knees, then entered her from behind, using his large damp hands to lave her breasts.

She was hot, flushed, and gasping for air. She was wet, slippery, and loving every moment of it. Tim's large hand cupped her lower abdomen, his fingers stroking the wiry curls at the base of her pelvis. He moved in and out of her, picking up the pace, and her whole body shuddered. Calloused fingers closed around her nipples. Rona wanted to die.

"Let go, babe. Let it come."

She closed her eyes and gave in to the feeling. Tim's lips nipped her neck and his breath caressed her skin. Lightning bolts jolted through her and the world stood still.

Tim Delaney was a keeper.

20

"Perfect," Erik pronounced. "Now don't move."

He buried his head in his sketch pad and continued to make deft strokes. Liza wished she could see how the drawing was going, but every time she'd tried looking Erik admonished her and stuck the pad behind his back.

Her limbs were cramping and her shoulders felt tense. She'd been lounging on an old couch for the last hour, one knee propped up and an arm under her head, while Erik, his brow deeply furrowed, continued to sketch.

Liza lay still and tried not to move. Her inertia reminded her of her modeling days when even the slightest shift of a pose brought with it retribution. She kept an eye on Buddy, who kept his eye on her, and let her mind drift. She'd been grateful to Erik for coming to her rescue the other night. Posing for him was the least she could do.

A cool breeze blew through the open attic window bringing with it the scent of fall. She and Erik had talked about going to the library later to research Syracuse's role in the Underground Railroad and any other relevant information they could find.

"Okay, I think we've done enough for one day," Erik said finally, setting down the pad and chucking a number-two pencil into a holder. He approached the couch, extended a hand, and tugged her up. Buddy sniffed at his heels.

Liza uncoiled long limbs and allowed him to assist her. She rotated her neck and flexed her shoulders. Erik's large hands kneaded her cramped shoulder muscles and she shook out her legs. Closing her eyes she leaned in to him, enjoying the pressure of his nimble fingers.

"Mmmm. Feels good," she said, when one arm held her around the waist and pressed her against him. "I could have you do this forever."

Eric's mouth dipped to kiss the nape of her neck. He smelled like soap. Soap and Erik. Then turning her around, he used two fingers to tilt up her chin.

"Hungry?" he asked.

"Famished."

"I'll make you something to eat, then we'll get going."

Surprised, she blinked at him, and then remembered the delicious brownies that he'd brought to the barbecue. He'd professed to be domestic. If he cooked like he baked she was in for a treat. Erik's finger traced the scars on her face and she forgot about eating.

"I could kill the bastard that did this to you."

She was confused by the emotion in his voice, totally thrown that he cared so much. She'd recited the events the other night leading up to her moving here, but hadn't discussed her feelings or the adjustment she'd made when viewing herself in a mirror. *The* Liza Hamilton had been perfect.

"You have no idea what I've been through," she admitted, and slowly began recounting the nightmare in more detail than she had the night before. Tears spilled onto her cheeks as she spoke. She'd felt helpless, inadequate, and vulnerable, as, held hostage by a knife, she'd been forced to strip.

Erik hugged her to him. "God, it must have been awful. You could have been killed."

"It was awful and I am forever grateful to those people who came to my rescue. Thank you for understanding," she said, kissing Erik on the cheek.

His powerful arms encircled her and made her feel safe as he kissed her back. She stood on tiptoe, twining her arms around his neck, brushing her taut nipples against his chest.

Erik kissed her again and time came to a standstill. She kissed him back, madly, passionately, and with an ardor she didn't know she possessed. He backed her up against the couch until her knees gave in and she sat down with a thud. He knelt in front of her, head bent, nuzzling her neck. She twined her fingers through the hair that curled over his collar and tugged his head back.

Erik's eyes were glazed, his lips wet. "Liza," he said, in a voice that sounded as if he were choking, "if I get started, I won't be able to stop."

"Kiss me again," she demanded softly.

And he did. She grasped the front of his T-shirt and attempted to pull it over his head. Buddy, realizing he was being ignored, circled and whimpered.

"Down, boy," Erik said. "Sit." The dog reluctantly skulked off to find a seat in the corner.

Liza's fingers trailed Erik's nipples. His muscles contracted and flexed, and his breathing became shallow. She ran her fingers through the patch of hair that formed a ridge across his pectorals. He buried his head between her breasts and his hands began working her nipples. Despite the cool autumn breeze, she was burning up. Liza began pulling her sweater over her head but Erik stopped her.

"Let me do that," he said, taking over.

Free of the confining top, Liza decided it just wasn't fair that Erik should remain in his T-shirt and slacks. A buff, beautiful body like his was meant to be seen.

When exactly had she begun to think of Erik as a sex object? From the very beginning. But it wasn't just a physical attraction. Erik had qualities that were rare. He'd come to the rescue of a troubled teenager, had offered to pay for the education of a sister he hadn't met until recently, and he'd been there for her when she needed him most.

She had come to love him with all her heart and soul.

"Do you want me to stop?" he asked, breaking into her thoughts.

"No, don't stop," she said, pressing her lips against his chest and pushing his T-shirt up farther.

Erik practically ripped the shirt over his head. Liza placed her arms around his shoulders. The smell of him was now even more pronounced.

He undid the clasp of her bra and pushed the straps down. Lowering his head, he took a nipple into his mouth. Buddy returned to lick the back of his leg.

Liza reached for the drawstring on Erik's sweatpants while he was still in a crouched position. He stood up abruptly and his pants fell to his ankles. Liza gawked. It was true. Large hands. Large feet. Large—What was she thinking?

He picked her up, slid onto the couch, and settled her on top of him. The furniture creaked under their weight. Liza wondered if it would break.

Erik rained kisses on her eyelids, cheeks, and mouth. He parted her legs and, using tender fingers, began to stroke. Sensations and disjointed thoughts swam through her head. She was conscious of Buddy whimpering, of a cool breeze blowing across her skin that did nothing to assuage this feeling of warmth. She was aware of Erik's arms around her and of feeling safe. Deep in her gut she'd always known that they belonged together.

Yet Erik was her brother. Forbidden fruit.

"Stepbrother," someone whispered as a gentle peal of laughter followed.

"What was that? Did you say something?" Erik asked.

He'd heard it, too. It wasn't just her imagination. As further confirmation the Labrador began howling and circling.

"I didn't say a thing," Liza said, clamping her legs around Erik's waist and sitting up straight.

"You're killing me," he said, propping himself into a seated position and laving her chest with his tongue.

"Then why prolong the agony? Put on your galosh and get on with it."

Erik's laughter came from deep within his belly. "I've heard a condom called a lot of things, but a galosh?" He roared again.

The sofa creaked as he rose and headed toward what Liza assumed was a bathroom. He kept condoms in his studio? She planned on quizzing him about that later. But not now.

Six feet four inches of solid brick padded back toward her. He handed her the condom, making sure that she understood what he wanted her to do with it.

And she did and apparently to his satisfaction, because he groaned, scooped her off the sofa and onto the floor. Erik positioned her on her side and with one hand wrapped around her waist, brought her up firmly against him. The other swept her body, finding all her hidden places. She loved every moment of it. Loved having him lie next to her.

He was inside her, filling her up, his hands stroking her breasts. His breath against her neck was a warm caress. Liza giggled. Buddy licked the soles of her feet before settling into a corner, emitting a doggy-like sigh.

The studio ebbed and flowed before her eyes. Then Erik placed another well-aimed thrust. Liza was overcome by numerous feelings, by the sounds and smell of him, by the warmth exuding from his body, and by the total feel of him.

She wanted to lie there forever with Erik holding her, with him nibbling her lobe and breathing into her ear. She let her hands explore the length and breadth of him. They moved rhythmically, letting a sensual rumba build. Hips slapped against each other, buttocks rotated, and spasms built.

Erik came to a slow, grinding halt inside her. The world stood still as the climax took over. They hurled over the top to a place where nothing else mattered but the two of them.

The library was a musty old place in one of the poorer sections of town. A few sleepy-eyed students hunched over textbooks or stared blankly at computer screens. They barely gave Erik and Liza a glance as they roamed around.

Erik and Liza approached the information desk where a small line had formed. After they waited several minutes, a smiling, blue-haired librarian beckoned them over.

"What can I do for you?" she asked.

"We're looking for articles or books about safe houses in Syracuse," Erik said.

"Safe houses?" the librarian said with a blank look on her face. "I'm not sure I know what that means."

"Safe houses were properties housing escaped slaves on their way to Canada," Liza explained. "They were also called stops or depots on the Underground Railroad. We'd like books or maps indicating where these properties were, and anything you have on their histories."

The librarian's stubby fingernails tapped the desk. The other hand played with her keyboard; after a while she scribbled some numbers on a piece of paper and shoved it at them.

"This is the best I can do. Try upstairs, you might get lucky. The woman pointed to a winding staircase leading up to the second floor. "If nothing turns up we have old newspaper articles that we've managed to scan. You might find something there."

"Thanks," Erik said, leading Liza toward the stairs.

She was still basking in the afterglow of their lovemaking, and what wonderful lovemaking it had been. Erik had taken her to places she'd never been before, physically and mentally. Just spending time with him filled her with a warm, wonderful feeling of contentment.

The upstairs had low slanted ceilings, leaving Liza about two inches of head space and Erik none. It forced him to hunch over. They stepped over young people sprawled on the floor reading, and proceeded to the section the librarian had jotted down.

The eight shelves they found housed voluminous books on Syracuse's history, and a glass bookcase held aging periodicals.

"How are we going to narrow it down?" Liza asked.

"Look for any titles that specifically mention the Underground Railroad. You take the bottom shelves and I'll take the top."

After ten minutes had passed they were able to find about a half dozen books on the topic. The glass bookcase also yielded three magazine articles complete with photographs.

Liza spotted a vacant table and said, "We'll grab that table and divide up our findings. One of these books has got to have an old map. Even if street names have changed we might still be able to identify our properties."

"Good idea." Erik laced his fingers through hers and drew her down to sit next to him. "Although I'd rather be in bed making love to you than in some old, musty library." He batted his eyelashes outrageously and made her mouth go dry.

Determined to concentrate on the business at hand, she swatted his arm playfully. "Bad boy. Now read."

"I can show you just how bad I am but there are too many people around," he grumbled.

Liza's already runaway emotions raced faster. What would it be like to lie in bed all night with Erik beside her? To wake up to a groggy Erik who was mealymouthed and had morning shadow? She needed to get her emotions in check and quick. While he had openly admired her he hadn't voiced one word about love.

"Come on, we've got work to do," Liza said, pointing to the neglected books and magazines.

A half hour passed while they flipped through pages and made notes on a legal pad Erik had brought. Having finished with her books, Liza turned to the periodicals. There was one article in particular that caught her attention. It depicted Syracuse then and now. Then being the mid-to-late 1800s. An aging map depicted streets that she'd never heard of and establishments that were no longer around. Liza tried to pinpoint the center of town. Using a finger, she traced a path, unsuccessfully attempting to find her house.

"Look, Erik," she cried. "Here's a map as well as an article of Syracuse past and present."

Erik paused in the middle of leafing through a large book. His hazel eyes roamed over her, lingering for a moment on her breasts then returning to caress her face. Liza flushed. To cover her confusion she slid the magazine his way. Those same large hands that had touched her in the most intimate places stopped the periodical from sliding to the floor. He examined the map, then said, "I think you have something here. This may be my house."

"Let's see," Liza said, peering over his shoulder, and inhaling a distinct scent that reminded her of their wild lovemaking. Erik had taken a quick shower, one that she'd shared. Despite that, he still smelled faintly of sex—sex and her perfume.

"Here." Erik outlined a winding route with a paint-flecked fingernail. "See this wide expanse? It represents an apple orchard that's now the park down the street. And this hill on the outskirts of town, near Sam's place, held an old cemetery. I wonder if it's still there. Now go down several streets a bit and you should find my house."

"What about my house? Can you find it?"

Erik scrutinized the old map, tracing a finger up and down several streets. "This might be it," he said after a while. "But I'm not sure." He began to scan the accompanying article. "Interesting," he said after a while. "You should read this."

Liza began speed-reading the article. It described Syracuse and the surrounding towns' role in sheltering escaping slaves. There were a few brief anecdotes about slaves who'd opted not to continue on to Canada and decided to make the city home. Many of them were in poor shape after the long and arduous journey from the South. Some clearly didn't make it. The cemetery that Erik had pointed out was where they were purported to be buried.

"Do you think Sam would know about the old slave burial ground?" Liza asked, a thought formulating in her head.

"Hmmm, maybe we should ask him." Erik glanced at his watch. "It's still relatively early. Let's head over to his place."

"Without calling?"

"Sam doesn't strike me as the type that would mind."

Before they departed, Liza convinced Erik that they needed to photocopy both the article and map. With that accomplished they took off.

Sam's carriage house looked abandoned when they pulled up. Every shutter was closed. Erik banged on the front door repeatedly, then gave up.

"Where to now?" Liza asked when they were again seated in his pickup truck.

"The man doesn't strike me as having an active social life," Erik commented, clearly puzzled. "We'll try Ned. He should be able to tell us where Sam is."

Liza leaned in to kiss Erik's cheek. "You're so smart."

"If I were so smart I'd be taking you home to bed," he grumbled, then moved his head so that their lips touched. Not just touched but welded together. As their tongues began an intimate dance, all Liza could think about was Erik. Erik and the way he made her feel.

21

"Those children should be walking through that door any second now," Sam said to Ned while sipping on his third cup of coffee that day.

Ned, who was seated across from him, yelled, "Liza and Erik are hardly children, old man."

Sam wished he didn't speak so loudly. The volume was enough to blow a man's eardrum.

"When you get to be my age, anyone under sixty is a child," he grumbled.

The front door banged.

"They've arrived," Ned announced as if Sam didn't know. "Hey, kids, come join us."

Sam had to smile. Children, kids, what did it matter? Footsteps hurried their way and Sam moved over, making space for one of them. Liza slid onto the vinyl seat next to him, smelling of autumn leaves and tantalizing woman. When the banquette creaked, Sam guessed that Erik had taken the seat next to Ned.

Erik's voice boomed. "How are you, Sam? Ned?"

Sam immediately picked up on Erik's aura. The query came from a happy man. It didn't take brilliance to figure out that he and Liza had obviously resolved their differences and were in the midst of a developing relationship. He envied them.

"Not as good as both of you," Sam answered, the smile in his voice hopefully evident.

Erik chuckled. "So you're really clairvoyant, eh?"

"Clairvoyance has little to do with old Sam picking up on your happiness," Ned interjected. "If my bones were younger and a woman was eager and willing, I'd be in a permanent state of lust."

Erik roared. It was one of the things Sam liked about him. He had a good sense of humor. Plus he was down-to-earth and wasn't afraid to show his feelings.

Ned's wife had passed away a few years back, and although it had been some time since he'd had sexual relations, he'd never lost his libido. Now his daughter, her husband, and their children were living with him in a rambling old farmhouse. They'd moved in supposedly to help out, though he needed little helping. Ned's movements were slow, but his mind was quick, and he was still able to appreciate a good-looking woman.

"What else you been up to?" Sam asked, guessing from the chicory smell permeating the air that Ned's granddaughter had brought over the coffeepot, and a good thing too, because he needed some caffeine.

"Is there tea?" Liza asked.

"Get Liza tea and bring us cake and cookies," Ned ordered.

Yes, yes, bring us food and soon, was all that Sam could think.

Erik told them about the break-in at Liza's home and how an unexplainable force had taken on the boys. Sam huffed out a breath. Hurrah for the spirits that had rescued his girl.

"We went to the library," Liza said.

Sam heard a clasp open and snap shut, then the rustle of paper. "We copied this old map. It has a cemetery on it. Sam, would you know if it's still around?"

"Matter of fact, I do." Where was that cake? He was starving. "It's on the property where I live, half a mile or so from the nursery school. Years ago the historical society identified some ah those graves. The ones they did, they put markers on, but for the most part the place has been neglected."

"Sam, do you think the slaves that died in the fire were buried there?" Liza asked, excitement making her voice go high.

He'd always suspected that that was the case, in fact he pretty much knew it. Where else would the slaves have been laid to rest? Whites had their own cemeteries, blacks had theirs. But slaves would have been segregated.

The banquette creaked as Erik stood up. "Come on, let's go. This is definitely worth exploring. Sam, you coming with us?"

"What about my food?"

"I'll buy you a huge dinner if this lead pans out," Erik said, waiting for the old man to get up.

"Okay, okay," Sam groused, allowing Erik to help him to his feet. "But, Ned, I need a couple of cookies for the road."

"You got it, old man," Ned grumbled. "The way you carry on you would think you were starving."

"I am," Sam said. "So help me out."

The sun was setting as they made their way toward the overgrown burial ground. They had abandoned the pickup truck when the path ended. Acres of untended grassland stretched ahead. The going was rough, made even slower by the hobbling old man. Sam, blind or not, had insisted he tough it out, and Erik was glad to have him there to show him the way.

"Turn right," he said, leaning heavily on Erik's arm.

Slowly they began trudging up the hill. Erik stopped every now and then to clear brambles from their path. Liza held on to one of his arms and it felt good to have her there. It was as if they'd known each other for years and years.

Sam stopped to catch his breath.

"How much longer?" Erik asked.

"Another five minutes or so. It's right over the hill."

Erik wondered if the old man would make it. His huffing and puffing had an asthmatic quality to it, but despite Erik's repeated queries he insisted they continue on.

Fading sunlight dappled the trees and drew patterns on the razor grass. Liza now danced ahead of them in a surprisingly upbeat mood. This was a side of Liza that he'd not seen, childlike curiosity and a joie de vivre. She threw her arms wide and did a little jig. Erik felt guilty for wanting to join her and for wishing that Sam wasn't with them. He wanted to hold her in his arms, to twirl her around and around until they were breathless and winded. He wanted to lie with her on that grass and make mad, passionate love to her.

Sam coughed. "Come on, boy, let's go," he said, his walking stick beating out a rapid staccato.

They trudged slowly up the hill, ignoring the uncomfortable brambles that sometimes scratched their faces. Finally, the top was in sight and Erik had to practically carry the old man the rest of the way.

As they attempted to catch their breath, Erik looked down on a field so overgrown that only the tops of the white crosses could be seen.

Liza remained ahead of them, her ankle-length skirt billowing slightly in the breeze. Sam seemed to regain renewed energy from somewhere. He hobbled along as best he could, grumbling under his breath.

"This place has been neglected. Abandoned," he said, his cane slicing through the overgrowth, punctuating his words. "Bet you if white people were buried here the place would be better tended."

Ironic coming from a white man. But Erik decided it was prudent not to answer. He hated to think that way, but the burial ground should have been an important historical landmark, a tourist draw, not this vast wasteland.

He scanned the area for a place where Sam could sit, and spotted several oversized boulders. Taking the elderly man by the elbow, he led him over and settled him on an uncomfortable-looking rock.

"Take a load off. Liza and I are going to poke around a bit," Erik said.

"Poke to your right," Sam said, munching on one of the

cookies Ned had given him. "Try under the elm trees. You might find what you're looking for there." He flexed arthritic legs and with his free hand rubbed his back.

Erik wondered if Sam's suggestion was just mumbo jumbo. There were several elm trees around, too many to even count. He offered his hand to Liza and she lifted her long skirt and carefully picked her way around the roots and debris. He was glad that he'd worn jeans and sturdy shoes. The heavy denim fabric shielded his legs from the scratchy thorns and brambles. But Liza could easily stub a toe or, worse, fall. Then what would they do?

How could the community let this place go to shambles?

Twilight had descended suddenly. The fading amber light cast a surreal effect over everything and blackbirds peered at them from the surrounding trees, adding to the eeriness. They chirped and cawed as if to say, "How dare you foreigners invade our territory?"

They passed several unmarked mounds, then stopped in front of a peeling white cross. Erik released Liza's hand to pluck the weeds at its base.

"Ouch," he cried, pulling a thorn from his palm and stopping momentarily to suck on the blood.

"You're hurt. Let me see," Liza demanded, a concerned expression on her face. She took his hand, removed a tissue from her purse, and dabbed at the tiny drop of blood.

"I'm okay," Erik said, retrieving his hand and returning to the business of clearing weeds. "Are you able to read what it says?" He pointed to faded lettering on the roughly hewn cross.

"Not really. I can barely make the words out."

Erik remembered Sam's advice and wondered if there was merit to his suggestion or if the old man was just rambling. He swore softly to himself.

"What's the matter?" Liza asked, using her toe to poke the vine-covered ground.

"Nothing. It's getting dark. Let's start with the elm trees as Sam recommended."

Liza started toward the closest copse, carefully sidestepping the neglected graves. Erik admired her sensitivity and liked that she showed respect.

"Yes, yes," Sam called, "you're getting closer. Try looking under the trees to your right."

Erik caught up with Liza, grabbing her elbow as she stumbled. Darkness was rapidly closing in; they needed to move fast.

The ground was lumpy and soft underfoot and the majority of graves unmarked. Erik decided to focus on those with white crosses.

"You start over there and I'll start over here," he said to Liza, pulling at vines with his hands.

There was a distinct chill in the air now and, despite wearing a bulky sweatshirt, Erik shivered. The crude lettering on the peeling wood was hard to decipher but he occasionally made out a name: Ezekiah, Henrietta, Thomas, Wilhemina.

"I may have found something," Liza called, pointing to three graves that were next to each other. "The markers say John, Jane, and Thaddeus Doe."

Erik squatted down beside her, ignoring the dampness in the air and the distinct rumble of thunder. A dark shadow spread over them and Erik shivered again.

"Tomorrow we'll speak with someone at the Historical Preservation Society, ask some specific questions and get as much information as we can."

Liza straightened, brushing remnants of soil and leaves from her skirt. "Good idea. There's got to be records, if not names, then descriptions of the slaves that are buried, and maybe some identifiable facts. There's got to be some information about that fire."

"You almost ready?" Sam called. "It's going to rain soon." As proof of that another clap of thunder followed and lightning filled the sky.

"Yes, we're on our way," Erik yelled.

Soon the place would be pitch-dark, and he had no clue how to get them back. They collected Sam and retraced their steps.

Tomorrow he would visit the Historical Preservation Society. Once he found out what he needed to know he would give them a piece of his mind and a great deal of money. One way or the other the slave burial ground was going to be restored. It was an important part of Syracuse's history.

22

"So what do you think of my article?" Quinn asked Delilah, holding his breath in anticipation.

Delilah pursed her lips. "It'll do."

"What do you mean it'll do?"

"Just what I said." She placed the paper on the counter separating them, and returned to the floral arrangement she'd started before Quinn arrived. "You didn't make me sound glamorous."

"You are glamorous. Glamorous and special." He tried reaching over the counter to touch her arm but she moved away.

To him Delilah was all that and more. She was way out there but he liked that. She was brash, beautiful, and confident in her sexuality. He'd never been big on skinny women, and Delilah represented everything he liked in a woman.

She stuck another calla lily into the vase, then picked up the newspaper and read aloud. "You call this flattering?"

No Gilded Lilies

Recently this reporter had the distinct pleasure of interviewing four of Syracuse's smartest, most entrepreneurial, and beautiful lilies (nothing gilded about these four, nothing jaded either as a matter of fact). All were forward thinking, industrious, and symbols of our brave new world, one in which women run successful businesses without depending on men.

The first woman I interviewed, a big, beautiful, outspoken sister with a mind of her own, was Delilah Kincaid, owner of the Gilded Lily. When you first encounter Ms. Kincaid she is as colorful as any flower in her shop. She is bubbly and vivacious and you can't imagine her having the patience to deal with indecisive, complaining customers. But Ms. Kincaid fixed me with these huge brown eyes of her and I immediately fell under her spell. She patiently answered the most mundane questions in a no-nonsense and forthright manner. And she flirted with me. This reporter especially liked that.

Ms. Kincaid freely admitted she had a limited budget but plenty of brass. That chutzpah caused her to research available loans and to open her flower shop with limited funds. "Taking a chance is what it's about," the delectable Delilah said, batting huge gold-flecked eyes that reminded me so much of the sunflowers she sold . . .

"Delectable Delilah, indeed," Delilah huffed, tossing the paper aside. "Sunflower, huh? Couldn't you have come up with other words, like stunning, memorable, or even unforgettable?"

"You're delectable to me," Quinn said, his breathing escalating when Delilah leaned over the counter and the deep valley between her breasts came clearly into view. She made his engine rev and his mind go foggy.

"Does that mean you want to sleep with me?" she asked, putting it on the line and backing him into a spot.

"I . . . uh—"

"Yes or no?"

"Uh, yes."

"Then let's go."

"G—go where?" Quinn sputtered.

"Into my back room. I do have a back room, you know, one with a very comfortable Murphy bed."

Delilah came around the counter and took his hand. Quinn realized it was now or never. He held her hand and walked with her toward the back.

Delilah Kincaid had both style and guts, qualities sadly missing in him. They would provide a good balance for each other.

Kalib's voice came at her over the phone. "Cassie, I'm no fool. I know you're bulimic. You need to see a therapist."

She wanted to clap her hands over her ears and shut him out. She should be angry, but Kalib was only echoing what she already knew. He'd caught on that she had an eating disorder, one that was running out of control.

"How long have you known?" she asked in a wobbly voice.

The cakes in the oven would be done soon and needed to be tended to before they became overcooked.

"I became suspicious when you started disappearing into the bathroom for relatively long periods of time, especially after you ate."

Oh, God, he hated her and was probably looking to dump her before they even got started. Most men didn't want women with issues. Cassie felt tears sliding down her face, felt her nose filling up, and her ears clog with cotton.

"I had been going to a therapist but I stopped," she admitted.

"Obviously you didn't bond. Try someone else," Kalib said with remarkable understanding. "Don't allow this thing to beat you."

"I'd planned on doing just that. I just haven't had the time."

"Make time."

She'd planned to. She didn't want to lose him just like she'd lost Jim.

"Then do it. Listen, I'm coming up next weekend. I'll stay an additional day or two. We'll take a ride to Ithaca or Binghamton, where no one knows you. We'll find someone you can work with."

We? What did that mean? Did it mean he planned on sticking around? Most men would have put on jogging shoes and run. She knew there was a reason she liked him.

"I'll look forward to seeing you," Cassie said, about to hang
up.

"And I, you. Hang in there, love. This will soon pass."

He'd called her "Love." If she wanted to keep him she
would have to be proactive and beat her bulimia before it beat
her.

"I will," Cassie said. "I miss you and can't wait to see you
again."

"May I help you?" a snotty-faced, thin-lipped woman manning the reception desk at the Historical Preservation Society
asked when Liza and Erik entered.

The building was an old colonial with peeling paint. It
needed remodeling in the very worst way. Liza guessed that the
aging debutante looking down her nose at them was one of
those society matrons with a prominent husband.

Erik was practically in the woman's face. "You most certainly can help us. We're here to ask for your help."

"And what kind of help would you need?" An arched eyebrow rose. She apparently did not recognize Erik. She looked
him up and down, wrinkling her nose slightly as if smelling
something unpleasant.

Erik was casually attired as he had a tendency to be. Today
he wore a red bandana around his head and a tiny gold hoop in
one ear. His hands were, as usual, paint-flecked, and the knee
of his jeans ripped. To Liza he looked both handsome and sexy.

"We aren't in a position to sponsor any charities," the matron continued in a tight upper-crust voice. "We are a not-for-
profit organization."

"We're not looking for you to sponsor anything," Erik said,
his annoyance clear in his voice. "We're here because we need
your help." He produced a crumpled card from his pocket,
slapped it down on the counter, and stuck his hand out. "I'm
Erik Price."

The matron brightened visibly. Her voice shook. "*The* Erik
Price? Oh, Mr. Price, it is so good to make your acquaintance."

"I wish I could say the same."

Liza tried not to laugh. A bony hand fluttered to the dried-up woman's tiny breasts. "Oh, my, and I thought you were a solicitor. How can I apologize?"

"By finding your boss, someone who can provide me with the information I need."

Erik had swiftly put the woman in her place, and who could blame him? People tended to stereotype; that was something Liza had learned from her modeling days. The companies that hired her were often surprised when they found out she didn't speak ebonics.

"Uh, Mr. Tilton, my husband, is on the phone."

"I'll wait until he gets off the phone. I have a sizeable check to donate to the Society if he's willing to speak with me," Erik said.

Mrs. Tilton visibly started and after an inward debate darted off to find her husband. "Wait right here. I'll be back."

Liza couldn't help laughing when the dry little woman disappeared.

"You were wonderful," she said, sticking a hand in the back pocket of Erik's jeans and giving his buns a little squeeze. "In fact you were marvelous."

He kissed her cheek and whispered in her ear, "If you don't want me to jump your bones, you need to stop right now." He stepped out of her reach, putting safe distance between them.

After a while, a pudgy, middle-aged man wearing an ascot waddled out in front of his wife. He beamed at them.

"Mr. Price. How nice to make your acquaintance. I'm Lawrence Tilton. I heard that you'd moved to Syracuse." He held out his hand to Erik. "My wife says you have a check."

"That I do, but first I'll need a favor from you."

"Anything."

Erik went on to explain about the information he needed.

Lawrence Tilton cocked his head. "It may take a little time, at least a day or so. We have a new computer system, and we're trying to get familiar with it. If memory serves me right there is some history about that ill-fated fire."

"Could you e-mail me anything you find?" Erik asked. "My e-mail address is on my card."

"Sure thing," Mr. Tilton said, patting Erik's arm. "Sure thing. Now what about that donation?"

"The sooner you get that information to me, the sooner you'll have your check." Erik took Liza's arm and led her toward the door. "I'm looking forward to hearing from you."

"We'll put a rush on it," Tilton said. "There's so much the Society needs to do and such limited funding."

"My donation comes with a condition," Erik warned, turning to eye the man slyly.

Mr. Tilton blinked while his dry little wife swallowed hard.

"But of course. We'll do just about anything to help you."

"Then that being the case, please make the old slave burial ground a priority. If you don't I will withdraw my offer."

As the Tiltons gaped, Erik closed the door behind them.

Liza wanted to break out in a wild round of applause. Instead she hugged Erik.

Less than six hours later Erik had the information he needed. He'd dropped Liza off at home earlier. Now he sat hunched over his computer printing out the message, which was two pages long. The information he'd downloaded confirmed what Sam already knew. It detailed the events of the fire.

Several slaves had died in the blaze, including a husband and wife who'd been split up and sheltered in different homes. The son they'd left behind later succumbed to pneumonia. The boy's name was Thaddeus, but no one was sure whether the name was real or something the minister had made up.

The old burial ground had been no more than a potter's field where for the most part unidentified slaves had been buried. It was speculated that the few names that were present on the graves had been made up. Lawrence Tilton had attached a roughly drawn map with Xs identifying the properties that were considered to be stops on the Underground Railroad.

After scrutinizing the properties with Xs, Erik confirmed that the house he'd inherited was one of the depots. He traced a finger down the street he believed to be Liza's, and found an X also marking the spot where her house stood. The old church, Rona's current nursery school, was also identified as a depot.

Sam had been right all along. He and Liza were connected. Glued to the page, Erik continued to read. The three properties that had housed escaping slaves were reputed to be haunted. Several sightings of ghosts were reported when the burnt properties had been rebuilt. Some had even claimed to see Harriet Tubman overseeing the work. Erik was so excited with his findings that he wanted to share them with Liza. Rather than call her he decided to take a ride to her house.

He headed for his pickup truck and turned back at the last minute, having decided to take Buddy with him. The Lab sat in the passenger seat licking Erik's ear and woofing intermittently. When he pulled up in front of Liza's house a soft glow coming from her bedroom indicated that she might still be up.

Erik debated tossing a handful of gravel at her windowpane but thought that might scare her. Better to simply walk up to the front door and ring the doorbell. Then he decided to call first from his cell phone to warn her that he was here.

He left Buddy in the car and headed up the walkway, pushing the preprogrammed number. Liza answered on the fifth ring.

"Hey, you up?" Erik queried.

"I'm up now," she answered in a voice heavy with sleep. "What's going on?"

"I downloaded the stuff we were waiting for. I've printed it out and have it with me. I'm in front of your door."

"I'll be right down," she said, no longer sounding sleepy.

Seconds later, Liza threw the door open and stood regarding him in a T-shirt that barely skimmed her knees and ankle socks with a lace border. Buddy, spotting her, began barking and scratching at the windshield.

"Better bring that dog in," Liza said, "before he wakes up the entire neighborhood."

Erik loped back to the truck and let Buddy out. The Labrador raced right by him, scooting through the open front door.

"Buddy!" Erik called

By the time Erik had made it inside, Buddy was already racing up the stairs to the second floor as if he lived there, wagging his tail furiously.

"Let him go," Liza said, laughing and pulling Erik into the house. She wound her arms around his neck, kissing him soundly and leaving him wanting more. She smelled like sleep and a fresh spring breeze. "So let's see what you have," Liza said somewhat breathlessly.

Erik waved the crumpled e-mail he'd printed out.

"The Tiltons came through. Amazing what the promise of money can do. This deserves a glass of wine."

Erik followed her into the kitchen and took a seat on a small wrought-iron chair that creaked ominously under his weight. "Uh, maybe we should find some place else to sit," he said, about to get up.

"Don't be silly. You act like you weigh a ton when you're a mass of sinew and muscle."

She opened the bottle of wine and poured it while Erik flexed his muscles and gave her a great big smile. "After we're done I'll show you more muscle," he said, winking.

Liza pretended to glare. Erik spread the papers out on the table and began to explain his findings.

"So Sam was right after all," Liza said. "We both live in houses that have a history and Rona's nursery school is a part of it."

"There's got to be merit to his beliefs and would certainly explain the strange dreams we're having. It even lends credibility to Sam's reincarnation theory. How else would you explain why we both ended up in these houses and why we were drawn to each other?"

"Hmmm," Liza said.

A floorboard creaked upstairs. They could hear Buddy circling and woofing excitedly, as if cavorting with a friend.

"Someone seems pleased that we've solved our little mystery," Liza said.

"Maybe we should go find that someone," Erik said, rising

and taking her by the hand. "Maybe I should show them how much I love you and that my intentions are sincere."

"Maybe you should," Liza said, preceding him up the stairs and stopping to pull her T-shirt over her head.

Erik's arms wrapped around her middle. He lifted her off the floor and took the stairs two at a time.

"I do love you, Liza Hamilton, and I intend to show you how much."

"Show me," she said, kissing his neck. "Show me with all that you have."

23

February 14 – Valentine's Day

"Thank you, ladies and gentlemen, for patronizing what will be our annual Valentine's Day ball," Lawrence Tilton boomed. "We hope you will enjoy the wonderful dinner and stay for the dancing afterward. I'm turning the microphone over to Erik Price, one of our new board members, who has a very special announcement to make."

To a loud round of applause, Erik bounded onto the dais, outfitted in a black tuxedo and red bow tie. Liza had never seen him look more handsome or sure of himself. He accepted the microphone from Larry and peered over the heads of the patrons, directly at her.

God, she loved the man. Loved everything about him. Not just his physical attributes but the thoughts that roamed around in his head.

It was Valentine's Day. At Erik and Liza's urgings the Society had thrown a fund-raising ball. Anyone willing to pay fifty dollars, or reserve a five-hundred-dollar table, had come. Judging by the number of attendees, the price should have been upped. The place was packed to capacity. The profits would be used to restore and maintain Syracuse's historical landmarks, especially those that were once stations on the Underground Railroad.

Erik and Liza were now on the board of the Historical Preservation Society. The money each had contributed ensured them a place and a say as to where the money would be spent. The first piece of business on the agenda was restoring the slave burial ground and making sure each grave had a pristine white cross.

Rona, who was seated on Liza's right, squeezed her hand. Tim was her escort and judging by the way they looked at each other the two were in love.

"I wonder what Erik's up to," Rona whispered.

Liza shrugged. "God knows. He's always a walking, talking surprise."

"And you love him because he keeps you guessing."

"That I do. There's never a boring moment with Erik."

And she did love him with a fervor and passion reserved for few. They'd grown close these last few months while they worked on a cause they were both fanatical about.

Elizabeth had made it clear that Liza would be a fool to let Erik get away. And Sara, handful that she was, now idolized her stepbrother and practically hung on his every words. And her grades had improved now that she knew that college was paid for.

"You two better stop gabbing and listen to the man," Sam, who was seated across from them, said loudly. "He has an important announcement to make."

"I take it you're privy to what he's about to say," Liza said to the old man.

Sam just smiled.

They'd convinced him to make a rare nocturnal appearance. Initially he'd hemmed and hawed, claiming he had nothing to wear, but Liza tempted him with the five-course dinner and he'd quickly agreed. He'd cleaned up beautifully and, after much arguing, had agreed to wear the gray tuxedo that Liza insisted he rent. Ned had convinced his granddaughters, Tiffani and Kelli, to be their dates. Both young women were dressed to kill in strapless gowns that had several men gaping.

Erik began by thanking the patrons for attending the ball and assured them that their contributions would be put to good use.

"Hmmmph, I should never have let that man get away," Delilah whispered, her eyes round. Quinn, who was her date, pretended not to hear.

"I'm glad you did," Liza answered. "Or I would never have stood a chance."

It paid to be gracious and keep Delilah on her good side. They'd been friends for too many years. Delilah went back to cooing sweet nothings in Quinn's ear while Liza listened raptly to what Erik had to say.

And Cassie, who was now engaged to Kalib, sat holding his hand as he catered to her every wish and looked at her adoringly.

All of Liza's friends were in this room. Her life was here with her three closest friends and the man she loved. She focused her attention on the dais where Erik now paused, his hand outstretched.

"Liza, will you please stand up?" he called.

"Stand, Liza, stand," Rona said, nudging her with an elbow.

Liza stood in a daze. She watched two burly men climb the steps. One carried an object draped in red velvet, the other an easel.

"There, ladies and gentlemen, stands my better half," Erik boomed.

A spotlight shone on Liza as one of the men undraped a canvas and placed it on an easel. She gasped. Erik had completed her portrait. He'd captured her essence exactly and he'd made her look beautiful. Not just beautiful but vulnerable too.

Awed, Liza blinked, and when she looked at the canvas again a turbaned woman with a huge smile was superimposed over her image. No mistaking the woman's identity. It was Harriet Tubman, Moses, savior of the people. Liza blinked again and her portrait came clearly back into focus.

The applause around her was deafening. And although Liza was used to adulation, used to people staring and gawking, she was suddenly self-conscious. She'd gotten over thinking that she was no longer beautiful. Erik had helped her achieve this. He'd assured her over and over again that her faded scars didn't matter, and that in fact they made her look exotic and human. Now today, Valentine's Day, he'd presented her with this gift— a gift she would always treasure.

Erik got down on one knee and crooked a finger at her. "Liza," he said, "please come up here and join me."

"Go," Delilah mouthed. "He's calling you, girl."

"Get up there," Rona urged.

"Move it," Cassie mouthed.

"Liza, Liza," the crowd chanted. "Go, girl."

In slow motion, Liza moved toward the dais. Then picking up the red satin skirt that swirled about her ankles, she practically raced up the two little steps and onto the dais. She floated toward Erik, who met her halfway.

Erik still held the microphone in one hand. His warm palm grasped hers as he pulled her toward him. To the audience he said, "You are my witnesses. I am asking this beautiful woman to be my wife. Liza, will you marry me?"

She took a deep breath and struggled to regain her composure. He was so sure of himself. So sure that he was willing to risk public humiliation. What if she said no?

But he was right to be so confident. The words tumbled out of her mouth. "Yes," Liza said. "Oh, yes, Erik. I would be honored to be your wife."

He kissed her and Liza forgot about everyone and everything. In her world all that existed was Erik—Erik and the two properties that had brought them together.

Behind them Liza heard the flutter of wings. She looked up to see shadows soaring. The ancestors approved and had joined in the celebration. Liza could only hope that they were on their way to heaven and had found peace at last.

She knew she had.